WINTER of BEAUTY

By Amy Hale Auker

Winter of Beauty

Copyright © 2013 by Amy Hale Auker

Night Riders Lament lyrics written by Michael Burton/copyright
Michael Burton Music, used with permission.

First Edition
Printed and bound in USA
ISBN: 978-0-9851274-9-7

Cover design by Adam Ritchey
Formatting by Kimberly Pennell

P

Pen-L Publishing

12 West Dickson #4455
Fayetteville, AR 72702

Pen-L.com

To my family, the one that got bigger instead of smaller.

A saddle built on a Will James tree hangs from the rafters of a garage and sways in the gloom, dancing with the dust motes. A pink arrowhead rests on a woman's dresser, and sometimes she touches it lightly as she passes by. A crystal decanter of scotch glows softly in the deserted study of a big house that once rattled loudly with love. An old cowboy turns the key in the ignition of an equally old truck, listens critically to the starter turn over, the engine roar to life as it does, once a week, as it has, once a week, for many years. Rain falls down and pools in a tinaja, a basin in the bedrock, a source of life in arid land, a place that captures and holds both magic and hope. Somewhere in a pawn shop, a drum set lies in pieces, dusty like the saddle, until someone sets it up and puts a yellow price tag on it. Bride Mountain unveils her face, sending her white cover rushing downward, baring her seeded breasts to the sun's insistent warmth. A couple makes love, and beauty is formed.

PART ONE : THE TINAJA

BRANDED

The padded booth in the dim restaurant swallowed Sunshine Angel Lewis and she held onto the table to keep from going under.

As a waitress with stick-straight hair took her drink order, Shiney silently cursed getting old, no longer limber enough to tuck one leg up under her ass to lift herself into a more dignified position.

And no, house scotch was not okay, not today.

In the interim between ordering Glenlivet and receiving her highball glass, Shiney regretted having chosen this fancy dining place instead of driving to the squat adobe house tucked into a dusty side street where a five-year-old piñata hung fading in the window and the Cinco de Mayo decorations stayed up all year. They didn't serve high-end scotch, but she liked Corona with lime just fine if it was cold enough. She'd have ordered the #7 platter: one enchilada, one chile relleno, and one beef taco, all swimming in beans and rice. Plus, since it was her birthday, if she had gone to *El Paisano* she would have substituted a stuffed relleno for the regular. Stuffed with shrimp. A garage sale painting of Madonna would have looked down on her as she ate.

She wrapped both hands around her glass. As it was still late afternoon rather than early evening, she was the only one in the dining room. The twelve-year-old waiter stumbled through his first recitation of the specials, but Shiney stopped listening after the veal, finally ordering baked roughy though only a fool expected good fish this far from the ocean. Ordering fish wasn't the only silly thing she'd done today. She pulled the new cell phone from her purse with two fingers. She'd have to get Monte to show her how the damned thing worked. The lady at the cell phone store had spoken fluent and rapid gibberish.

Shiney felt foolish as she ate her salad. She should have stayed at the ranch, worked at her desk in the office, kept to her normal routine. Lately she had been doing a lot of things that were out of the ordinary. Like using Google, damn her foreman's hide. And damn the satellite dish on the office roof. She wished she'd never typed "female midlife crisis" into the little search box. Dangerous little box. Sunshine Angel Lewis had clicked out of the screen just as soon as she saw that there really was such an animal.

By the time the roughy arrived – too much food, smothered in white sauce, sprinkled with peas so green they looked plastic – Shiney wasn't hungry. She put her fork down after three bites and sipped at the familiar scotch, peopling the rest of the table in her mind. They were all ghosts, but she sat them around her like jewels, invited them to join her for her party. She wondered who she could have invited that was alive. Well, Rafe, of course. And Monte.

Nothing was as it had been, and she wasn't sure what she was moving toward. There were so many things she'd never done, and she was tired of doing the things she'd always done.

Sunshine Angel Lewis hit her thigh on the edge of the table rushing out of there. She drove toward Bride Mountain just as the sun began to sink. She raced to the only thing she'd ever known. Tonight of all nights, she couldn't miss the sunset.

And so, sunset found her, this silver-haired lady, tough as leather on the outside, soft as the rich river bottom on the inside. On the second story of a many-windowed house, graced by the sun's evening angles, she poured another scotch and looked out over the country to which she was given in matrimony on the day of her birth, the country that was her heart, her child, her double-gendered parent, her identity. The country that ruled her life, both with love and weather, three hundred square miles of tyranny and cradle.

For over sixty years Shiney Lewis had looked out over, or ridden over, or driven over, or – even once – flown over this land, had reached her hands toward it when nothing else made sense – this country where cows kept eating the grass and turning it into beef, where an ever-changing cast of cowboys moved them down to the low country in winter and up into the pines in summer, and where, for many springs, two big bands of mares gave birth to short, athletic, rock-footed, cow-watching ranch horses that attracted buyers who drove out to stand and spit and bargain. That heyday passed, as most do, and the buyers' tastes changed, and too many people started breeding horses. Now, simple nostalgia allowed a few old mares to stand around the headquarters and crop the dry winter grasses, bellies swelling.

Almost every day of her life the silver-haired lady has walked to the tinaja north and west of the big house. The tinaja — a place where men, women, children, deer, skunks, mountain lions, the rare elk come down to visit the low country, always a squirrel and a coon, sometimes a sure-footed horse, often a cow, went for the absolute peace of the place. Or a drink of water. In August it is almost certainly dry, but, oh, hope drives one to scramble over the boulders and through the brush anyway. In January, it is almost certainly crusted with ice. Then there are those times when the basin, and sometimes two or three basins of water in steps, are full and edged with the lace of small animal tracks and the deeper impressions of big ones, like coats of arms pressed into wax wafers, mud atop the rock. The eccentric old lady, as she now thinks of herself even if others do not, walks to this place via a faint path through the junipers and oakbrush, one she could have followed in her sleep.

Sunshine Angel Lewis started out life with eccentricity as the norm. Her mother was a pale gray child bride from back East who went straight back east as soon as her baby was born. The accepted story was that she had health problems, but no one in the West ever saw the lady again. She left the infant behind with her large, loud husband who walked into the hospital room the evening of his daughter's birth with an armful of flowers and a snootful of whiskey, booming, "She's my sunshine angel, by Gawd, my own little sunshine angel! We'll just tack her old pappy's last name to that, and brand her as Lewis stock!"

It took him a lot of talking the next morning to convince the nurses that he really meant it, and several of them quietly consulted the mother who lay pale on her pillows looking east. Some of the nurses didn't blame the woman for leaving the big red-faced man, but they did wonder at a mother who could get on a train without her newborn. But in the end, or rather, the beginning, the little girl was Sunshine Angel Lewis, "Shiney" by her second birthday, and no one delighted her more than the father who toted her out to live in the shadow of Bride Mountain when she was one week old.

No one knew where Paul Amato Lewis came from originally, just that he showed up in the Southwest with a pocketful of money and an English backer who rode out on the train every fall to sit in the old hotel beside the depot. There the Englishman ate one well-done steak (putting him immediately in a questionable light with the locals) and drank one whiskey with "Punch," as Paul Lewis was known by then. There was considerable speculation as to whether the Englishman just went on back to wherever he came from or whether he went on to the next cowtown and then the next because he had ranches all over the West. Whatever the case, everyone was so used to having Punch in the community that they forgot to notice when one year the Englishman didn't come, not then, and never again.

Punch Lewis had earned his place among them by putting together one of the largest ranches in the state with the help of Ernesto Chavez. Nesto was Punch's best friend, his foreman, and his cow boss, and if a man didn't want to work for a "Mexican," then in Punch's opinion, that man could go on down the road. Nesto was widely considered the best cowboy in the country.

When Punch brought his newborn daughter home to the Tinaja, he had the foresight to bring along Damaris, a petite but decidedly round young woman with long blonde braids wrapped around her head, a strong Norwegian accent, blue eyes, and skin that was apt to turn bright red whenever she was mad or embarrassed or overly warm. She set herself and the infant up in Punch's cabin while Punch moved into the bunkhouse with his cowboys and stepped up the pace of construction on the Big House that was still half-built.

Damaris was more than a baby nurse. She was Sunshine Angel Lewis's mother right from the beginning. She was everyone's mother. She mothered Punch, mothered the cowboys, mothered the barn cats and the dogs and the dogie calves. The only person she didn't mother was Nesto, and she was likely to throw her apron over her face as if to disappear whenever he came around. This behavior puzzled Nesto considerably and puzzled Punch, too, but when Shiney was almost a year old, the odd couple, Damaris, short and round and golden, next to Nesto, tall and thin and dark, went to the ranch owner and told him they were getting married. Punch went roaring out of his makeshift office in the bunkhouse, hunted up the construction foreman and demanded that the blueprints for the Big House be altered immediately. He added a whole wing expressly for Nesto and Mama D, as she had become known, and before too many months had passed they all moved into the monstrosity. The newlyweds immediately began filling their part of the house with little Chavez offspring, siblings for Shiney. The whole passel of kids looked alike except that when each one popped out, no one could be sure if it was going to have black hair or blonde, blue eyes or brown.

Mama D got rounder and rounder as the years went by, mainly

because she was constantly frying, roasting, harvesting, rolling dough, and pouring batter, though Shiney always wondered how she got so fat because she was always moving. No one could remember her ever filling a plate for herself, much less sitting down to eat. She had a huge garden, a noisy and underfoot flock of chickens, and the Big House was always spotless. She still threw her apron over her face when Nesto teased her, but she reigned as unchallenged queen over the Tinaja.

Mama D learned to speak Spanish just as fast as Nesto, and louder, though with her old accent intact. The two of them and Punch spoke Spanish as often as they did English until Shiney started school, and then Punch demanded that only English be spoken at meals, which they ate together at a big trestle table.

"Family!" Punch would roar. "Family is what you make it, and by Gawd, this is a family!" And he would bang his fist on the table where Shiney even now drank her coffee of a morning. And it *was* family – a big mixed-up colorful family. The only custom that set the ranch owner and his daughter apart from the noisy Chavez brood was Punch's after dinner habit of disappearing into his library where Shiney joined him. There the two of them sat in big red leather chairs, and Punch read aloud to his girl from books he ordered, ones that came in the mail wrapped in brown paper. Later on, she did her homework while he worked on correspondence and read livestock journals. Shiney learned to love the smell, and later the taste, of fine Scotch on these evenings with her father.

Shiney rarely saw her real mother, and then only when Punch took her east expressly for that purpose. She never talked about those visits. When she was fourteen, for reasons that only Punch and his wife knew or understood, Shiney's father sent her to her mother for the summer. She had been gone two weeks when Mama D burst into the ranch office where Punch was working on the accounts. From the beginning she had called Shiney "My Baby." Even after she started popping out little rainbow babies of her own, Shiney was always My Baby. Mama D was fascinated by the ranch's new telephone that rang simultaneously in the Big House and in the original old cabin that had become the ranch office. Rarely did anyone else get a chance to answer it. On this day, she had answered its ring in the kitchen as she stirred a big pot of green chile stew, so if she was red-faced because of that, or because it was June, or because of indignation, who knew. She stamped her fat little foot at

Punch and declared, "My Baby is miserable back there in that East, and I am going to get her! My Baby needs to come home." With that and a string of Spanish curses uttered in a Norwegian accent, she turned and waddled back to the house, yelling at one of her boys to get her suitcase down out of the attic. Punch followed as fast as he could, but by the time he found her again, she had already packed her bag and had her "going to town" hat pinned over her braids. It became something of ranch legend how he bellowed at Mama D to "take off that hat and calm down!" Punch ended up retrieving Shiney from "that East" himself, but from then on, when someone wanted to tease Mama D about her temper, they would yell, "Take off that hat, Mama D, and calm down!" Everyone would laugh uproariously, except Mama D who would threaten the teaser with her wooden spoon.

When Punch brought Shiney home that summer, the girl went straight up to her room, put on her cowboy clothes and never wore a dress again. Ever. Three days later she walked into the kitchen carrying Mama D's sewing shears. Mama D gasped, "My Baby. *Pobrecita. Venga*, let me help you." When she'd done the best she could with what was — left, Mama D waddled to the barn where Punch was doctoring a sick horse and said, "Now you listen to me. My Baby has cut off her hairs. And you will tell her it looks nice. Do you hear me? You will say that she is just beautiful with her hairs like a boy's. I mean it, Punch Lewis. *Muy bonita.*" Mama D kept Shiney's hair cut short for her from then on.

Punch Lewis got word that his wife had died when Shiney was eighteen, and many said that with that word he also became the trustee of a large sum of money that Shiney inherited on her twenty-first birthday. By that time, Shiney had gone east again, this time to college, and no amount of pleading from Mama D on My Baby's behalf could bring her home. During those years, Shiney would visit the ranch on holidays and ride her horse for hours, very often sleeping up on the slopes of Bride Mountain, but she rarely spoke in detail about her life at the elite women's university where she spent her other days. After four years, Shiney walked into her father's office, put her leather-bound diploma on his desk.

"I did what you wanted. Now I am going to do what I want."

And she went away again. She spent two years going through a newly established ranch management and animal husbandry program at a Texas university, the first woman to ever do so, and then, Sunshine Angel Lewis came home to the Tinaja for good. She split her time between the ranch office where she fought huge and bloody battles with her father about modernizing the ranch's accounting system and outside horseback with the cowboys where she worked as hard as any man.

All of the Chavez children grew up and moved away. Punch Lewis made sure that they all went to college and they all earned master's degrees. Two of them earned PhDs. One by one, or in little clusters, they drove out to the Tinaja to see Shiney around Christmas. They all loved Shiney Lewis.

No one ever knew of Shiney having a suitor, a lover, or even going on a date. There was an old faded ranch rumor that Nesto's oldest son had loved her, but if so, he went away never having done anything about it. Shiney always referred to the Chavez children as her brothers and sisters, even if she was the only child to have her own bedroom in the Big House.

Shiney became a true orphan when she was thirty years old, on the day that Punch Lewis died of a heart attack while helping gather the River Pasture. Punch rode in to the hold-up with the biggest wad of cows of anyone, and when he got there, he slid off of his big bay horse and onto the ground, dead before anyone could get to his side.

Shiney was the first one to reach her father, kneeling in the dirt, her hands like birds fluttering above, but not quite touching, his chest. Nesto and one of the other men knelt there with her until Nesto looked up. *"Está muerto, niña. Su papa está muerto."* None of the eight or so men there that day ever forgot the young woman's eyes when she raised them from her father's body.

Two of the hands followed her tracks back to headquarters. They found her horse unsaddled and in the corral, but they didn't see Shiney. For several weeks, no one did, other than Nesto and Mama D, except on the day of the funeral, for just one hour, as she stood with her head down and her cowboy hat on beside the woman who raised her while they buried her Papa on the knoll overlooking the tinaja.

Legend on the ranch also had it that on the day Shiney finally did come out of the Big House, she came down to breakfast and sat down across from Nesto. "Nesto, I have been drinking one scotch with Papa every night since the day I turned eighteen. Last night I had two. It's time I got horseback again. Someone's got to run this ranch."

And Shiney Lewis has been running the Tinaja ever since . . . and she is tired.

OLD OWL

April 24 – Started riding fence up around the Lower Mountain. Damned cold wind robbing us of our good spring.

Rafe Johansen accidentally wrote poetry. He was not a cowboy poet, not someone who ever read poetry or even thought about poetry, but he accidentally wrote it, almost a poem a day. He had grown up at a boys' ranch after his parents somehow couldn't keep him fed or safe, and had gone to work for Dan Pogue right out of high school. Mr. Pogue demanded that his young employee keep a record of each day's tasks so that he could glance at it on payday, an accounting of time, an accounting for the dollars paid, only $75 a month and a box of groceries in those days. That was the only year that anyone ever saw Rafe's entries, but it became a habit for the young man, one that continued into his early years of being an old man though he still felt nineteen. The entries were less than a diary, more than just tally marks. He wrote down what he did each day. He kept a log of projects accomplished, weather, cows seen, and miles ridden in spiral bound calendar books with the year foil-stamped on the front, shelved each January above the rod in his clothes closet, a row of spirals facing the light each time he opened the door. He ordered them from the same address that he'd copied from the inside cover of that first one, though he shook his head every November at how the cost had climbed. This last one was $24.95, even with the clip-out coupon from the year before. He'd paid $2.13 for the first one. Didn't take an accountant to do those figures.

Not only were the words written in Rafe's notebooks the truest history of the Tinaja, or at least Rafe's part of it, but the pages were also scattered with jewels of poetry amongst the cow numbers, records of hay bales stacked in the barn, logs of when the windmills got greased, and documented repairs on ranch trucks.

May 21 – Tied in stays at Precious Camp water lot. Old owl watched me all day.

Rafe Johansen was proud of his horses. He was sure of his way with cows. He loved the boy he and Nell raised. He took careful care with the products he delivered out of his leather shop, and he was proud of the good reputation that the Tinaja Ranch had earned through the years. Most of the cowboys in the region had worked there at one time or another, in one capacity or another, on one wagon or another, either for Punch, back in the wilder days, or for his daughter after that day he slid off his horse and died. Coffee shop and feed store and saddle house talk often turned to a man's days on the TJs, as it was known casually. Tinaja cattle wore a T with a J-hook, a clean, simple brand high on the left hip, a brand that Rafe never ceased to admire, plus a crop out of one ear, a cut Rafe was deft at making, right ear on the steers, left ear on the heifers. Punch Lewis had been smart to adopt the brand as his own when he bought the initial herd and the block of country that made up the core of the ranch, back when the mountain was still wild.

Rafe remembered Punch as the kind of man other men wanted to work for, and his reputation, like the ranch's, had been solid, but not tame. Punch Lewis was anything but tame. A tame man could not have put together a ranch the size and caliber of the Tinaja. Only a few men spoke of Punch with anything other than respect, and those who had something bad to say had probably tried to cross him and lost or had some character flaw that caused Punch to ask him to move on down the chuck line.

Those who had known Punch were respectful of his daughter. Those who had worked for the daughter felt as if, in a way, they had also worked for her father. Unfortunately, some men have a hard time saying anything nice about a woman in authority.

Most big ranches were places where people, horses, trends, management styles, and even owners came and went, the camps and bunkhouses gaining and losing cowboys with regularity. But Rafe Johansen wasn't a comer and a goer. He was a stayer. And a doer. And those, he thought, were favorable attributes, even if he occasionally had to be reminded that there was a whole wide world outside of work, outside the boundary fences of the ranch. He knew the ranch as intimately as some people know their hometowns. The Tinaja *was* his hometown. He knew not only the roads and the watering holes and the fence lines, the domesticated animals that were his purpose in life, but also the wilder places and animals, the hidden trails off into the canyons, the paths through the boulders and back out the other side. He often frustrated newcomers with his easy descriptions of how to get around in the rougher country, assuming they'd see each ridge, each haired-over cow trail, each obvious (to him) landmark. To the uninitiated, the ones who drive only paved roads, stay plugged in to cell phones and GPS devices, he was an enigma, an antique, or a non-entity. He'd worked now for a quarter of a century for the lady who drank scotch and watched the shadows creep down the side of Bride Mountain as the sun set each evening. He counted her as one of his best friends.

Rafe had come to the TJ bunkhouse the same year Shiney came home from ranch management school. He had stayed a long time in a bunkhouse where men usually spent only a season or two. He was there some years later when Punch died, was there that day, and for the days that followed as the ranch kept on going without the big blustery man who had put it all together.

He recalled distinctly the day a few months after Punch's death when Shiney Lewis and Nesto Chavez stood with him out at the barn, all three of them leaning on the top rail of the colt pen, and offered him Old Sally Camp.

"Uh, Miss Lewis, I'm not married, and I don't have an intended. Not even the prospect of one." He knew that the cowboy at Old Sally had recently given notice, but Rafe had never expected, as a single man, to be offered a camp job. Those were traditionally reserved for men with wives and families.

Shiney, he remembered, had rolled her eyes. Not too ladylike, he guessed, but sure enough straightforward, something he admired then, and continued to admire all these years later. "I don't think being joined in matrimony is indicative, Rafe, of a man's character or qualifications for doing a job." She did a little sideways grin at him, one of many they shared over the years, and something he looked forward to every time he saw her. Shiney might be a lot of things, he always thought, but she was not dumb.

He'd lived at Old Sally for several years before he met Nell, long enough to convince himself that he was lonely, though he often looked back on those years alone with an odd nostalgia. He'd done pretty well, living at the lower camp during the winter, staying up high on the Bride in the old cabin at Precious Camp most of the summer. His map of the

Tinaja Ranch was a summer one, and all he had to do was close his eyes to see the whole thing from Tip-Off Point. He could close his eyes and look down upon the map of his life. He could see the long ridges that spread like skirts around the Bride, down down down to the lower country where the canyons widened out into wet bottoms and rolling pastures beyond. He could see where headquarters was nestled, though not the actual buildings. He could see the long ribbon of blacktop on the far eastern side, the old Zanders homestead that Punch Lewis had acquired and renamed Farm Camp. Rafe could see down onto the long flat mesa that rose up from Old Sally Camp, the one he rode across to the trail that led up to the Bride's steeper slopes. He looked over to the west side of the ranch where the country was more broken up, rougher, harder to work, and south to where town lay on the other side of the horizon, where in Rafe's mind, the stars and sky ended.

During the winter, Rafe worked in his leather shop, chopped ice and put out block for the cows, trailed up a lion or two. Talked to himself. Talked to his dogs. In the summer, he lived high with the cows, keeping the fences up, riding for long hours in the mountains, coming to the cabin tired and ready for a toddy and a sittin' spell so he could watch the sun go down before lying on top of his bedroll until almost dawn, then doing it all over again. After he got married, he would come down off the mountain most weekends, mainly because he figured it was the right thing to do, riding down of a Friday, back up the old familiar trail of a Monday morning most of the summer.

July 1 — Cows watering early, shading up under the pines. Water dropping out except in the deepest canyons. Saw a zone-tailed hawk today, and his cry made me lonely.

The summer Bride wears pearls, white rock set in deep green blousiness. She carries an ever-changing bouquet that ages with the months, from the honeyed manzanita blooms to the dark black August chokecherries that delight the birds. In summer the mountain's jagged peaks rip holes in the clouds. After one heavy thunderstorm that overflows the creek banks and basins, toadstools of every color push up through the duff beneath her oak trees, crowd into the crevices of rock overhangs, living and dying in puffs with no human eyes to witness their glory. The cicadas screech and saw in her trees while from the edges of nests fledglings stretch their wings and complain that they are not ready to fly. Gophers bring up fresh dirt and laugh into the afternoon.

The Bride in summer is the heavy ponderous mother of all, the benevolent keeper of cows and secrets and seeds and seasons. She knows nothing of tallies, of spreadsheets, of markets. She does not know when she is threatened, taking even the furious thunderstorms as right, as natural, as part of her walk down the aisle. She cradles full and exploding ovaries, multi-colored exhibitions of fertility, and on her slopes calves suck hard at udders, stripping the rich milk.

CAN OF PEACHES

Rafe went through the wire gate into the water lot at the barn without dismounting, taking his time, letting the colt figure things out, going slowly, carefully, keeping the young horse's feet out of the wire, his mind out of the panic. He guessed he was one of the last to still build those wire gates loose enough to open and close one-handed, without getting off his horse. Rafe was also one of the last to check all his waters horseback. Earlier in the year, when the men had gathered on the cookhouse porch, he'd caught a little hell about it, Levi saying that Rafe's riding instead of driving made the rest of them look bad, "And besides, I like to have my tools with me in case there is a problem. Can't do that horseback."

Blake had laughed, "Nah, Levi, you just like your air conditioning like I like my tunes!"

The way Rafe figured it, if he left out at sunrise and was back before midday, then he still had time take the truck and go fix any problems he found along the way. It was just as fast as bumping the whole circle over miles of rough pasture road and kept his pickup in better shape to boot. Besides, some of his waters up in the higher country were impossible to get to in a truck, not like the country that Levi and Chris looked after down in the bottoms.

Rafe enjoyed the added bonus of putting miles on a young horse, giving him time to figure out the whole deal without a bunch of cows to chase.

This little sorrel horse was ready for anything now, he figured. He let him stand, facing away from the barn while he rubbed his neck in appreciation for how well he had done coming through that scary gate. It had been a good summer up on the mountain, and Rafe had spent a lot of time with the colt. Since he had come down to Old Sally for a few weeks, getting this country ready for winter, he'd made several big circles on him, coming to take the colt's good disposition for granted. Rafe was considering handing him over into Monte's string. The sorrel would be one of those that stayed solid, the kind a man could lay off for weeks and he'd be just as gentle when you stepped back on him.

Rafe stripped the saddle and pad in front of the open saddle house door but didn't remove the bridle just yet. He took some extra time to examine the colt's sweaty back and rub some green grainy salve into a two-day-old bite mark on the colt's rump. "Sorry old alligators." About that time, the rest of the Old Sally remuda came charging around the corner of the barn, stirring up a cloud of dirt that enveloped the cowboy and his horse. With what passed as a shout from him, Rafe said, "Get back! Get back!" The colt eyed the rest of the horses warily and then trotted out to join them after the cowboy slid the headstall over his ears.

Rafe gathered his kack up out of the dirt and carried it into the cool interior of the barn. As he latched the door behind him, he said over his shoulder, "Not a bite! Go eat some of that grass out there, you chow-hounds." He turned and pointed his finger at an older bay horse with a head like an ironing board, standing a little apart. "You! Quit chewin' on the young'uns. Mean ol' cuss." Truth be known, Rafe loved the old horse, depended on him, caught him out when he needed a full-on partner, one he didn't have to worry about being there to do the job. Lately, though, he'd been sparing him the hard days. He was getting a little age on him and having a hard time keeping flesh on. Rafe figured he'd find time over the winter to carry him to the vet and get his teeth floated, give him a little boost.

Rafe noted that his wife's car wasn't in front of the house as he stomped the dust off his boots on his way up the back steps. The kitchen and dining room were dim and cool, a note under the sugar bowl on the table.

"Gone to town to make deliveries and have lunch with Kenzie. Call if you think of something. N"

Nell went to town once a week and went to headquarters every Thursday. She tried to be home at noon except on those days. Ranch life was something that hadn't come easy for her in the beginning and Rafe had tried to see things from her point of view when he first moved her and Lance out to Old Sally. Had tried to see how hard it must have been, cooped up with the baby inside that drafty little house they had lived in those first few months before Shiney bought this pre-fab and set it on the new foundation ten feet away from the old one. He still missed the old frame house, the concrete foundation of which showed in a rectangle through the grass.

Secretly, he had thought it would be luxurious to be given license to hang out with Lance, cook good things in the kitchen, fold clothes warm off the line, read all the books you wanted, take a nap with that relaxed little body beside you. But every week, without fail, Nell buckled Lance into his car seat and went off to town for the day, the afternoon, the weekend even. He was glad she had her Avon business, the one she'd started a couple of years after they got married. He figured it gave her something that was all hers, something to keep her busy.

Raised as a charity case without much of a real family, Rafe felt honored to have been able to raise that boy. He guessed he could have been a better provider if he'd gone into some other line of work, but he'd never wanted to do anything but punch cows. He padded his savings every month with money he made in the leather shop, the orders steady now, not sparse as they had been in the beginning years when he made up blanks simply to show so that people would think of him when they needed spur leathers, a belt, a breast collar, or even just a pair of latigos or bridle reins.

When the boy got bigger, Rafe had good memories of working with Lance on what they called "project trailers" that he bought cheap and they refurbished together. They would scrape off the old paint, tear up the rotten floorboards, rewire the lights and brakes, smooth on fresh paint, pull it to town, and put the same old bedraggled "for sale" sign on it . . . if it wasn't already sold. Which it usually was. Last time he came out to the ranch, Lance had mentioned that those were some of his favorite memories, too.

"Dad, I realized that all of those evenings and weekends we spent on horse trailers, it wasn't because you were just hunting up something for us to do together, but because you were showing me that if a guy wants to work, he can make a little money, any time he really wants to try. That's why I am changing jobs right now. Because you showed me that there is always a way. And this job is a good way for me to make money, be happy, plus the company is going to train me in some technical stuff, send me to some different schools. And I like the work I'll be doing."

Rafe washed his hands at the kitchen sink and dried them on the towel from the hook. Lance was a good kid. Kinda skinny. Not sure who he was yet, but he was making his way. He'd have a retirement account someday. Rafe was sure of it. Not that Rafe ever intended to retire. He liked to work too much, and this ranch was more than work to him.

Nell was a good wife, had been a very good mother though she seemed to struggle with this grandmother thing. Rafe had to admit some disappointment in how things had been since Lance got big. He had always thought that when the boy no longer needed his mother's constant care, when he went off to school every day, Nell would show more interest in the ranch, in riding with him, in the day-to-day nuts and bolts of his job. But she had her own stuff, wasn't much interested in horses and cows stepping on her toes. She had never gone up on the Bride with him, said she was scared of bears and lions and missed phone calls about Lance needing her.

Rafe had been alone most of the hours of his life, and he liked it, but sometimes he wondered what it would be like to have a companion, someone to silently take notice when a badger lumbered along the path or an eagle flew overhead or he rode up on a new pair, the calf just beginning to get his feet under him. Rafe thought about how bad his habit of talking to himself was getting and how much fun it would be to bounce his ideas off of someone real. Wondered what it would be like to have someone lift the other end of something heavy, even if it was just an interesting thought. Wondered at having someone to share the miles and the weather. The moons and the seasons.

Nell always wanted him to take trips, go see something besides the Tinaja, relax, but what she didn't understand was that when he saddled up a horse and the pack mule and went up the trail to the high part of the ranch, it was a great trip for him, a vacation. He got to see things no one else ever saw, and he did relax, just him and the dog by the fire, a good book tucked into one of his packs, a can of peaches at dawn, each cold slice fished out with the blade of his pocketknife.

Rafe didn't hate much, but he had to admit to hating holidays, to looking at the calendar in dread. He hated those red and green or picnic-colored squares when everyone expected everyone else not to work, to gather around a tree or an arena or a courthouse square or a full table or a television screen. Rafe hated the blankness of a holiday, the way the hours stretched before him, no jobs, no tasks, no country to see, nothing getting done, and the only acceptable chore was feeding the horses.

Once he tore apart his ranch truck on Christmas Eve, hoping to get a new water pump installed before he had to clean up and be sociable in the house where several of Nell's kin and close friends were gathered. He didn't get plumb finished, so after eating ham on Christmas Day, in mid-afternoon when everyone was playing new games, taking naps, and eating some more even though they weren't hungry, he'd snuck back down to the barn. He'd gotten the water pump bolted in, but he'd also gotten all greasy, and Nell brought it up every holiday since then. Now he tried to stand with a beer in his hand and look out the window, present and accounted for.

Today he stood with the fridge open, pondering. Soon he had spooned a bowl of cottage cheese and made a sandwich out of a piece of leftover chicken fried steak, lots of horseradish smeared on the bread. He poured tea over ice and found his book from beside his chair in the living room. He propped it open with the sugar bowl and the napkin holder, ate his lunch in the quiet.

September 9 — Killed a timber rattler in front of the cabin. Must have been born mad. Wish I could have let him go but he was determined to get under the floor. Shady there. Rode over to Bull Water Canyon today.

LIME AND ICE

Before he came to the Tinaja, Monte Wells had felt like a minor player in his own life. Seemed like someone else was always the star and he was always the supporting cast. He'd felt that way as Matt Wells's son, for sure as Pam Schaffer's husband, but now, as Shiney Lewis's ranch manager, he felt like he'd finally grown up and gotten a real role in life. Maybe he was a late bloomer.

Monte had always done the right thing, the expected thing. He'd spent years in front of a computer or on the phone and many of his days listening to very important people complain about things that were beyond his control. After going to college and marrying his equal in brains and ambition, he'd had a series of jobs with agriculture lending firms where he wilted under the tedium of days and sterile lighting, feeling as if he were a stick figure in some vast charade. In his late 30s he'd decided to get back in touch with real livestock rather than their numbers on paper and had gotten a job running a large horse complex from which a world class reining horse trainer, an equally qualified cutting horse trainer, and a world championship calf roper all ran high-dollar clinics. For a decade he did what he had been doing before, listened to complaints, answered the phone, and punched keys on a keyboard. He'd done a lot of hand-shaking and a lot of head-nodding. He'd acted as liaison between numbers and dirt, opinions and reality. He'd been everyone's friend. His life had been symmetrical, all of the pieces fitting together except for one black fuzzy spot on his heart when he looked down on the arena through the hard clear walls of his office.

At the end of the day, he walked downstairs to the bar with cowhide stools and overpriced liquor. At least there he could smell the cow and horse manure through the open door.

Pam had worked alongside him when she wasn't riding cutting horses herself, and he knew that some of her bitterness was warranted when he walked away from that world of over-trained horses and a bejeweled social whirl, that 20X beaver-felt hat existence. And walk away is exactly what he had done when the black spot got too big. One morning he did not go to work. Instead he walked off into the hills, sat on a boulder all day, and rearranged his life.

The next morning he handed in his resignation and asked his wife out to dinner.

He had leaned across the table, his drink forgotten amidst the debris of the meal, and spoken of a life connected to real things, real animals, real people, real decisions about things that really mattered. About producing something of value. About a life away from where money buys everything and people are measured by their cell phone ringtones. He had rambled on about standing in the sun instead of the shadows, and rather than understanding, he saw disbelief, concern, and faint humor in his wife's eyes. By the time a week had gone by, that look had turned to genuine and concentrated scorn. Even now he felt powerless to turn it back into the affection that he remembered from their earlier years. Maybe it had never been Love, exactly, more like Agreement, as if they had shaken hands at the altar instead of making vows and kissing. Now his marriage was just another part of his life turning black.

One week after Monte quit his job, he drove out to interview with Sunshine Angel Lewis, took a cut in pay so big as to be unimaginable to his wife or any of their friends, and became manager of the Tinaja Ranch. He traded an ordered life that made him drink gallons of Pepto Bismol and too many tequilas every night for one that was real.

He still drank tequila.

In a very short time his philosophy of having switched to a less-stressful job was shot all to hell. For about ten minutes he had been able to hold onto the outdated picture of his own father drinking coffee while reading livestock journals, cussing last week's cow prices, stepping out onto the porch each morning to search the sky for signs of rain, listening to the AM radio as he drove around the ranch, making cow deals on a handshake.

In contrast, Monte drank his first cup of coffee every morning in front of a glowing screen, checking the global news for hints of where oil prices were headed, looking at the stock market to see how light the American consumers' pockets were going to be, throwing darts in the wind trying to figure out if the demand for beef was going up or down. He watched the Doppler radar, clicked on the ten-day forecast as the sun came up.

In his ranch office, he spent even more time in front of a computer, but he found that he liked trying to sort out the tangled books and come up with workable budgets and income projections. He liked stepping back to see the whole big picture of people, animals, and land, and trying to do the best for each of them. He loved the challenge of keeping the ranch operating in the black, figuring out what made money and what didn't. He looked at every expense, followed every lead on doing a better job marketing TJ cattle. In the last few months, he'd done more to move away from being a price taker. The down side was that the numbers haunted him, woke him up in the middle of the night, and sometimes he wondered if he was doing the best for any one of the big factors, especially the people, the ones working for wages at the bottom of the sponge.

On this evening, Monte had the ranch office all to himself. He stood in front of the large laminated map thumbtacked to the wall. Even if he had stood high on the side of the Bride beside Rafe, he would still see this printed map in his head, would not have recognized Rafe's view of the country below their feet, highlighted with histories and people long gone who were yet present in Rafe's memory.

Monte's map was peopled more with worries and dilemmas and the current cast of faces. Monte saw Half-way Camp to the south, Levi and Velma Jo Anderson, with two teenagers, Chad and Haley. Levi was a good hand with a hot temper, a little hard on his horses, but responsible and dependable, a man who worked hard without having to be asked. Monte knew that in spite of his redneck rhetoric and patriotic bumper stickers, Levi was conflicted by Chad's decision to join the Marines after graduation. Velma Jo worked as the school secretary in town and seemed pretty high maintenance for a cowboy's wife, always trying to outrun her old last name of Sisneros or Gonzales or something like that. Monte didn't know her very well.

To the east was Farm Camp, with his newest employees, Chris and Annie Merritt. He'd really only intended to hire Chris, but had been paying Annie day wages on occasion and in some ways she was a better hand than her new husband. Monte knew that right out of high school she'd spent a couple of seasons as the only woman on an outfit in the Ruby Mountains of Nevada. Chris was one of those simple plodding men, already getting a little overweight, the kind of cowboy who was prone to taking a nap on the couch instead of getting right back out there in the afternoon.

In the center of the ranch Monte imagined the hot complicated stew of headquarters: himself and Pam in the house on the hill, Shiney in the Big House, Sam and Sue scurrying like ants in and out of the cook house, and Joe in the bunkhouse.

The far west side of the ranch, West Camp, was home to Blake and Brenna Davis, a big family in a hungry little house. To the north of headquarters, tucked into the lower folds of the Bride, was Old Sally Camp, home for many years to Rafe and Nell Johansen.

The ranch was more than bookkeeping, accounting, and numbers to Monte. Rather, it was people – cowboys and wives and families.

And that fed his one regret . . . his regret that he'd never be just one of the cowboys, never be just a ranch hand living on a cow camp, drawing one new colt a year, coming in at night to a wife who made food that smelled good. A cowboy whose most important numbers were the tallies he kept on how many head were in each of his pastures. He'd shot his own self in the foot because he'd gone to college expressly so he'd never be just a damned old cowboy after hearing his father say, all his life, that cowboying was a "great way to live, but a piss poor way to make a living!"

Monte wore his spurs every day, but he spent more time spurring his chair around the office than riding a horse. Some days the closest he got to being horseback was to walk down to the barn and rope the dummy in front of the saddle house a few times to relax.

As a solace for his regret, he had two things. Shiney Lewis and The View. There wasn't, really, an ugly spot on the whole of the TJs, but as far as Monte Wells was concerned, the foreman's house at headquarters sat in the very best perspective. The front of the house with its lawn and garage and small functional porch looked down on headquarters from the top of a sloped driveway like a pretty woman with her makeup on. But Monte would have traded the whole manicured business of the front lawn for the back deck that faced out over the canyon, looked out west where the sun set, looked out over the rim to where the deer, and occasionally low-browsing elk, came to catch those final rays of day. The tinaja was off to the north.

Nothing man-made impeded The View which both aroused and soothed. It was the *real* Monte had been seeking when he left that glassed-in office in the suburbs. It was this view that Monte had counted on to sway his wife to congeniality after he took the job and possibly to enjoying being his partner once again. He had imagined evenings on that deck, eating, grilling, drinking, talking. But, it hadn't worked out that way. Pam had immediately signed a contract to sell veterinary supplies for a nation-wide firm. She was rarely at the ranch long enough to enjoy The View and rarely sat still long enough to even try. She got a glazed look in her eyes when he tried to talk about the ranch, his worries, his care for the different pieces that made up the whole puzzle. Still, he had The View, and it was fine enough to enjoy alone, any season of the year. It was The View that vanquished the black spot if it ever started graying back into being inside of him.

Tonight Monte switched off his computer after one last look at the forecast, hoping that the 20% chance of rain a week away would grow to 60% or even 80% as the days marched on, as the calendar advanced toward fall. They'd been lucky. The bitter cold winds of spring had turned into a warm summer blanketed with frequent afternoon thunderstorms. Now, a few weeks away from fall works, the calves were fat, and better yet, the cow prices were decent. Just that afternoon, in spite of Shiney's misgivings, Monte had called a contact who had agreed to come out and bid on the calves to be weaned, bypassing the local sale where TJ calves had been sold for years. Monte hoped that by going directly to the feedlot, they'd get five or six cents more for those fat calves. Going this route would also cut out the freight costs, plus yardage and commission at the sale. They might have to hold the weanlings a little longer, beating up a few of the holding traps, but that was a sacrifice he was hoping would pay off.

He liked the ranch office this time of day, all dim and old-fashioned looking without any glowing screens, the way it must have looked when Punch filled up its corners. Monte wished he had known Shiney's Papa. He wished that once in awhile the ghost of Punch would show up for a cup of coffee, sit down and give him some advice, but perhaps it would have been futile. Things had changed so much since the old man's time.

He pulled the heavy door closed behind him. The cook house windows were already lit up, while the Big House windows were still dark. Pam was on the road and would be gone for another two nights. That suited him. He had a phone call to make, and he was looking forward to hearing Liz's voice.

Just before he went inside, he glanced up at the Big House again and saw a single light go on upstairs.

Because they didn't have children, he and Pam had each commandeered one of the extra bedrooms as home offices. Pam often remarked at how cozy it was, both of them working, their desk lamps the only lights on in the house. He never agreed with her, but Pam didn't need anyone to agree with her. She was happy being right, happy and sure with her own ideas, and she rarely asked to hear anyone else's.

She was on the road as much as she was home, selling her products out of a van, flying to conferences, attending fairs where she slung her leather bag over her shoulder and talked about animal health with a confidence and flair that had quickly made her the top saleswoman in the state. Sometimes Monte felt like she used up all the good parts, the energetic parts, the shiny parts of herself, at work, bringing home only the wrung-out, tired shell.

Monte often hesitated to make noise when he was home alone, except for the friendly clink of ice into his glass. Tonight he skipped the beer and sliced a lime on the cutting board to garnish his drink. Tonight was definitely a tequila night. Drink in hand, Monte toed his boots off in the kitchen and padded his way down the hallway to his home office, turned on the shaded desk lamp. His first sip of tequila went down smoothly, but then, it should. It was expensive tequila. The lime and ice just made it friendlier. His desk chair squeaked as he got comfortable and picked up the phone.

"Happy Anniversary."

Liz's laughter at his greeting warmed up his whole evening. "You're horrible! You know I can't talk about this with all these rug rats and the love of my life listening in! Let me retreat . . . ."

He heard her wading through the sea of children, making an excuse to her husband, and finally, shutting the bedroom door. He imagined her in a small oasis of peace, though he knew her well enough to know that not one surface of the master bedroom was free of clutter, that in order to sit down, she'd have to push a pile of clothes off of the bed or chair.

"You are terrible, you know. How many brothers remember such a strange anniversary date?"

He laughed. "Oh, it's the guilt thing. I'll never forget." He asked after his nieces and nephews and let her chatter on and on. He talked to his younger sister, really only eleven months younger, at least once a week, but every year, on this date, he didn't fail to call her unless he was entrenched in fall works, and then he always managed a card mailed the week before.

She was right. Not many brothers remembered the anniversary of when their little sister got her first period, but he'd never forget it. And would probably never fully forgive himself for the prank he had pulled as a youngster. For years, Liz had blamed it on their mother, asking what good mother would have let her son know that her daughter had finally become a woman, but Monte blamed it on his best friend Rusty until he was adult enough to shoulder the true blame himself. After all, he must have divulged the information to start with. He still didn't totally remember whose idea it was to get in the other boy's truck after school instead of riding the bus, make a quick dash to the local market for a huge box of Kotex, the thick cheap kind, and a bottle of ketchup, the thin cheap kind, and hurry to beat the bus out on its rural route. He wished he could remember how in the hell they'd had the guts to go through the check-out line. He did remember squirting ketchup on each pad while Rusty stuck them all over the spines of the cactus garden in front of the foreman's house, right where the school bus would pull up to drop off the rest of the ranch kids.

He would never forget the completely shamed and wrecked look on his sister's face when she stumbled down the steps. He would never forget how she ran into the house and he didn't see her again for two days. He would never forget the horror he felt at his own actions, how he didn't even recognize his own meanness, and how he should have known that she had a crush on Rusty. The joke never seemed funny, ever, from the moment he saw the yellow school bus bouncing over the cattle guard. To this day he hated the smell of ketchup, and never again wanted it to touch his skin after he had cleaned up the mess in the cactus garden, thrown the garbage sack into the burning barrel, and washed his hands at the bathroom sink, the silence from Liz's room the loudest sound he'd ever heard. Even his mom's yelling at him wasn't as loud. Sometimes he wondered if the failures in his personal life, his failure to be the kind of partner who got true intimacy and love in return, hadn't started with his thoughtlessness on that day.

Liz had forgiven him long ago. "So, Pam gone?"

He told her his own news, as little of it as there was. When Liz got all quiet and sisterly, he knew what was coming.

"You and Pam ever going to make me an auntie? You know I'd really like that. You spend way too much time alone, you know. Marriage isn't supposed to be like that."

"Sis, not everyone can live in the kind of chaos you seem to thrive on. I need my peace, and so does Pam. Besides, this ranch is teeming with kiddos."

They chatted a few minutes longer about the ranch, people they knew in common, their parents' health, but he could tell that Liz was becoming distracted by what was slowly building in her own home. "Monte, you know I'd love to talk longer, but Chase needs help with algebra and Mandy is building an igloo out of sugar cubes. I didn't even know they still made sugar cubes, did you? Anyway, she's probably eating more than she's gluing, and Hank is hopeless at dealing with more than one kid at a time. Yeah . . . I love you, too. Don't be lonely! You hear me?"

She was still screeching sister stuff in his ear when he hung up.

The house was brilliant in its silence when the phone beeped off.

Monte took a long swallow of tequila.

COUPLE SETS OF AUGHTS

The oldest building on the Tinaja Ranch was the cabin where Punch Lewis had brought his delicate bride so long ago. Damaris and infant Shiney had lived in it, too, while the Big House was being completed. After that, it became the ranch office, and then, when the long low addition was added, the core cabin became the commissary. The new wing had been both ranch office and post office back when the headquarters had been on the map with its own zip code, something Punch Lewis had been inordinately proud of. In Monte's eyes, the post office was no big loss, but the loss of the commissary in the early 90s when the tax laws changed was a crying shame. At least back then a foreman could be sure that his camp men and their families were eating well even if the shelves had only held the basics, staple groceries with the occasional case of chocolate pudding to sweeten things up. Monte wished he had been there when the commissary shelves still groaned with bags of sugar, flour, cornmeal, rice, and beans, plus cases of canned fruits and vegetables, buckets of honey and lard, and tins of spices and nuts during the holidays. Now the dusty shelves were almost empty, holding only horseshoes, empty burlap sacks, boxes of shoeing nails, rasps, and sometimes a coil of new lariat rope if Monte found a bargain. He felt bad for doling out shoes and nails, but it kept everyone honest, and he sweetened the deal by furnishing rasps.

When Shiney Lewis hired Monte, one of her stated objectives was the modernization of the ranch bookkeeping. Monte had walked into the Tinaja Ranch office to find no computer and row after row, box after box, of binders – green, 16-column pads, filled with neat penciled numbers recording transactions in the same fashion they were recorded in 1929 and before. Some, stored in the commissary, were mouse-chewed and musty. In spite of Shiney looking all furrow-browed and concerned, he had immediately ordered a computer and called a variety of internet providers. He had nightmares about all that was modern and relevant wiping away all that was traditional with a sacred historical precedent.

Maybe not so dramatic as all of that, but Monte had felt it begin the moment he sat down at the ancient old desk, had run his hands across the scarred top. Decades of decisions had been made right there, thousands of entries had been jotted into the green books, and none of them had anything to do with Quicken or Peachtree. The desk didn't care about double journal entries or single. Monte made a silent vow to that desk to erase the old habits without erasing the feel of this place full of history and ghosts.

It had taken him two years. Two years of moving a mountain with a teaspoon, all while trying not to dislodge something precious and beautiful. One of his main hurdles had been adapting software meant for businesses far removed from ranching, modifying it to suit his purposes. Monte finally had the last five years' accounting keyed in, the payroll semi-automated, and his boss using e-mail. The third item had started out complicated. It had been difficult justifying internet access to a woman who still boiled her coffee over a blue flame and refused to own a cell phone, but after the technician had mounted and positioned the small dish on the outside wall, it had been fairly easy. To his surprise, Shiney liked e-mail. Shiney liked convenience. Shiney liked not having to talk on the phone. Shiney liked no hassle and no waste. And Shiney liked Google. Of course, they'd had to buy another computer.

Monte's desk commanded one end of the ranch office, and Shiney had its twin at the other end. They often sat together in the brown leather chairs on the old Navajo chief's blanket that served as a rug by the coffee pot and small sink. She still persisted, though, in sending him e-mails when he was right across the room that now felt like a blend of old and new.

Introducing Shiney to modern communication, changing the bookkeeping from ledgers to Quicken and finding a bank that accepted journal entries had been one thing. Wading through the blinding red mess of the insurance drawers had been quite another. Monte had actually seen red when he realized that there were vehicles still on the policy that the ranch hadn't owned in ten years. He didn't fault Shiney so much as the agent, a squirrely little man who had stammered and stuttered through what had been an interview so uncomfortable that Shiney had fled. In fact, Shiney fled a lot of things the first year Monte was around, and he got the impression she had been fleeing for quite some time. The brush along the path to the tinaja would rustle or the curtain would twitch at a window way up on the second story of the Big House.

Monte had discovered one perk of cleaning out all of those wooden file cabinets when he found the old commissary records. For a week he'd spent his evenings, and his drinks, in the ranch office, carefully turning the crumbling pages of those hand-written records. Never in a hurry to go home. He did his own fleeing.

There was still much work to be done in the record keeping and efficiency departments, but for the most part, he had solved some mysteries and fixed some wasteful drips in the budget. The only thing Shiney had balked at completely was turning payroll over to an outside company.

"Jesus, Monte. I don't have so much arthritis that I can't at least sign a dozen paychecks the first of every month. A few more at Christmas. Besides, there is something about having a boss sign your paycheck, pay you a set dollar amount each month. I like the idea of it, the feel of it, not some big impersonal machine that mails them out come hell or high water. I want to dole out a little *more* come hell or high water. I don't mind all of the other new stuff, but Papa's chairs are staying, and we keep passing out paychecks the old fashioned way."

Monte had to admit that seeing the messy scrawl that meant Sunshine Angel Lewis had picked up her pen a few days before payday had come to mean something to him as well. And he liked the old custom of actually getting to see each employee on the first of the month when they came by the ranch office. Liked being able to hand them their checks, see them face to face.

"The best thing we ever did was take on Sam and Sue."

Shiney looked away from her computer screen and over at her foreman, tall and dark and a little too rugged to be truly handsome. "Yes, I know."

Monte turned toward her from where he had been looking out the window. "I mean it!"

Shiney liked the way Monte talked sometimes, as if he was trying to convince himself of his own thoughts. "Why do you say?"

A chugging noise rattled the glass in the window. "There goes Sam. Off on the backhoe. I told him yesterday that the creek crossing close to that playa was really rough, and there he goes. He is actually going to fix it. And Sue. Damn. That woman can cook. She made chile rellenos for dinner. You should have joined us."

Shiney sorted through the outgoing mail, a pile that continued to get smaller and smaller now that they were "modern," to make sure she had it all and fished in the bottom drawer for the leather purse one of Nesto's boys had made her for her birthday twenty years ago. She took her reading glasses off of her nose and let them hang by the silver chain she'd been forced to wear around her neck after she realized that she was spending the majority of her time searching for them.

"Chiles give me heartburn. I was happy with my lunch. Now, if you will excuse me, I am really and truly going to town." She wasn't actually going all the way into the town but to the wide spot in the road where there was a post office and a gas station. Fifteen minutes earlier the UPS driver had called to say he had left a package at the little country store beside the gas pumps. Monte and Shiney both knew it was the vaccine they had ordered for the mares and that someone had to go get it because last fall the clerk had forgotten to put a similar shipment in the refrigerator case. Shiney and Monte had a running joke about how the UPS truck on the television bounded across the dirt roads of Australia's outback but refused to come down the five miles of gravel road leading to Tinaja headquarters. Nothing about the internet solved the problem of delivery men who didn't want to drive down country roads.

"Did you read that e-mail I forwarded from Greg Mackey?"

Shiney slapped the drawer shut and looked around distractedly for her glasses. "Who?"

"The guy with the conservation group. Mountain Top Preserve or something like that."

"Oh." Shiney touched the silver chain around her neck feeling foolish. "I saw it but didn't read it all the way through. Maybe I will tonight. They probably just want my mountain." She made it to the door, but turned back when Monte said, "Don't forget your phone." She glared at him as she dropped it into her bag.

"Bring me a Kit Kat!" but Shiney didn't answer, just thumped the office door behind her. If Monte'd had to make a wager on whether or not he'd get his candy bar, he'd have called it a toss up.

Monte was pleased, an hour later, when he saw Rafe's ranch rig pull up and park across the lane at the machine shop.

Monte was glad that no one was ever party to his private conversations with Rafe. No one would have believed them. Monte himself was not always sure, when one of them was over, exactly what had been said, or exactly how the line had been carved, but carved it always was. One thing that Monte was beginning to understand was that Rafe spent a lot of time alone, away from technology, input, content, distractions, alone with his own thoughts. And when he came to headquarters for tools or supplies, the way he had this afternoon, he often brought a head full of ideas that had been percolating for days. It didn't do to rush him when he settled into the chair opposite or, as they were wont to do, settled onto the boards of the porch looking off down the way.

Today was no exception. An hour later Monte stood at the window looking at Rafe driving away, at his dust disappearing toward Old Sally Camp, and had to admire what was only genius, the genius of the older man's thoughts about a situation that had been worrying Monte for a while now. When Rafe first got to headquarters, he dropped his stock trailer at the shop to get the center gate welded up by Levi's kid, who, though he was only a senior in high school, was by far the best welder on the ranch. He drove over from Half-way Camp to work on various projects most Sunday afternoons. It was one of Monte's favorite tasks, figuring Chad's paycheck each month, paying him about half what a welder in town would have charged, knowing that the kid was good at what he loved and that the skills he was practicing now would stand him in good stead in the future. And the whole ranch benefited when Chad got creative, using old bits and pieces of metal from the junk pile, plus most of the used horseshoes, to weld up lamps and hat racks and other items that he spray painted black and gave away generously. Monte figured the benefits outweighed the cost of extra welding rod.

Rafe was a slight man, and he walked like a shadow. Once, Monte had watched him move through a pen of steers, and not one of them had looked up from eating alfalfa as he passed. He'd heard his dad describe an old cowboy years ago, saying he was made of "whang leather!" Monte wasn't sure what that meant, but any time he was brought up against the knowledge of Rafe's wiry strength, he thought, "whang leather."

As he came up the steps, Rafe had nodded at the offer of coffee and said, "Need a couple sets of aughts, too, if you got 'em."

When he looked askance at the coffee pot, Monte said, "Decaf."

Rafe grinned as he settled into one of Punch's chairs, "Can't have leaded this late in the day anymore."

When Monte had come to work for the Tinaja, Shiney Lewis said, "Your biggest asset will be Rafe Johansen. He's been here going on thirty years. If he wanted it, I'd give him this job, but he doesn't, and I don't blame him. You'll put in more office days than you will horseback ones, and that wouldn't suit Rafe at all. He's not simple, don't get me wrong. But Rafe is happier up on the Bride and wouldn't want to be saddled with all of the details that go into running an outfit even though he pretty much runs that part of the ranch independent from the rest. I'm not sure he even knows how to turn on a computer and can't help us on that end. But trust me . . . if you want to know something, about the country, about the cows, about weather patterns, about which plants the cows eat, about these horses – or hell – even about me! Rafe is the one you'll want to ask. Rafe is good about knowing people, too."

What Shiney didn't say and what Monte had learned, was that Rafe Johansen was probably Shiney Lewis' oldest and dearest friend.

Sandwiched between the two of them, Monte hadn't felt entirely comfortable for over a year. But he admired the friendship, admired Shiney's decision to bring him in here this way, make him a part of the team. She was right about Rafe. Monte admired the way the old cowboy gave his share of the advice, gave it in such a way that a man could think he had thought up the ideas all on his own, though if Monte picked back over their conversations, he could see how deftly the seeds had been planted. Today was no exception, only Monte hadn't gone to Rafe this time. Rafe had come to him.

"Did you have a good summer, Rafe? I'll bet the mountain looks good what with all of the late rains."

"I got you a surprise. That little Lisa May colt, you know the one. Sorrel with one white foot. Been showing him a lot of country, and I think I'll bring him over here for you if you want him. Maybe after fall works. I call him Jack."

Monte grinned across his cup. "I've got more than I can ride now! But I thank you. Maybe I'll put Bonner into the bunkhouse string if you think that's a good trade."

Rafe nodded, blowing on his coffee though he secretly thought those drip pots never got it hot enough. "West Sally looks good. Lots of tall feed. Sideoats really seeded out. Think I'll pick up ol' number 76 when it's handy. Showing his years, moving pretty slow. I found him off by himself the other day, got whipped off of the spring by that new Braford bull. Oughta ship him before he has to go through a hard winter." Monte agreed and told Rafe that when he got the old bull in the trailer to just haul him on in to the local sale. They discussed the new bulls to be delivered in late fall and how Blake ought to feed them through the winter so they were in prime condition to be scattered out in early spring and how many Rafe thought he'd need with 76's imminent retirement.

"How many are going over to the west side do you reckon?" Rafe asked.

"Hell, I'm not sure. Haven't really gotten a good report from Blake lately on what all he's got over there, on what all he'll need. Or even how the heifers look for that matter."

Both men sat quiet for a bit. Monte refilled his cup just to be sociable.

Blake Davis had been on Monte's mind a lot lately. He had a whole houseful of kids, a round little wife, and he could play the hell out of the guitar and the fiddle and the Jew's harp, really just about any instrument he picked up at a pawnshop, even an old accordion he had jiggled around the other day on the bunkhouse porch. Tall and thin with almost red hair, he'd looked like an almost clown as he'd wrestled with the armful of noise. More of a Howdy Doody than a firecracker. He'd been with the outfit going on six years, a long time for a big outfit cowboy to stay around, especially one as young as he was, but lately, Blake had been doing some bellyaching, some complaining, sounding a note of dissatisfaction. Given his position as not quite one of the hands, Monte hadn't been able to pinpoint exactly what the cowboy was unhappy about.

The truth was, Monte was a little unhappy with Blake as well. High electric bills from that camp, plus the constant expense of keeping Blake's ranch truck repaired kept taking little bites out of the budget. Little bites that added up alarmingly. He was considering a new policy where every ranch hand had to sign the repair tickets on their trucks just so they could see what their occasional carelessness or recklessness was actually costing. Monte couldn't seem to impress on the easy-going cowboy that the well of money wasn't bottomless.

Rafe leaned forward, put his elbows on his knees. "She has you doing double duty, don't she. Foreman and manager? Or is there a difference?"

Monte had a hard time making the shift. "Well, my official title is General Manager, but I guess I fill the slot of foreman as well. Little call for there to be both on an outfit this size."

"Yeah. Yeah." Two yeahs were a lot for Rafe.

"You know, on big outfits, they used to have a manager and a foreman. But sometimes they called him the cow boss or jigger boss or wagon boss. Remember that?" Monte nodded his head and waited for a bit more clue as to Rafe's conversational direction. "Sometimes there was a foreman who couldn't always be out with the wagon the whole time, so he'd designate a straw boss or wagon boss to act when he wasn't around. Lots of titles for boss. Lots of words for someone who leads."

Rafe stopped talking, and the two men sat in silence once more. Monte knew to wait, that Rafe had a point and would get there.

"Sometimes it's good for a man to be singled out, given a little boost in his responsibilities. Makes him take aholt when he wouldn't otherwise. Around here we've no call for another boss atall, but I know one outfit where the big boss designates a drive leader. Just a man to lead the drives when they gather, someone to drop everyone off best he sees fit, someone who knows the country. Someone who's been there long enough to understand the lay of the land. I don't think he gets paid any more than anyone else, or anything."

Monte was getting the picture and already starting to see its merit. "You've been here the longest. Want to be drive leader, Rafe?"

The older man waved his hands in front of his face. "No, no, not me! I'm not interested in all that nonsense." The two men laughed comfortably, both completely sure that they were understood. Rafe got up out of the chair and stretched his back on his way to the little sink to rinse out his cup.

He spoke over his shoulder. "Talked to Delbert Lincoln on the phone the other night. Did you ever know Del?"

Monte shook his head. "No, just heard stories about him. And I think he worked for Dad a time or two."

"He said there's a boy been working for him, Cash Neil's kid, and he might need a job down the road. Thought you and Shiney might hire him. Don't know how Joe likes it here, but wanted to pass on what Del said. Shiney knows Del."

Joe, the single man currently in the TJ bunkhouse, was plenty unhappy, looking to move on, eager to find another place, probably a camp, but Monte just nodded, sure that Rafe already knew the whole situation even though he'd been up on the mountain all summer alone. Monte asked a few questions about the kid as the older man thumbed through the stack of empty burlap sacks on the commissary shelf.

"Goddamned old puke . . . that ol' bay horse tears up more morrals than he's worth."

Now Monte stood at the window watching Rafe's disappearing dust and smiled at a possible solution for Blake's discontent. Now why hadn't he thought of that? He wondered if he could work the electric bill into the conversation as well.

APPLE SLICES

They'd never meant to make a habit of coffee together in the mornings, at least Shiney hadn't. She'd had several foremen through the years and never thought of them when she made breakfast, never added extra pieces of bacon to the pan, never kept an extra coffee mug by the pot. Mama D would rise from her grave and walk if she could see the cheap electric drip machine Shiney and Monte poured from in the office, but here at home Shiney still used the old heavy enamelware pot that sat in a place of honor on the back burner of the cookstove. Shiney enjoyed the ritual of preparing the coffee pot at night, putting a clean half-sheet of paper towel down with two coffee mugs on it, ready for morning. It was Sue who got her started on the little half-sheets. Shiney had always bought the cheapest brand of paper towel until she saw the ones Sue used, the good kind, and perforated so you could just tear off that little half size. What *would* they think of?

Shiney rose early, but rarely made the bed, something that had always made Mama D fuss. Every morning she took a shower, toweled her hair dry fiercely, and dressed in clean clothes. People who wore the same clothes day in and day out were just plain slovenly. Most days she could hear Papa's voice in her head. Those echoes were all Shiney had now.

She put the coffee on at six o'clock each morning, even on weekends. Any later would have made her feel like a slugabed. Maybe this coffee and breakfast thing with Monte had started because she had offered him some one morning when he came by earlier than usual, or perhaps she just hadn't felt like eating her meal and had pushed it across to him. Most mornings now, he ate a piece of toast and two slices of bacon as if he were doing her a favor, as if he were just cleaning up her leftovers like some faithful dog. Not a Lab, though, more like a German shepherd. Sometimes she'd wait to fry her egg until he opened the screen door and took off his hat, and then she'd fry him two. Did her good, maybe, to share a meal with someone.

This morning it was still warm enough to leave the door open, the sounds of the birds filtering through the screen. Shiney set some apple slices out on the table. She knew he'd make polite noises about her not feeding him and then eat every one. Monte had huge hands and she liked to see the younger man lift his coffee mug, swallowing it up in his palms.

"Morning, Shiney." His eyes looked tired.

"Good morning, Monte. Coffee?" She always asked, as if he had just accidentally dropped by.

Monte rested his hat on the long bench that for so many years had held a jumble of hats and gloves and syringes and tools and pieces of baling twine and sometimes a child's toy, always a rope and often a water pump or some other greasy part that Mama D insisted should rest on newspaper. Now it served for Monte's hat each morning, and the rest of the time looked strangely bare. He always sat down at the foot of the table and Shiney sat to his left looking out the open back door. She had been sitting at this spot since the house was built. It was her "always spot."

"Well, Joe quit. Just like we thought he would." Monte sipped his coffee with enough air to help cool it off.

"Last night or this morning?" Shiney sat back in her chair.

"Oh, last night. He came over to the office after you left. I was going to come over and tell you, but I didn't see a light on up here, and I figured this morning was soon enough. Head count down by one . . . ." Monte saluted in the direction of their humorless accountant's office.

At the beginning of the summer, Shiney and Monte had sat in uncomfortable chairs in that office and listened to both the good and the bad news. The good news had been that the man had done what could only be described as a happy dance about Monte's new bookkeeping and computerization of the ranch accounts. Shiney thought it was all six of one/half a dozen of the other, but Monte had gone from manually filing payroll reports and making tax deposits at the local bank, to e-filing reports and drafting the ranch account for tax deposits. The CPA looked like he wanted to hug her big manager for his efforts. The bad news had been the bottom line, operating dollars down and a serious need to "reduce their head count." He didn't mean livestock.

Monte took a bigger gulp of coffee. "Bad time of year to lose someone though. He gave two weeks, but I told him to go whenever he was ready. I'd have him a check. Is that possible?"

"Yes. I'll cipher it out this morning first thing. So what do you want to do about fall works?"

"It's not just works. It's sending someone to help Rafe for a couple of weeks on the mountain, it's an extra driver in a rig, it's a lot of things. And pencil to paper, a full-time employee is still cheaper than day help."

In the fall, they always worked the upper country first, the stuff that broke away from the flats and foothills and rose up into the mountains. That way, the snow could fly early if it wanted to. One of the most efficient things about Rafe was that if Monte would give him some help, just one man, for two weeks prior to bringing the whole crew, Rafe could have most of the cattle moved down out of the mountains and into the lower holding traps. Monte was always amazed at how the remnant was very often standing around the salt blocks at the upper gates, waiting to be let through when the cowboys went to clean out the traps. But now they were faced with no single man at headquarters and the camp men trying to get their own country ready for fall works.

Shiney rose and turned to refill their cups. She had resigned herself years ago to the fact that there would always be personnel issues.

"What about hiring someone for the bunkhouse just until the end of works? Try to make it through the winter empty."

Monte nodded. "Yeah. Been thinking about that. Maybe this time we'll hire someone younger. Rafe was saying that he knew of a kid who was looking for a job. Really young. Like nineteen or so, he thought."

"That might be too young."

Monte grabbed a piece of bacon. "Maybe. Might be just right. Might not think painting pipe corrals is beneath him."

Shiney grinned. "You just don't like to paint, Monte Wells."

Monte's voice was a bit louder and higher pitched than usual, his grin wider, "It just doesn't make sense, boss! We're always going to have to do it again, eventually!"

Shiney stiffened her back and got up from the table again, no excuse really, but she knew that the younger man was flirting with her, and it made her restless. Made her restless that a man twenty years younger, okay, so fifteen, was her friend, not just her employee. She did something meaningless over by the sink with her hands before answering. "Humph."

Monte finished his bacon, wiping his hands on the cloth napkin that Shiney always thought of as "his" now.

"Anyway, thought I'd tell Rafe to see if the kid would at least give me a call. He's living with Delbert Lincoln right now, might could get here in time to go up on the mountain with Rafe in the next couple of weeks."

"Del Lincoln!" Shiney turned back in Monte's direction and laughed. "Why I haven't seen Del in years. Del Lincoln! I swan. He went through several wagons here. So what's Del doing with a kid living with him? He never married so's I knew of."

"Rafe said something about it being Cash Neil's kid."

"Cash Neil's kid." Shiney spoke with more wonder than nostalgia now. "Well, you make that call then. This should be interesting."

Monte grinned at his boss. "The two of us are going to give that accountant a heart attack. I've got to order all of the vaccine today and try to contract for hay for next summer. Don't want to put that off until the brokers price us out of the game. And, I think I'll go over to West Camp, check in with Blake in person. I want to look at the pasture where we are going to put the new bulls." Monte patted the table beside him. "Don't worry! I'll leave plenty of shit for you to do, too."

Shiney sat back down. "This old lady doesn't need help finding stuff to do nowadays, 'specially since you are going to desert me in about three weeks anyhow." She knew that she even sounded old.

Monte leaned back in his chair and swallowed the rest of his coffee. "Who's old? You? Give me a break." He grinned over at her. His eyes were soft, but he slapped his hand down on the table again with his next thought. "Oh! And another thing I've been thinking about. Totally off the subject. How about having the Christmas party over here this year?"

Shiney brushed some toast crumbs from the table into her cupped hand. "We always have it here. What are you talking about?"

"No, I mean here in the Big House. Make it kinda fancy. I am sure Sue and Nell would help you. Do all the hard parts. Don't look at me like that! It's a good idea. It'll help morale."

Shiney snorted a very unladylike snort at this, sounding, if anyone who could remember had been around, an awful lot like Punch Lewis. "Morale, my foot!"

Monte held up his hand. "No, now listen. I've got Blake looking irritable and grouchy, for him, Levi sighing over what Chad is going to decide about the military, Chris and Annie all new and not yet a part of the group. I am trying, oh boss of mine, to create a cohesive unit here. Help me out, and let's invite them up to the Big House. Show them a little bit of history or heritage or something. Anyway, think about it. Don't answer right now."

Again, Shiney had an opportunity to say, "Hmph. You seem to have it all figured out." She got up to dump the crumbs from her palm into the sink. "Pam leave?"

"Yeah. She left early this morning. Four or something. Surprised you didn't hear her drive out. She'll be gone awhile this time. Not only her normal circle, but then she's riding a couple of three-year-olds through the futurity in Fort Worth. I don't remember when she'll be back. Got it on the calendar somewhere."

The rest of the talk was back and forth, weather, horses, brake pads for pickups, medicine doses for weaning calves. When Monte got up to leave, his hand hovered in the air as if to rest on his boss's shoulder, but didn't, quite. The big man turned away, grabbing his hat off of the bench.

"See you in the office." And he was away, the screen door slapping gently behind him.

Shiney sat for a longer time than usual, trying to remember the last time anyone had touched her or she had touched anyone else. Last Christmas, she guessed, when some of Mama D and Nesto's kids had drifted out to say hello and bring too many empanadas and tin cans full of popcorn. Months. The thought of all of that lonely made her shoulders ache.

Shiney stood to start cleaning up the kitchen. Today was Nell's day. She always came on Thursdays to clean. Shiney liked the way Nell did it, no nonsense, no snooping. Shiney had once had a girl who lived in the cook house cleaning for her, and she was always missing something from the pantry afterwards, a tin of smoked oysters, a packet of English water biscuits, something little every time, and she didn't care about the stuff so much as the idea of it all. She didn't like how it made her want to go in and count the bottles of soy sauce, become miserly and weird about her things. Of all the housekeepers they'd had since Mama D died, Nell was the best, the easiest to have around once a week. She just came and did her job and went home. No hanky panky, no long conversations necessary. No fancy shmancy anything. One housekeeper she'd had put these smell-good plug-in things all over the house, and it reeked. Shiney had pulled them out one by one and thrown them into a waste paper basket and put the basket out in the garden shed until the cleaning lady came back. To Shiney, the Big House should always smell of Papa's pipe tobacco. Sometimes she woke in the night to smell it, pungent and fresh, floating up the stairs.

Shiney always cleaned up before Nell got there. No sense in anyone knowing what a slob she really was. Oh, Mama D had known. Mama D sure had. Mama D had known everything about Shiney. Had known about her slovenly ways, had known the shape of her *café au lait* birth mark, had known what size shoe she wore. Had known why it was so hard for her to think about getting married and having babies. "Who am I going to marry, Mama D? Some nice school teacher who comes out to the ranch on weekends or wants me to move to town? Some cowboy out of the bunkhouse who will be boss by default?" Mama D had always clucked and fussed during these discussions, but she didn't argue, just looked sideways at Nesto who smoothed his thick mustache with the back of his hand, first one side and then the other, and shook his head sorrowfully at his coffee cup.

Sometimes at night when the Big House was dark and so still she could hear herself breathe in all of the corners, Shiney wondered about her choice to forego a traditional relationship, children, grandchildren all for her dedication to this piece of land, her love for a mountain in its many seasons, but she always came back around to a life that had been, and still was, full, meaningful, chockfull and running over with love even if it wasn't the Hollywood, romance novel kind. And as far as children went, sometimes she felt like everyone's mother, having so many people looking right up the ladder at her, trusting her to keep them paid, fed, safe.

In some ways, Monte was the first man to be in her life, really in her life, since Papa and Nesto. Christmas party in the Big House. Bah. The things she did for her manager! She'd realized early in the conversation what it was all about as well as the fact that losing the man in the bunk-house was not the only thing making Monte's eyes look tired. That man's personal demons were going to eat him alive if he didn't watch out, and she wished for their demise, hoped that it worked out the way Monte wanted it to. Dammit, but Pam Schaffer was a stupid woman.

Cash Neil's kid. Shiney shook her head in wonder as she rinsed the coffee cups.

PART TWO : THE LAD

MOTEL ROOM BLANKETS

There came a day when Jody Neil no longer wore his dead daddy's hat. The old-fashioned boots had only fit him for about six months right in the middle of his growth spurt in high school. He still put his feet on the Navajo blanket that had been spread beside his bed since he was ten years old, and he still carried the yellow-handled Case pocket knife. He had spent hours honing its edge in Del's saddle house. He drove the old truck with the stock racks and slept in the bedroll tarp patched with his father's clumsy stitches. The Copenhagen can of arrowheads still rested on his bedside table. He'd never seen a photograph of his father, but he still rode Cash Neil's Chester Hyde saddle.

Del had given him the bedroll the week he turned fifteen. Up until then, Jody had been using an old green manty with some blankets rolled up inside, tied with a piggin' string. He felt almost offended when Del dragged something as personal as Cash's bedroll out of the rafters of the barn five whole years after he'd started coming out to the ranch. Five whole years, a piece of his father denied to him. Del's curt explanation of "all things in good time" was coupled with a little sermon about how some things are earned, especially in the cowboy world. He did his usual ramble about how Jody should know that by now, had worked with Del on enough crews around the area to know that you didn't get cut any slack or given any good horses to ride until you proved you were trying, on and on the same things Jody had been hearing for so long, and they only made the teenager irritable.

He was sullen about the whole deal until he unrolled the bed for the first time, smelled what might have been his father, brushed a couple of ancient juniper berries and a pointy leaf of oakbrush off the canvas. He couldn't lie down on it. Instead, he rolled it back up and propped it in the corner of the back bedroom for a few weeks longer. When he unrolled it again, he folded up the greasy sheets and put on a fresh set he'd taken from the Las Lomas linen closet, added a better pillow.

Del poked his head in the room where Jody was contemplating the blankets, one orange and ratty, the other green and pilled. "Cash always took the motel room blankets when we went to town. I think he took that green one the time we went straight from the Rocker B wagon to Frontier Days in Coalville. We'd spent all week wet and freezing our asses off and didn't even bother to roll our beds or teepees. We had to be back to jingle horses on Sunday night, so we just went straight to town, bought new sets of clothes at the feed store and got a motel room. Wore the same clothes all weekend with a fresh shirt for Saturday night. Woooo eeeee, we had a good time! Woke up not feeling so great midday on Sunday. We was loading up the truck, getting ready to head back to the wagon, back to freezing our asses off, and Cash just throws the covers back on that motel room bed and grabs that blanket. We'd paid cash for the room, you see, so he figures no one can do anything about it, and he needs that blanket on his bedroll."

Del left grinning and left Jody grinning, too.

FOR SALE: HAPPY MEAL TOYS

Jody owed a lot to Delbert Lincoln, arguably the ugliest black man who ever lived. Truth was he kept Jody from being the loneliest white boy who ever lived.

Because of Del and a new bike, Jody got a life the summer he was ten, way before most boys really start living. It wasn't anything as prosaic as freedom, the wind in his hair, the friends he made down at the local swimming pool, the chance to be out of the house that the wheels afforded him Friday through Wednesday. Jody's real life started when he accidentally pedaled up onto the big smelly chaos of Thursdays, the parking lots full of muddy ranch trucks, the maze of pens full of animals and shouting men, the quiet street turned thoroughfare by belching blasting cattle trucks. He stood on the fringes of that real life for weeks before he ever went inside the building where the auctioneer shouted and money changed hands. It amazed him to think it had been there all along, every week, his whole life, only six blocks over from his house where on a normal street there were only people and houses and cars, no signs of a cow or horse anywhere.

The sale barn parking lot was full of cowboys – or at least that's how Jody thought of them at first. He figured out later that some were farmers, some were ranchers, some were ranch managers. There were cowboys with jobs, cowboys without jobs, horse traders, cattle buyers, truck drivers, farriers, horse trainers, and craftsmen. From the Thursday he first discovered the crowd of ranch rigs and pens of bawling animals, he rode over every week. He loved how on that one day the whole compound was a large, loud sound and stench – the cacophony an antithesis to his lonely. He went back on a Friday and a Sunday and a Tuesday only to find a few dark-skinned men walking through the empty alleyways and one lady walking to the sole car in the parking lot at the end of the day. It was as if the whole compound were holding its breath, waiting for Thursdays. Things would begin to stir on Tuesdays, and by late afternoon on Wednesdays be prepared for the full roar of Thursdays only to end in the dead silence of Friday mornings.

Jody figured he had been lonely pretty much every day of his life. His mom worked or slept every day of her life, or cleaned. Sometimes she shopped but, when she shopped, she went with her friends to boring places like malls or craft fairs. She always brought back bags of things that smelled like girl stuff and didn't make sense to Jody. After a big shopping trip, his mom rearranged the living room or redecorated the bathroom or cleaned out her closet. He would lug things to the car for her to take to Goodwill or to the garage so she could have one of her garage sales.

But mainly his mom worked. Most times at the hospital, sometimes over at the new nursing home on the edge of town.

He could have turned into a TV zombie or a computer nerd or a bookworm. Instead, like Del said, it turned him into someone who watched. He watched the neighbors come and go and live, watched other kids play, watched houses get torn down, watched houses being built. Watched the brown bird build a brown nest up under the eaves of the house. Even watched his mother's plants grow. And that's what he did the first three or four Thursdays after he discovered the sale barn. He sat on a side street with his new bike between his knees and watched. He might be there still – Del said that sometimes he lacked initiative – he might be there still except for the cattle truck that got a flat and had to be moved onto the side street to wait for the tire fixing truck to come and Jody had to move out of the way. He found himself up on the sidewalk in front of the Tri-Co Livestock Auction and Horse Sale (first Monday of the month). He parked there under a big old shade tree every week after that where he could see people up close, hear what they were saying, see how they were all alike, see how they were all different. The ones he liked the best were the ones who were real cowboys, the ones in tall-topped boots and real cowboy hats, not like the one the preacher wore or the ag teacher or the bank president. Real ones with sweat and dirt on them. Real ones shaped over steam kettles by the men who wore them. Those men told stories and laughed or said serious things in quiet voices. Their language and jokes meant nothing to the skinny blond-headed kid, but he paid attention to which ones smoked, which ones dipped and spit, which ones had boys of their own who came running up and then away again, as if they were on stretchy cords. Jody liked to watch kids with dads. All he knew about his own was that he got sick and died when Jody was a baby.

One Thursday Jody sat under the shade tree all afternoon and watched a group of cowboys on the tailgate of two pickups in the parking lot, trading and smoking and spitting and laughing. He heard one of them asking everyone who walked up about where he might find a job. Another threw a new saddle over the side of the truck and acted like he wasn't proud of it, but Jody could tell that he was.

As the boy eavesdropped there, a thought began to pull at him until the afternoon drew to a close. When he finally started toward Las Lomas, the street where he lived, he pedaled as fast as he could because he only had about half an hour before his mom got home. He slowed down long enough to lean his bike carefully against the front porch, to the side, not so visible from the street, and lock it to the railing. When his mom gave him the bike she lectured him about how if he left it in the driveway and she ran over it, no more bike. If he didn't lock it up tight and someone stole it, no more bike. She was real serious about responsible stuff.

Jody ran into the house and through the kitchen, flipping on the wall switch that lit up the dim garage full of items his mom was selling in the next Saturday garage sale.

It was all very organized. Boxes of neatly folded clothes. Boxes of silk flowers, baskets nested one inside another, framed paintings of more flowers, other pretty stuff. Folding tables that she used to display things. Markers. Tape. Price tags all especially ready for writing on. Sometimes he wondered why she kept buying stuff if she was just going to sell it in the driveway a few months later.

The saddle hung way up in the rafters. Until now, it had never really registered with the boy. It was just there, had always been there, hanging like a dusty shadow, hanging by the horn with a short piece of rope. He had never asked about it. Not in his ten whole years. But now, Jody gazed up and saw it, really saw it, for the first time. Cobwebs swung gently between the stirrups.

Mattie Neil rarely looked closely at her son, just enough to make sure he was alive, wasn't bleeding, wasn't visibly into some sort of mischief. On this night, she didn't notice the gray-brown dirt smeared on his shirt or how many cobwebs were in his hair. She just noted that he was home, asked perfunctorily about his day and whether or not he had finished his chore list, and was relieved to see that the only mess in the house was beside the kitchen sink where he had made one of his numerous peanut butter sandwiches.

"Do you want chicken cordon bleu or hot wings for dinner, Jody?" She poured a Diet Coke over ice and dropped a bag of frozen mixed vegetables on the floor. For the past six months, ever since the hospital board of directors had voted her a raise, she'd thanked them and God for the Schwann's truck. Jody chose hot wings and then scooted to his room until he was called.

He'd need a knife. Yeah, that was it. A knife. He'd climb back up there and saw through the rope. He'd found it impossible to lift the saddle from his precarious perch in the rafters. He lay in bed awake for a long time that night, thinking about the saddle, thinking about a box in the attic that he remembered having a real cowboy hat in it, wishing it wasn't so long until Thursday came 'round again.

By the time the saddle crashed down onto a box of garage sale stuff the next morning, Jody's face was red from exertion and decorated with streaks of dirt, his arm was aching from sawing a steak knife back and forth across the rope, and his knees were sore from hanging on so tight to the rafter. He'd had to climb back down once because he'd chosen the wrong kind of knife. Later on, like in the next few months, he'd learn that it is hard to cut a rope with a slick blade and that a good packer always carries a serrated blade with him, sharp enough to saw through any old rope and keep his livestock and himself safe. Jody had never heard the word *serrated* until Del used it one evening, gesturing with a wicked-looking knife while he cooked dinner. Jody traded his mom's butcher knife for a dinky-looking steak knife, and he dropped it when the rope finally gave way. Mattie found it two weeks later and wondered how in the world it got there, between the boxes.

She never looked up.

The saddle was much heavier than Jody expected, but he finally got it lugged into his bedroom where it lay on the floor, and made him feel like crying. It didn't look cool or useful. It looked like a bug he had pulled the legs off of. Later, after he got to Del's and saw how Del often leaned a saddle up on end, balanced on the horn, he wished he had known how to do that. Instead, the saddle just lay there awkwardly, all splayed out. Jody got a piece of old towel from Mattie's rag box and tried to dust it off. He wasn't sure if water would hurt the leather, but when he used some spit on what he learned later was the cantle, it shone so pretty that he dampened the rag just barely and finished cleaning the whole thing. Later, weeks later, in Del's saddle house, he rubbed almost a whole tin of R. M. Williams into the leather – made it really glow. When the saddle was less dusty, he tried to arrange it in a less forlorn posture, but he sat back on his heels, defeated.

He didn't wonder then who had once owned, once ridden that saddle. Del didn't let him ride it for several years, making him ride some old kid saddle, bought for $45 at the end of the tack sale before a first Monday horse auction. But the saddle, stamped *Ch. Hyde* was never dull again; it always shone with cloth and attention.

The truth was that when he went to the attic to look for the brown-patterned box he had once seen up there, he was only thinking of the hat, not the men's clothes in which the hat lay nestled. Before it was all done though, the whole box was in his room, the stairway to the attic was sunk back up into its hole, and the pull rope had stopped swinging. The box smelled like someone Jody wished he knew.

The hat fell down over his eyes, perched itself on top of his ears. The clothes were too big and the boots flopped around on his feet, but he loved how they sounded on the wood floors his mom had gotten the floor guys to install everywhere except in the bedrooms several months before. Except one of the guys had told Jody that they weren't *real* wood.

The items in that box immediately became a part of Jody's life. An empty leather wallet, a set of keys on a copper ring that looked like an Indian charm, a coffee mug with the Grand Canyon on it, a folded-up scratchy blanket that felt warmer than a normal blanket, but best of all, a pocketknife. It was yellow with a tiny silver plate that said Case. Jody sat cross-legged on his bed, the things all around him, the knife heavy as it slid against his knee. He held a Copenhagen tin in his hand, bits of black snuff still stuck to the waxy inside, and dumped a handful of arrowheads onto the bedspread. A few were just pieces of arrowheads. Some were black and shiny, some were green or pink or brown and translucent, but the most perfect one was white, long and slim, sharp as a knife on the edges. He put the tin down, scrambled off the bed, and stomped his way in the too-big boots into his mother's bedroom. There on her dresser, beside her jewelry box and a vase of fake flowers, was a pink arrowhead, wide across the base and familiar, one he had seen a million times and never thought about. Like the saddle.

Many years later, an older Jody would lie awake in a lonely bunkhouse and wonder about all of the things that a boy who watches can see without really seeing.

Back in his room, starting to get worried about his mom coming home, Jody opened the drawer in his nightstand, the one where he kept every Happy Meal toy he'd ever gotten. The Copenhagen can looked out of place beside a plastic Buzz Lightyear. He got an empty shoe box from the garage and donated all of the toys to the pile for his mom to sell. She always told him that he could sell any of his things in one of her garage sales when he was tired of them, and she gave him real money afterwards, folded over, not flat. Without the toys, the snuff can and the pocketknife and the wallet looked very grown up in his nightstand drawer. On the side of his bed away from the door, he spread the blanket over the carpet, thinking as he did that it would look better on a real wood floor. He put the boots side by side, shoving their toes under the edge of the bed. Everything else he put back in the box, sliding it into his closet among the shoes and Lego sets. He kept biting his lip, looking at the saddle, wishing there was a way to hide that, too. Mattie rarely came into Jody's room, or rarely did more than stick her head in, and he hoped it would be a long time before she did that.

Jody Neil knew his mother would not want him to have these things.

He slid the saddle over to rest on the blanket, as close to the edge of his bed as he could get it and then stood at the door of his room where his mother usually stood. Not too bad. He crossed his fingers, and he crossed his fingers again every time he closed the door to his room religiously for the next several weeks.

Jody didn't wear the hat where his mother could see him, but he wore it every moment that she wasn't home. He wished he had Wranglers or Levis like the men at the sale barn wore. And he wished for a pair of boots that fit.

Shaking Hands with Lemon Pie

The next Thursday, mid-morning, Jody parked his bike beneath the shade tree. He had to tilt his head way back to see out from under the brim of the hat, and he'd had to pedal slowly to keep it from blowing off. The pocketknife bumped heavy against his leg. He'd only been there long enough for his breathing to return to normal when a big black hand closed over the handlebars of the bike. Jody tilted his head back so he could see the man standing there.

"Hey, boy." It was the first time anyone had spoken to him, it felt like, in his whole life.

"Hello." The old black man he'd seen almost every time he'd been to the sale barn looked down with no expression on his face. "You Cash Neil's kid?" In the box of clothes there had been a stamped leather belt with the name Neil tooled across the back. Since Jody's last name was Neil, he guessed he had known all along that the stuff was his dad's, but he hadn't let any of those thoughts come to order in his brain. He was happier when they were all fuzzy.

Cash. His dad's name had been Cash. He'd never known anyone named that before. Didn't even know it *was* a name.

Jody wasn't about to admit, especially a stranger, that he didn't know his own father's name. He squinted up. "I'm Jody Neil." The old man's face broke in two – like before it had been solid still night and then the sun came booming over the hills in one huge gush. That's what Del's smile was like, and it never stopped being a surprise to Jody.

The man stuck his hand out. "Delbert Lincoln." The boy tentatively placed his hand in the huge black one. The smile left Del's face. "That ain't no way to shake a man's hand! Like your hand was a limp old rag or a dead fish! When you shake hands, why SHAKE!" That was the first lesson Delbert Lincoln ever taught Jody Neil, and he never forgot it. From then on his grip was firm, sure, conscious, and he looked men in the eye when he greeted them.

"Boy, how come you never come inside? Let's go watch some calves sell." So Jody stowed his bike up against the side of the sale barn and hurried to follow the man inside.

The building was cool and smelled of animals and ammonia and coffee. As Del led the way up a long concrete staircase, Jody saw a brightly lit, busy office behind glass doors that reminded him of the lobby of a bank with ladies like tellers behind the counter. To his left he saw and heard the jangling door to a café. A café! He registered the social atmosphere inside with a kind of shock. All along the way, men nodded their heads and said, "Del." The old man nodded his own head and said names, too. At the top of the stairs, a man with a gray mustache, a little silver hat, and a cigar held the door open for them as he was coming out the opposite way.

The auction ring had only been an echo to the boy before, one he heard through the opening and closing of the front doors and the big heavy sliding doors around back. Now it was at full roar, the previous sounds and smells magnified and assaulting. Del and Jody stood against the wall at the top of a concrete stadium and looked down on the ring below. A door on the left slid open and crowds of cattle came rushing in as if propelled from behind. They milled around and around, looking for a way out until the door on the right slid open, spilling them back into the sunlight. Jody had no idea what happened in between. During his initiation that day, his baptism into agriculture, the auctioneer's voice was just so much noise, the crowd disconnected from the process. Jody loved the energy that came from the animals, the total male energy of that place.

He stood by Del Lincoln and belonged. He could have come in here at any time, but he hadn't known that, and never would have done so on his own. Del was his ticket into this world, and though Jody didn't know it, to another where he would have to pay some dues, pay a lot of dues. A world where he would fit, though, without even trying.

When Del was ready to leave, they walked back down the steps and out into the waning day. Jody was surprised at how late it had gotten and said quickly, "I gotta go." He was going to have to hurry to beat his mom home. Del shook his hand again and said, "Better." Then he said, "You tell Mattie I said hello, you hear?" He'd pedaled for two blocks before Jody realized that Del meant his mom.

Jody never got around to telling his mom about Del, but he began to live for Thursdays even more than he had before. The next week he rode over to stand breathless under his tree until Del, who'd parked on the other side of the building, stuck his head out the door and said, "Hey, stash your pony and come in, kid!" Jody stood by Del's side in the lobby while he talked and laughed with the other men. They all seemed to like Del, to be friends with him. This time they didn't climb the stairs right away. Instead Del said "You *quiere* a soda, boy? Me, I need some pie." That was how Jody found himself in the café with a tall red plastic tumbler of Coke on the Formica table in front of him while Del ate a huge slice of lemon pie. The meringue was thick with yellow droplets oozing up through obvious pores. Del drank very black, very hot coffee from a white ceramic mug that never got empty because a waitress with an old face and a young laugh kept coming by and pouring more out of a round clear pot. The boy was careful to put his hat upside down on the booth bench just as he saw the men do.

When people stopped by the table, Del would nod and say, "This here is Jody," and the men would nod and say his name, "Jody." That first day, Jody wished he had not turned down the offer of pie and wished he had ordered coffee instead of Coke. He had no way of knowing that his first cup of coffee with Del wasn't very far off.

Del asked all of the questions that day. "How's your mama," which made him feel guilty. "How old are you now?" the answer eliciting a small sigh and a head shake. "Has it been that long?" "You like horses?" "Where does yo' mama work?" "Where'd you get that bike?" "You still live on Las Lomas?"

"Where'd you get that hat?" Jody ducked his head, so he missed the explosion of happy on Del's face when he said, "It was my dad's."

"Hell, I know that! It's how I knowed you was his kid! I'd know that hat anywhere . . . ."

The boy's head came back up immediately. "So you knew him? You knew my dad?"

Del wrapped one hand around his coffee cup. He picked up a napkin with the other and wiped his mouth. He put his fork back on the empty pie plate and pushed it aside. He looked Jody right in the eye in a way that few grownups ever did. "I did. He was my friend."

The boy and the old man met every Thursday. Jody figured out that Del ran a little three hundred cow spread out north of town, that he came to town once a week to run errands for the ranch, buy groceries, and eat lunch at the sale barn. He didn't understand why Del was embarrassed about this fact, as if the coming to town was an indulgence like too much ice cream or sleeping late.

"Silly old man, thinks he has to come to town for some comp'ny when he should stay hisself at home and work. But a man gets to talking to hisself, you know." Jody nodded his head. He talked to himself all of the time.

Del wondered sometimes if the kid understood anything at all, or if perhaps it was the opposite and the kid understood everything there was to know. He was a hard little nut to crack, a quiet pale big-eyed kid who didn't seem to really care about anything, but he showed up every single week without fail, for the rest of the summer, and the two ate not only pie, but lunch together every Thursday.

When school started, things changed. Every Thursday at 3:30 pm Jody would ride home as fast as he could, grab his hat and his knife, and then peddle furiously to the sale barn because Del had started putting off eating lunch until the boy got out of school. He could have saved himself seven blocks total if he had ridden straight over, but then he wouldn't have had the hat. When Del figured out that the hat was too big and blew off if Jody rode too fast, he used an awl out of his toolbox to poke a hole on either side, up close to the crown, and with a string of leather begged off of a saddle maker set up in the parking lot, made him a "stampede string." Jody watched the process in horror until Del said, "Look, kid. Your daddy would have wanted you to wear this hat, but not for it to blow off any time you picked up speed. Cash Neil *liked* speed."

Jody thought it was only fair that if his friend waited until after school every Thursday to eat lunch, so would he. He skipped going into the lunch room and went instead to the playground where he leaned against the bike rack with his stomach growling and thought about sale barn burgers.

And so, a friendship was established between the old cowboy and the lad, one Thursday at a time, and it went along great until Jody committed a felony.

FELONY IN HIS POCKET

Mattie Neil came bursting into her son's room.

"Jody! What in the world happened to my freshly painted wall?" She stopped. Her face paled as she stared at the saddle, no longer looking like a dead bug on the floor, but sitting proud and beautiful astride a wooden sawhorse Jody had found in an alley. Unfortunately, he had scraped the wall as he shoved it along the hallway.

Mattie took Cash Neil's things away. She locked them in the garage, telling her son that he had no right to take things that weren't his. She'd called him sneaky and underhanded, not to be trusted. She said it was time to get rid of those old things anyway. She hadn't found the knife because he had slipped it into his pocket moments before she opened the door to his room. Jody hid it under his pillow where he could sleep with his hands around it, no matter how sneaky. And he carried it in his pocket when he was awake.

For almost a week no one at school realized that the quiet boy had a knife in his pocket. He didn't mean to break any rules, but he didn't have room in his head for caring about what a kid could or couldn't carry onto school property. On Thursday, he headed for Del. He didn't ride home first but pedaled straight to the sale barn, the knife bumping against his thigh as he rode. The hat, the saddle, the boots, the wool blanket, the box of personal items . . . they all had sticky price tags on them.

Del was already seated in the café when the ten year old boy walked in and laid the yellow-handled Case pocket knife on the table with less than a slam, more like a thump. Del looked up from the menu in surprise, peering over new reading glasses purchased at the drugstore a few days before. He always studied the menu even though it hadn't changed in fifteen years. He always ordered one of two things, either a burger and fries or the chicken fried steak platter with mashed potatoes and cream gravy. And always, a side salad with thousand island dressing and several packets of saltine crackers. The familiar cup of coffee steamed in its saucer. The conversation in the café swirled around the table, punctuated by the rhythm of the auctioneer's muffled song as the door opened and closed, and the cow bell smacked against the glass like a tambourine marking time. A red plastic tumbler full of crushed ice and Coke rested at the place opposite the cowboy, a straw in its paper sleeve lying on the table beside it.

Del's looked from the pocket knife to the boy's face. "Where's your hat, boy?"

At those words the boy's eyes and lips bulged, full dams, almost full to bursting. Del looked at him for a long moment before folding his glasses into his shirt pocket, reaching for his own hat propped in the booth beside him, and waving his hand at the passing waitress.

"Cindy, me and the boy have some bizness to tend, but we'll still be wanting our table in a few. And we will bring this back." Del picked up the soda, donned his hat, and guided the stiff boy toward the side door with a strong steadying hand on his shoulder, the only thing that kept the dam from breaking.

By the time they got to Del's truck one tear had escaped, and it ran its lonely way down Jody's face, a single flag of distress. Del ignored it as he lowered the tailgate and sat down. The boy turned around backwards and with a mighty heave of his thin arms, muscled himself up to sit beside his friend, almost blue from holding his breath along with the tears.

"Let me see that knife." Del held out his huge hand with its pale palm. He opened the big blade and tested the edge with his thumb, grunted. In response, Jody finally sucked in a big breath because the tear was lonely no more. His whole face was wet with them, and he turned away from his friend.

Del sat still, looking at a pen full of old shipper bulls awaiting their turn in the ring. Finally, Jody rubbed a sleeve over his face, and reached in his pants pocket for a crumpled piece of newspaper which he shoved at Del. Del spread it out on his knee, placing the knife, still open, on the tailgate beside his thigh. He reached for his glasses again and read the ad aloud.

Garage Sale: 1430 Las Lomas. Clothing, household items, cowboy gear. Everything must go. Early birds welcome and rewarded. Cash only. Handmade saddle, Ch. Hyde, 1990.

Del never saw the value of anger unless he had to get a little mad to get some no-driving bitch of a sulled-up mama cow out of the bushes. But anger grabbed hold of him now, and he had to breathe some long breaths before he could find his way through it.

"Huh. I take it she didn't know you had his things." Jody, done crying, shook his head vigorously. Through the end of his tears, the boy saw his savior coming just in the way that Delbert Lincoln held the clipping, still gazing at it through his new glasses.

"Why don't you tell me what happened . . . all of it."

Jody started talking, softly but more intensely than Del had ever heard him. The speech was loaded with a juvenile litany of injustice that was, in spite of the boyishness of expression, quite legitimate, especially since the old black man (middle aged, really, but old enough to feel old) had come, in a few short weeks, to love the boy, one soda, one cow sale, one hamburger at a time. Del had never had a child, never had much family in his life, never been intimate with a mother other than his own, and she'd died a few years back after getting crankier by the second since she was born.

He sat still and quiet for a long time, it seemed to the boy, after the story was over. Del imagined Mattie's pain when Cash died, leaving her with a baby boy to raise alone. Del imagined her saving some of Cash's things. Del imagined the boy Jody finding those things, hoarding them in his room, wearing his father's hat, carrying the heavy yellow knife, dusting the saddle with spit and tap water, and putting his bare boy feet on the Navajo wool. What Del could not imagine was why Mattie never told Jody about his father, why she took it all away, why she hated the thought of the boy wearing Wranglers instead of those trendy baggy things that Del was sure were in all of the catalogs and stores. Why a mother would take away the only pieces of her son's father that were available, at least as far as she knew. Del knew where there were more.

Jody looked like a wet puppy as he gazed up at the big man. Del snapped the knife closed in one fist. "Reckon I'd better keep this for you, just 'til the ruckus is over, don't you think? Just safekeeping. You'll get it back." Del slid the knife into his own pocket. In that moment, Jody's pocket felt a little less lonely.

"May I?" Del indicated the little scrap of newspaper in his hand.

"Sure." Jody nodded.

Del tucked the ad into his shirt pocket along with the damned reading glasses and looked at the sky, at the pens full of animals, nodded his head at a passerby, and finally said, "I allus get up early, with the birds. Don't you?"

When Jody had been a little boy, only five years old, he'd gone swimming with one of his friends and his friend's father. The father had stood bare-chested in the waist-deep water and thrown the boys in the air, letting them land with huge splashes. His stomach felt like that now, as if it had gotten left behind. Jody had counted his coins and creased dollar bills over and over. Had even imagined getting a loan from a bank. But the idea of Del showing up on Las Lomas Drive on Saturday morning had never entered his mind. His two worlds were about to meet over the top of a Chester Hyde saddle and a beat-up felt hat.

He took a big swig of the soda, swung his legs from his perch on the tailgate, and listened to Del talk about how Mattie wasn't being cruel or mean — insensitive, maybe — not meaning to do anything but protect her child, who she loved, and how memory can be a painful thing and how sights and smells of the past can bring old hurts up fresh and new. Jody Neil let the words flow over him washing away the panic of the last few days, his savior sermonizing while both their stomachs growled.

Soon they were back in the red Naugahyde booth, cheeseburgers and fries on heavy porcelain plates in front of them, fresh coffee in front of Del, a refill in the red cup. Jody put mayonnaise, ketchup, and mustard on his burger, passed his onions across the table as usual, and for the first time did not have to make himself choke down the last four bites of the huge meal. He polished off every one of his fries with salt, pepper, and ketchup, just like Del ate his. There was nothing stuck in his throat anymore.

FLESH AND BLOOD

The sun went down on the little house on Las Lomas Drive where soon the boy would sleep like boys are supposed to sleep. Delbert Lincoln was too old to expect to sleep like a boy, and besides, the heavy yellow Case knife in his hand would keep him awake, or the memories of its previous owner would, or perhaps the ghost of those memories, made flesh and blood ten years before, this sweaty real-life honest-to-bejeezus in-your-face-someone Del had forgotten existed until just a few weeks ago. This boy. This boy who was so much like the friend Del had known before, and lost.

Del wasn't given to analytical thinking, wasn't much given to examining life because, hell, most of the time he was too busy living it. But tonight he held the pocketknife in his hand, thought about the crumb of a story he had heard that afternoon, a crumb of a cake whose baking he had witnessed years before. And in that hearing had been handed a role in the story all because he had recognized the crease and sweat stains on a felt hat. No longer a witness, but a participant, Del wished he were a hard drinking man. Only hard liquor would help him sleep tonight.

Early Birds Welcome

It wasn't until Jody's boyhood began to ripen into manhood that he could look back at that autumn garage sale and the next ten years with any real understanding. And even then he wondered, and would always wonder, what sort of woman his mother really was.

The night before the garage sale Jody slept deeply and soundly, but he redeemed himself by waking up earlier than he ever had on a Saturday morning. His mom already had a cup of coffee in her hand, had already lifted the garage door, and was dragging things out into the dim mild barely-blushing air. She was still mad. Jody trailed along behind her, eating peanut butter toast. He kept chewing and swallowing even after he saw Del's truck parked across the street, two houses down. Del was the earliest of early birds. Jody's mom slid the sawhorse with its burden out onto the driveway, the hat hanging from the saddle horn by the stampede string.

She placed the boots side by side, the price tag dangling in the breeze, and flung the wool blanket over the back of a chair, raising a little puff of dust into the rising sun. Jody found it harder to swallow now that his father's belongings were out in the light where anyone could walk up with cash and buy them, but from the direction of that same sunrise came Del. Mattie shaded her eyes with her arm and squinted up at the big man.

"Miss Mattie. It shore is good to see you this morning."

"Del? Delbert Lincoln!"

"Yeah, Miss Mattie. It's me. You didn't think you could put that Hyde saddle in the paper without me seeing it, now did you?" Del had a smile on his face, but not in his voice.

Jody had never seen his mom nervous, had never seen her stutter or stammer. "Well, now, Del, I didn't really think about it. It was just gathering dust and taking up space, and well, you know . . . ."

Del pulled out a big wad of bills. "How much for his things?"

Mattie turned her back on the now bright sun and Del came around to stand beside her. "I haven't added it up, but I was asking five hundred for the saddle."

Del pulled some bills off of the roll and handed them to her. "I reckon six will buy me all of Cash's things, then, don't you?" He walked over to the saddle and picked up the battered gray felt that hung from the saddle horn. He turned to Jody and put it on his head.

Only then did he nod at the boy. "Jody."

Mattie got stiff and still. "You two know each other." It wasn't a question.

Del finally grinned for real. "We do."

"I see." Since Jody knew Mattie much better than Del did, he knew that there was a world of meaning behind that "I see."

Del and Mattie sat on either side of the kitchen table with cups of coffee in their hands. Del didn't really consider it coffee after he tasted his, more like hot colored water.

"Jody's a good kid."

Mattie's mouth got hard and tight. "Del, you don't have to tell me about my son. Just like you didn't ever have to tell me that my husband was a thief."

Del leaned back in his chair and sighed. Was the whole conversation going to be this hard? "Cash was a damned good hand, Mattie. Was a good man. Would have made a good husband and father if he had gotten the chance. He was a good friend, too."

Del had forgotten how angry Mattie could get. She didn't look like the young woman she had been back when Cash Neil was doing everything he knew to please her. The lines around her eyes would have been a sexy addition, but the bitterness around her mouth rendered her nondescript.

"Good? He got shot, Del, shot by someone he was stealing from. Shot because he was dishonest. He left me with a kid to raise."

"And a house."

She stood up and slapped her hand hard against the table. "Don't you tell me about this house! All Cash Neil did was plant a baby inside me and make a down payment . . . with money that wasn't his! Don't you tell me about a house that I have made payments on every month since then, payments I work my ass off to make with an education I worked my ass off to get. Don't, Del. Don't come in here and pretend to know anything about my life. I told you to stay away then, and I don't believe I have issued an invitation back." There was an almost musical rhythm to Mattie Neil's speech that made Del wonder if she had given it to herself over and over and over for the last ten years.

"I just want to spend time with the boy. That's all." Del stood up, his hat in his hand. "Why'd you keep his things, Mattie, if he was all bad?"

The kitchen was silent as the two stood mired in sepia-toned memories of the same man, or maybe it was two different men. Mattie had spent whole nights with him, not sleeping, had made a whole new person with him. Del had spent days and weeks with him, working and laughing and sharing beers, jobs, stories. And outside on the lawn, wearing a hat stained with sweat containing DNA that floated in his own blood, was the boy who had no knowledge of the man who had sweated, the man both adults had loved.

"Sit back down, Delbert Lincoln. You are welcome in this house." Mattie turned her back and stood at the sink, not staring out at the perfect fall morning but gazing at a daddy longlegs spider that had drowned and now rested crumpled in the sink trap.

"Mattie, I am going to ask you a personal question. Not pretending to know anything about your life. How long has it been since you went on a date, since you thought of anything besides work? Or since you went out for a drink with anyone besides your girlfriends?" Del's voice was soft and gentle, the one he used for young horses.

She turned back, the smallest of smiles allowing him to see the beautiful girl she had been a decade ago. "You asking me out, Del?"

"You know I'm not. I's just saying. There's bound to be more men in this town than an old black man – who's beautiful, I *know* – but too old for you. Why don't you let Jody come out to the ranch some weekends, spend some time doing man things, learning things, and you stop working so hard and have a little fun?"

Mattie Neil had a garage sale to run.

It was late that night, before the disk of moon finally came up, that Mattie allowed the tears she had been holding all day to fall, tears she had held back that morning while she agreed to the odd friendship between Delbert Lincoln and her son.

Cash Neil. That name, that man, had caused her nothing but pain, and she usually avoided thinking about that closed off portion of her life. Most of what she remembered from those days was a heavy dragging weight even after she no longer carried the child inside her and a nagging anxiety whenever Cash Neil was out of her sight.

She had met Cash at the grocery store, not somewhere glamorous like a rodeo or a bar. Instead she had met him at her job bagging groceries. The little blue-haired lady in line in front of him had been carefully sorting out coupons, and Mattie had rolled her eyes at him in apology for the delay. All he had in his cart were beer, snuff, and a bag of Fritos. No one needs a bagger for a roll of snuff and a case of beer, so Cash grabbed a handful of candy bars from the display case and threw them on the conveyor belt. She'd stayed, the conscientious little employee, and put them all in a plastic sack. He'd winked at her. The next time he came in, he'd asked her out, a fact she found strange since he'd only ever seen her in her blue apron at the store.

At the time, Mattie was already enrolled in nursing school. She had sworn off of men the moment she walked across the stage with her high school diploma in hand. All her life she'd been watching small town girls who never left the small town, never achieved their dreams, never saw anything of the world, all because they were having some cowboy's baby. Or maybe he was a truck driver or a gin worker or a miner or a diesel mechanic or one of those guys driving the heavy equipment out on the highway job. But it was the same story. Pregnant, married and mopping floors, broke and bored, long before any dreams had a chance to come true.

It was Cash Neil who wasn't the same. He was the new story. He was perfect. He was beautiful. His laugh made other people laugh, even if they didn't know why. Everyone wanted to know him. Everyone loved him. He promised Mattie everything, gave her a pink arrowhead with a blush just as pink and a lot of dreams that seemed to match her own. Cash could do many things well, but he was best at dreaming. One night they lay on top of his canvas bedroll in the back of his truck and looked up at the stars while he told her how he was only cowboying to get a start, intended to own his own horse training facility someday, intended to build his own house, intended never to look at the ass end of a cow again unless it was in the cutting or reining pen. Cash Neil intended to *be* someone.

A week later she slept with him.

For her, nothing was the same after that. His big dreams seemed to evaporate into the stars he had been speaking to, but his words had taken root in her mind, grown at a pace much faster than they seemed to in his, just as his seed had taken root in her body after it left his. He kept right on drinking with his buddies, right on working on the big ranches, right on driving too fast. It was when she found out she was pregnant, when she started throwing what had only been little seeds of dreams back to him as full grown plans with the potential to bear fruit through much work that things had gone wrong.

Things had gone so wrong. Mattie figured out that Cash had never intended to do any of the work to make all of those dreams come true. They had a justice of the peace wedding, but Cash Neil still slept at the ranch most nights rather than in Mattie's mom's house in the bedroom where her senior year homecoming corsage hung on the wall. When he did come to town, he was so damned quiet, so tired looking. After Mattie showed him the fixer-upper house on Las Lomas, he stayed gone for almost three weeks. When he did come back, he was flying high. Like a whirlwind, he dragged her to the bank, put a down payment on the little house, and took her out to eat, insisting that she order shrimp, the most expensive thing on the steakhouse menu. He threw a few more dreams around, but they sounded forced and hollow. Cash Neil had changed.

Jody was born a few short months later, but the father, out on the Daniels Ranch wagon, missed all of the action. He spent a week that Christmas with them, holding Jody like a football in the crook of his arm, rocking back and forth in his high-heeled boots, looking like he had finally found something he had been missing, but then he was gone again, leaving her to wonder when he'd be back.

Cash Neil never came back.

Now Mattie wondered if her son would disappear into the same void and wondered what kind of mother she really was when she thought of weekends alone with a kind of relief. The deal with Del had been brokered simply with, "No horses, Del. Keep Jody away from the horses," and the understanding that all of Cash Neil's belongings stay out at the ranch. Except the hat. There had been some negotiation, and Jody got to keep the hat.

FRIED EGGS AND FRIED POTATOES

Someone once said that teenagers don't really care what adults do as long as it doesn't intrude upon their own lives, as long as it isn't a hassle for them. So when Jody's mom started dating, the truth was, he barely noticed. From the day of the garage sale on, he spent over half of his time when he was not in school out at the ranch. Sometimes Del picked him up on Fridays, his dusty truck an incongruous addition to the shiny SUVs parked on the street by the crosswalk. Sometimes Mattie drove him out north of town to the small gray mailbox beside the shallow cattle guard where Del waited. Mattie never drove on down that dirt road to Del's camp, not ever, which made the little cluster of buildings – house, hay barn, saddle shed, chicken coop, boxcar full of feed – feel as if it belonged to Jody, a private place for his own joyous growing up.

The first weekend that Jody spent at Del's he felt out of place. He had never been in a house where no woman lived. Everything was clean and plain and useful. There were no silk flowers, no carpeting besides some woven horse blankets on the old cracked tiles, no knick-knacks except some faded Charlie Russell and Will James calendar prints on the walls. In the bathroom a propane heater burned from early fall until late spring, making it a sweltering place to be, sometimes a comfortable swelter. The heat didn't keep Jody from spending some of his time in there after he discovered that the magazines stacked on the floor beside the toilet were all either *Playboys* or *Western Horseman*.

One of Del's favorite things to do was to say, at odd times in the middle of the day when he and the boy were working, "God bless February!" or insert some other month, especially when Miss Whatever happened to be a woman of dusky color. Or one with a tattoo. Del liked the women with tattoos. Jody just liked the women.

That first evening, Del made fried eggs and fried potatoes with cream gravy from a package and poured Jody a glass of the sweetest iced tea he had ever tasted. It was Del's favorite and most frequent meal and one the boy came to adore as much as the old man did. Del also cooked canned biscuits with sausage gravy some nights, or hamburger patties with a side of canned corn or canned green beans swimming in butter, or sometimes a steak and baked potato, a meal that made the evening feel like a party. Del bought pimento cheese spread in large plastic tubs, and he ate it on white bread with Lay's potato chips in the middle of the day. And sweet pickles. Del loved sweet pickles.

Del teased Jody about being a scared little rabbit, sneaking around door frames and being careful not to breathe, but that was only the first weekend. It didn't take Jody long to discover that he loved being at the ranch. He loved climbing the haystack under the creaky shed that sounded like a marching band in the wind. He loved feeding chickens, gathering eggs, pounding nails, the smell of horses, the mean old black cat with a crooked tail and one missing ear. He loved that Del swept the saddle house every evening as soon as he had poured out grain for the horses, hollering out the open door at the ones who insisted on fighting instead of eating peacefully out of the bunks they'd been assigned, the chickens dodging beneath their feet pecking at stray grains. He loved the heavy feel of tools in his hands and showering after a long day, going into the kitchen with wet hair to where Del was making dinner. He loved dog paddling in the concrete reservoir in the summer, feeding the wood-burning stove in the winter after he learned to split wood with the maul out by the woodpile.

That first weekend, Jody slept on the couch in the living room, wrapped in a blanket that smelled faintly like the propane heater in the bathroom, but the next time he came out, Del had moved some things out of the back bedroom, set up an old iron twin bedstead, put new sheets on it, and spread the freshly-aired wool blanket across it. That was Jody's room from then on. Sometimes at night Jody would wake to the smell of cigarette smoke. Del said that old men had trouble sleeping and a cigarette helped ease his bones. Jody loved that not quite awake feeling, the knowledge that he wasn't alone.

Del broke his word to Mattie early on. There was no keeping Jody from the horses. He didn't just like how they smelled. He loved how they had a pecking order. He loved how their eyelashes looked. He loved how they sounded as they ate. He loved how they rolled in the dirt, their feet flailing at the sky.

Besides, after a few weekends of hanging around headquarters, it made sense to see more of the ranch. On a horse. And pretty soon it made sense that if they were on a horse, they might as well check on some cows or ride some fence. Jody fit into the life without trying.

One night as Del lay in bed smoking his lonely cigarette, he realized that he wanted to teach Jody everything he knew, pass along everything he had learned about cowboying and about life to this boy who was like a dry sponge. It wasn't long before the weekdays seemed longer and lonelier than they ever had before, for both of them.

Jody never forgot the first time he and Del camped at Screw Worm Trap #27. Jody had dreamed of the day when he would get to be part of packing in to the farther country, sleeping on the ground, had lived it in his mind many times long before it was a reality. Getting up before dawn. Packing the old solitary mule. Saddling up and riding out as the sky turned pink. Del cobbled him together a bedroll out of a green manty and some blankets, and the boy's heart pounded hard under his shirt for the whole six mile ride to camp. He was finally doing things, real things, things other boys just dreamed about.

That night after the campfire had simmered down to a glow, after they had eaten chili out of a can with rolled up tortillas to wipe their bowls clean, they moved the sticks and rocks from the ground and rolled their beds out. Jody was startled when the old man stripped naked right there in the big night. Del laughed loud and long at the look on his face. "Don't be scared, boy! An old black man don't have nothing to do with a scrawny little white boy like you! You're safe! Now get yourself in bed!"

As they lay there under the stars, Jody felt like a king. That was the last time the boy went to bed with his clothes on, always thereafter stripping down naked and proud, just like Del. He did a lot of things, in his lifetime, just like Del.

Those were the years when Jody not only watched, but learned to pay attention. He was finally getting his hands dirty. He liked learning to move cows. Liked learning how to rope, spending hours with Del swinging and throwing at the dummy, learning to rebuild his loop fluid and steady. Jody liked the way Del talked about shoeing horses and teaching a colt a thing or two. What surprised Del the most was how much Jody liked building or fixing fence. Jody loved the task for one secret reason — because when the two of them were moving along a stretch of fence, tying in stays or setting new posts, fixing a water gap washed away by the rain, Del talked, told stories, and Jody always steered him to talk about Cash.

To hear Del tell it, back when he and Cash were partners, the cows were wilder, the horses were wilder, the land was wilder, the women were wilder and more beautiful. The dogs were meaner and tougher. The winters were colder, the summers hotter, the days longer, the nights lonelier. And Cash Neil had made it all fun. He had made everyone laugh. He could ride anything with hair on it and catch anything in his rope. Del liked to tell Jody about Cash as much as the boy loved to hear it.

Sometimes, Delbert Lincoln felt like all he'd ever done was watch Jody Neil grow up, like all he was ever meant to do was be here, alive, for this boy, at this time. The only problem was, he had no idea how to tell the kid the truth, and so he didn't. He just watched that boy eat, and grow, and learn, and work, and look more and more like his dad every day, except Jody's good looks were softer, less movie star, more "trust me, I am good." Del was glad. The way he saw it, sometimes too much beauty in a person upsets something on their insides. Perhaps looking in the mirror is so fine that what happens away from the glass isn't so important to them. Del, with all of his ugliness, didn't know how it was personally, but he knew from watching that sometimes beauty hurts a person.

Del couldn't bring himself to tell Jody the story of Cash's end – so he told him everything else. Del told the truth.

"There was only one thing your pa complained about and that was the wages the outfits paid cowboys. Your daddy thought it was criminal for the money-men to expect a man to work as hard as a puncher did and then be grateful for little more than a bed and grub and a mount. He always said, 'None of these outfits pays worth a shit,' and you know, I guess he was right. He was always dreaming, your pa. Always dreaming of something bigger. And he'd a got it, too. He'd a got it, too."

Del's voice would trail away and then pick back up.

"Your daddy could shoot a gun, ride a horse, drive a truck, rope a steer, train a dog, court a woman better than any man I've ever known. And find an arrowhead, wooo eeee! He could just *sense* an arrowhead was around, and he'd go to looking. We was allus having a contest, who could find the first arrowhead. The man who got off his horse to look at a piece o' flint that wasn't a point had to buy a case of beer. The man who got off his horse to pick up a honest to Gawd ar-T-fact, well, everyone had to buy *him* a case of beer. Good thing your pa was generous, 'cause if he'd hogged alla that beer, he'd have been a drunk mother-fucker!" Del cussed around Jody from the moment they drove over the cattle guard onto the ranch and then stopped the minute they crossed it going the other way. He held Jody to the same standard.

"And if your pa had kept every arrowhead he found, why, you'd have a valuable collection, fit for a museum! But did he? Hell no! He was always giving 'em away to the pretty girls. And the ugly ones. Your pa liked them all, even the little blue-haired ladies that cooked at the café!"

This made Jody think of the pink arrowhead on his mama's dresser. And wonder how many women had Cash Neil memories scattered amongst their girl stuff.

When he showed Del the snuff can, Del got awful quiet and said, "Take care of 'em, boy. Them are little pieces of treasure from your pa."

And Jody did. He took care with every piece of Cash he could find.

The biggest treasure had been the truck. The already-old-fashioned-when-he-was-born truck parked out under the shed on the south end of the barn. A '56 Chevy with stock racks that Jody ignored or didn't see for a few years, but that Del gave him when he turned sixteen.

"I start it every week, and I've kept the dry rot and mice out of it. It's yours now, kid. I'm tired of being responsible. It was old when your daddy was alive, and it's way older now."

Jody had driven it home from Del's after he got his driver's license, and his mother had pursed her lips and turned away from the sight of it.

Mattie often felt that when Delbert Lincoln bought Cash's saddle, he also bought her son. It wasn't true, of course, but sometimes it felt that way. Mattie didn't agree with her son on the subject of college or the old truck that held so many memories he would never share, but there was one thing both Mattie and Jody agreed firmly on after Jody got old enough to become aware of the starve-to-death wages Del was living on. He went straight to his mother, just a twelve-year-old boy in a too-big nasty hat, and explained how Del always had things that Jody liked on hand — sodas, boxed mac and cheese, breakfast cereal. He told his mom how he was worried that the old cowboy spent every extra penny he had on luxury things for the boy, like a sale barn kids saddle, the extra hamburger from week to week, and how much it must have cost him in savings to have bought the Hyde saddle. It was one of the only times that Jody could remember when it felt like Mattie Neil truly listened to him. After that and from then on, his duffle bag was heavier going out to Del's. For one thing, he took food that he stopped to unpack into Del's pantry first thing. For another, he always had some folding cash that he gave to Del when they ate at the sale barn. At first Del blustered and fussed, but in this matter, he was no match for Mattie Neil. She laid it out firmly, explained in definite terms that if she did nothing else in her life, she was going to feed her own kid. And one afternoon, when Del came by the house to get Jody, she gave him $600 in a white envelope, buying back Cash Neil's belongings for her boy. The three of them never talked about money again.

But the beer, well, that was between Jody and Del. The first time he and Del gathered a good-sized group of cows by themselves, branded all of the calves and sorted off the shippers, Del offered Jody a barely cool beer while they watched the cows pair back up with their babies over flakes of alfalfa. Just offered it to him without explanation or preamble. Jody was fourteen. Of course later Del said he would pull Jody's pecker off if he told his mom.

"When a man does a man's job, he deserves a little something." That was what Del said about the beer. The sun went down. The men walked to the house. The fried eggs and fried potatoes spilled their scent out into the night.

THE OLD BROAD

Jody leaned over the low fence of the dog pen and watched the puppies play. They were just cow dog puppies. No fancy pedigrees or abilities. They were the accident of a weekend when the cowboys weren't thinking of anything but drinking beer and swapping plunder. Somebody's bitch in heat got with someone's, evidently, blue heeler male, and now the bitch lay panting in the early autumn afternoon surrounded by a betrayal of her six weeks earlier travails. No longer were they cute and squirming, all eye slits and fat bellies. Now they were bundles of too much hair, needle teeth, and enough energy to sap the strength of six mamas. She was tired of them. They either bit, growled, tumbled, and chewed on her lips and ears, or they sucked her dry and lay in stupefied sleeping piles, attracting flies and ticks. In fact, Jody realized that if he picked out a puppy, he'd have to de-tick her immediately. Wouldn't do to go to his new job with a tick and flea infested partner riding on the seat beside him.

One little girl pup bit her brother on the nose when he tried to take her spot in the sun. Lifted her little lips and growled at him. When she settled back in to sleep, she yawned wide. Her mouth was solid black on the inside.

Later, with the now fully awake pup under his arm, Jody walked over to where the bitch's owner and Del were finishing up their smokes. Jody had never taken up the habit, mainly because Del had warned him almost daily how horrible it was, and also because he listened to Del cough hard when they were doing something strenuous, had been listening to it since he was ten years old. Del never offered him a smoke, and Jody knew he never would.

Jody and Del got in the truck, headed for home, tired horses in the trailer behind. Del sometimes got day work for the two of them on neighboring ranches since the little outfit he ran didn't keep them busy all the time. It was good for both their bank accounts since Jody was careful not to turn in too many days for pay to Del's boss. Didn't want to abuse the hospitality. The pup was heavy on Jody's lap, whining in protest, watching Del out of big eyes. She must have sensed he was grouchy.

"You don't need no pup. Just be a hassle – weigh you down. Eat a hole in a man's pay." Del had already given Jody several speeches about job hunting and living on single man wages. Jody had been out of high school for over a year, living primarily with Del, day working around. He'd grown into a tall, slender, fair-haired man with long tapering fingers like his father's and the same inability to grow a decent mustache. Mattie had a full-time boyfriend now and had put the Las Lomas house on the market, planning on moving soon, closing the door on this chapter of her life. Jody had known for some time that he had to leave Del; both of them knew the younger man needed a full-time gig. About halfway home Jody broke the crusty silence.

"Thought I'd tell you. I called on that TJs deal last night, the one you said Rafe Johansen told you about." Del stared down the highway, a little more hunched over the steering wheel than he had been a year before. "Hmph." Jody let the silence crust back over, but pretty soon, Del's face softened, and he said to the windshield, "Shiney Lewis. A fine lady."

"Nah, I didn't talk to the old broad. I talked to Monte Wells."

Del slowly turned his head, all softness gone. "Shiney Lewis ain't old. And never refer to her as a broad again. Your balls ain't been dropped long enough to saddle that *lady's* horse, you hear me?"

Jody nodded. He didn't care if Del was mad as long as Del was talking. "Sorry."

Del looked back at the highway until he turned off onto the dirt road. "Now Monte Wells. That would be Matt Wells's kid, I reckon. Knew Matt when he was running the Aught Eight. Good cowman. Not a cowpuncher, mind you, but a good boss. Knew when to get out of the way. Knew when to get outta his own way, too. That's the mark of a good cowman. What's Monte sound like? I know Rafe speaks highly of him."

"Smart. Busy. Nice enough, I guess. He said call back in a couple of days and he'd tell me when to show up."

"Headquarters deal?"

"Yessir. Bunkhouse. But with a cook, too."

"Well, a man can get used to that. What about horses? They got plenty?"

"Yeah. Said they'd mount me. And I can bring the pup. I already asked." Jody rubbed a soft ear gently between his thumb and forefinger. The little girl snored, her sleeping form heavier on his lap than her awakeness had been.

Del snorted. "They pay worth a shit?"

Jody grinned over at Del. "Nossir. They don't pay worth a shit."

Anyone observing the two would have been startled at how similar their smiles were.

PART THREE : FROM THE WINDOW SEAT

At the "Cheat Yourself"

Brenna Davis put her hands on the steering wheel and sat very still. Cars came and left from the parking spaces around her. People pumped gas, bought sodas and chips, left again. Only Brenna sat very, very still. She had parked her truck after getting gas, gone in to pay, and bought some Junior Mints with the private joy of knowing she wasn't going to have to share them. They lay on the console unopened. Having all four children in school this year meant that Brenna could do a lot of little things like buy a candy bar, walk through a gift shop, take a nap in the middle of the afternoon, eat a handful of crackers for lunch when Blake was eating at headquarters, watch an R rated movie while she ironed everyone's church clothes or folded laundry.

Today, because of the sign in front of her truck on the wall of the building, Brenna had gone back inside the store. The steel building was built a couple of years before when several downtown merchants decided that rather than see their clientele continue to dwindle, they'd close up their main street windows and move out here to the intersection of the two major highways through town. They all paid one light bill. The businesses converged into a convenience store/gas station, what Blake always called a "Cheat Yourself," plus a gift shop, pizza joint/deli with an ice cream counter (twelve flavors – the kids had counted), a jewelry store, and a pharmacy. Brenna thought the long elegant jewelry cases with their hidden light bulbs looked odd under the same roof with the racks of shapeless cowboy hats, "I ♥ the West" t-shirts, and Shell Oil travel mugs. At the beginning there had been a selection of fabric and household items before the owner of the previously Olsen's Dry Goods had put everything on clearance and started a more profitable movie rental business in his section.

The sign in front of Brenna's truck read: Two Brothers Pizza $1/slice. The idea of digging in the coffee can full of change in the console and having one slice of greasy cheesy pizza had made her stomach move in anticipation. She was digging for elusive quarters when she remembered how much she had craved pizza when she was preggers with Bradley.

And that thought had lead to a profound gratefulness that her current birth control method seemed to be working, something that hadn't always been the case since some of the hormone-laden ones made her violently ill.

And that lead her to wonder where the hell her period was and do a mental check of the number of tampons under the bathroom sink at home, since she was close to a store . . . .

And that had led to her drag out her checkbook and look at the calendar.

Shit. Two weeks. Her period was two weeks late.

She tentatively touched her breasts. Sore. Swollen. Achy.

She checked out the second time in the back of the store at the pharmacy register, wishing that the pharmacist wasn't a member of her father's church, but she didn't feel like driving to the huge Walmart on the outskirts of the city thirty miles away. Besides, she was already spending nine extra dollars from a budget that was sensitive to every ripple, and she didn't need to add more gas money to that. Once back in the truck, she had removed the wrapping from the stick with its clever absorbent tip and cutesy little window, stuffed all of the paper and cardboard into the sack along with the receipt. Brenna didn't bother to read the instructions. She put the stick in her purse, dropped the garbage in the can on her way back through the front doors, and waved breezily at the clerk who had sold her the Junior Mints. She peed on the stick in a stall in the bathroom at the back of the store, replaced the cap over the absorbent tip without looking at the window, and shoved the stick back into her purse. The instructions about laying it undisturbed on a flat surface for five minutes be damned. She'd never once peed on a stick that turned out negative. Maybe this was her lucky day.

She washed her hands, brushed her hair, applied lip gloss, and filled a gigantic waxed paper cup with Dr. Pepper at the soda machine. The liquid felt too heavy for its flimsy container and she wondered why the largest size was the cheapest as she dumped another handful of change in the zit-faced clerk's hand. But she smiled her "no big deal" smile and went back to the truck.

She'd been sitting there ever since. Sitting very still. Her purse might as well have contained a scorpion. Not that she didn't love babies. She did. Loved carrying and having Blake's babies. Loved how sleepy being pregnant made her. Loved how Blake treated her, how he ran his hand across her belly for nine months, how he sat and watched a new baby nurse, how he fetched and carried for her while she recovered from childbirth. She had to admit that he also did more housework during those times, and it was kinda nice.

There were two things she hated about being pregnant, though. The money part was one of them. The never-enough, stretch-every-dollar, how-will-it-cover, just-let-the-littlest-wear-the-nicest-of-the-hand-me-downs, eating-ramen-noodles-at-the-end-of-the-month and now-there-is-another-one-coming kind of fear. Since the moment she started puking with Bliss, she and Blake had been counting pennies.

Puking. The other thing she hated about being pregnant.

Brenna stayed still but her mind whirled to touch on each previous pregnancy.

Puking.

With each one there had been weeks of pale shaking sweating nausea that started the moment of conception and ended firmly sometime during the tenth week. It always ended just like that. Snap. One moment she was puking at even the smell of her shampoo and the next she was a happy, sleepy, hungry blob, glowing and sweet-tempered.

Brenna grabbed for her purse. No nausea equaled no baby. No baby equaled no shitdamnfuck finances. Brenna pulled out the stick, hoping to see a blank window on the test.

But no. The blue line was perfectly clear. No nausea but still a bright blue line. Positive. Perfectly positive.

Brenna envied women for whom peeing on the stick did not mean WIC, pitying glances from the whole community, food stamps, thrift stores, charity. The pity had been bad enough that first time when she was still a teenager, and pretty bad the third and fourth times. She cringed to think of how gracious, and yet condescending, all the church ladies would be now as they planned yet another baby shower and discussed how "best to help the family."

Five kids. All her adult life, Brenna had been the poor little knocked up girl. Time number five was not going to be any easier. She wondered if Shiney knew about the food stamps and WIC and Medicaid or if Monte signed the forms without telling her. Damn. They'd have to start going to her dad's church again, if only for the hand-me-downs.

The crunchy granola homeschooling rhythm-method crowd truly did think she was one of them. Last time she got pregnant, one of them had come out to the ranch for coffee, trying to sell her a kindergarten curriculum that looked, as far as she could tell, like taking a walk every day out in the pasture. The lady had also been peddling a line of cloth diapers and accessories made of organic cotton. Not only was the initial line (no-leak covers printed with peace signs or smiling sheep) more than Blake made in a month (twelve easy payments), but Brenna couldn't imagine adding every wet or poopy diaper to her already unmanageable mounds of laundry. She listened to the lady's speech about landfills and how things bio-degrade or don't. Finally she asked why organic cotton was so much more expensive than regular cotton and was subjected to a passionate sermon about aquifers and nitrates and chemicals in our environment (even the clothes we wear!) as well as one of those poor-Brenna looks she despised, as if the lady thought she was a dumb ignorant girl rather than a grown woman. Brenna plastered an understanding smile on her face, but inside she was wondering who the fuck was going to organic the diapers into the washer, organic them into the dryer, organic them onto the bare ass of the baby for that matter. She wondered who was going to organic the diaper pail smell out of her and Blake's bathroom. She wished she could do more for the environment, but sometimes she wished the world could do more for her.

Brenna left the "Cheat Yourself" parking lot in a daze, headed home to West Camp on the TJs. It was four days before she got around to telling Blake about the baby.

FIGHT SONG

The summer Bliss was fifteen, she was obsessed by two things: toothpaste and dirty words. Since her birthday was September 1, she always ended an "age" with a summer.

While the girls from her school lay on the concrete apron of the swimming pool in town and dreamed of boys and dates and an even tan, surreptitiously sniffing their pits to make sure they weren't sweating noticeably, Bliss lay on her bed in front of the swamp cooler, hoping her mom wouldn't call her to do yet another chore, and dreamed of order, of clean, of neat, of new, of private.

Her reality was messy, sometimes even dirty, tubes of toothpaste minus their caps squished in the middle, dehydrated worms of paste on the edge of the sink. Her reality was full of little boys, what with being the oldest in a family of four kids . . . and her the only girl. Bliss longed for the day when she would buy her own toothpaste, stand in the aisles of Walmart or Safeway in front of the shelves of slim gleaming boxes and choose exactly the one she wanted to live with for the next several weeks – not the cheapest, not the one she had a coupon for, and definitely not the fruit-flavored kind with Elmo on the box. She would never squeeze the tube in the middle or leave the lid off. Her mom thought the whole thing was stupid and refused to buy Bliss her own tube, insisting that toothpaste was a silly thing to get upset about. Too bad her mom didn't have to share *everything* with three little brothers.

Bliss guessed she'd always remember that summer because it felt like she had finally started separating herself from the melee, the craziness her parents created, and then, in one evening, she got sucked back into it all.

Early in the summer she had moved all of her toilet articles out of the bathroom, zipped them up in the makeup bag her grandma got her for Christmas, and stashed them in the top drawer of her dresser. She had divided the bedroom into halves with two old sheets hung with thumb tacks in the ceiling so she and her youngest brother had some privacy, not that he cared. He just thought it was fun to jump out from behind the barrier and scare her. If he jerked too hard and the sheets came untacked, he roared with laughter and wrapped himself up in them even when Bliss got angry.

Bliss was also obsessed with dirty words. They floated through her mind, intruded on her thoughts all day long. Shit. Fuck. Asshole. Son of a bitch. Boob. Pussy. Goddammit. Screw. Dick. Jack off. Even when she wasn't quite sure what they meant, they floated around in her head anyway. Cunt. Cock. Suck. Nympho. Erection. She never said any of the dirty words aloud, or even the ones that weren't dirty. Vagina. Breast. Penis. Anus. Intercourse. Arousal. Those were the words she knew that just referred to dirty things. They swam around in her head, a mean and sexual soup, a silent telling-off of the whole world.

She didn't even direct them at anyone. It wasn't like she called her mother a sucking whore in her head when she had to do the dishes. Or her father a dickwad when he teased her about the zit on her chin. It wasn't like that. The words just floated there, little pieces of dirt in the stream of her thoughts.

Bliss was a good girl, and she always thought of that with a little sneer. She was one of those that all the adults trusted and liked, and the other kids were friendly to. Good. Nice. Sweet. Responsible. A dirty-minded fucking little cunt whose boobs were lopsided, who wondered if she'd actually enjoy sucking dick. The first day of school she walked up the front walk of the high school. Bucket of steaming shit.

When she lay on her stomach at night in the almost silent house, her hand between her legs, she thought of the one pornographic picture she'd ever seen for maybe like two seconds before her brain switched over to the cover of a romance novel she'd seen in the library – a bare-chested man in a cowboy hat, his arms around a big-boobed woman with her back to him, her red hair flying around them both. Bliss would imagine what he was saying in her ear, and how it felt to press up against him, backing into the deal. "I want to suck on your breast." That always worked for sure, sometimes too well. The only time it didn't was when she substituted "nipples" for "breast" and then it reminded her of breastfeeding and her mother's cracked and bleeding nipples from the last time. A total turn-off. The other way it wouldn't work was if she substituted a real guy in place of the fake cowboy in the stupid hat. She'd tried them all, back when she was worried about possibly being a lesbian. All of them. All the boys in her school. All the male teachers, especially the baseball coach who said hello to her when she walked by his class-room during passing periods. All of the cowboys on the ranch. Even Monte who was pretty hot for an old guy. But none of them worked like the dude on the cover of the book.

She sat in math class and thought of flipping over on her stomach, pistoning her hips just a little with her eyes closed and her thighs spread apart enough to allow her hand access. Her face flushed when she thought of doing it with everyone watching. At night she dreamed of a darkened classroom, brand new tubes of toothpaste, and everyone's hips rising and falling as they chanted the school's fight song.

Bliss was sixteen now. September first had come and gone. It still felt like summer outside even though Bliss had school books piled on her bed and the new denim jacket with rhinestone spangles she got for her birthday hanging from a hook on her closet door, waiting for the first cool morning. But for Bliss, it was no longer summer in any way, and she was no longer fifteen.

It hadn't been the start of school or even her birthday that marked the boundary so much as her parent's casual-seeming conversation with her the night before. They'd sent the boys outside with dripping popsi-cles after dinner, and when she stood up to start clearing the table, her dad said, "Oh, sit down, pardner! I'll help you with those later. Let's have a bowl of ice cream."

As the three of them sat there at the table, the coldness hurting her teeth, she found out about the new baby due in the spring. All of her dirty words flew away. No fucks, no humps, no pokes, no damns. No pussies or heads or even an anus. Just blankness in her brain. She felt old all of a sudden – much older than her parents, who looked and acted like two kids sent to the principal's office. And all of a sudden she realized that for them, too, there would never be the joy of new toothpaste.

OBLIGATION

Music was part of Blake's skin and melodies swam in his blood. Blake often felt as if all conversation should be in rhythm, like his brain was a constant waterfall of song, as if his guitar grew from his hands. In fact, if he wasn't holding his guitar, he felt like a part of him was missing. Once in awhile something came along that took that bereft feeling away. Like when he reached to undo his rope string and started building a loop. Like the night in high school when he first danced with Brenna. Or the morning he first held Bliss in his arms, marveling that he had helped make such a strange little red creature. It had been wonderful to hold each subsequent baby, of course, but he never felt that total sense of wholeness that he felt with Bliss.

Besides, the babies seemed to come so fast. By the time Brenna and Blake had been married ten years, a few months shy of Blake's thirtieth birthday, there were four of them. Bliss, Brice, Brian, and Bradley. The all "B" thing was Brenna's idea, and when she was seventeen, looking like an obscene china doll, waddling around with Bliss in her belly, her hair in two pigtails, it had seemed like a completely harmless and simple indulgence to say, "Sure we can name all of our babies with B." Now it felt like some huge cosmic joke, too precious and ridiculous for words.

Blake was usually good at looking on the bright side of things, but he had to admit to himself that life was pretty bleak lately. And this mother-fucking hot wind wasn't helping any. The hot winds were seasonal, characteristic of fall, but he hated the way the dirt blew across the road and the gusts buffeted the truck.

Blake was good at being happy, at singing, at drinking a cold beer in the shade, at writing songs about baby calves and "good spring rain." He was a springtime kind of guy – always young, always looking for the good stuff, looking for the fun. Autumn with its decline toward entropy just didn't match his approach to life. Happy go lucky. But – damn! He didn't feel so lucky today.

Another baby. He was sure there were people who would say that the news of a new baby was the best news ever – joyous tidings and all of that. But he had to admit that the cloud of happy he'd ridden through the first couple of pregnancies was wearing thin beneath his feet – given as how there was never enough money to go around. Most of all, Blake hated the old conversation that echoed between his ears at times like these – a conversation that had only been spoken aloud once, but was repeated silently every time he saw or talked to his father – or his mother for that matter, since in some ways they were one and the same, his folks. The conversation had taken place long ago, but its prophecies and its echoes had become Blake's story.

"That girl will just keep on having babies if you let her, and cowhand wages are going to spread pretty thin. We'll help you go to college, and help you get on your feet, but you'll have to focus. It can't be all about horses, cows, and music."

Young-and-Stupid Blake had wondered why not? Why couldn't life be about doing a job you loved in an industry producing food and articles of value for society and playing a few tunes that made people happy, maybe even want to dance? Back in June, Blake thought he'd finally put the echoes of that conversation to rest when he drove down this same road, pulled up at this self-same mailbox, and found a tan envelope between a credit card bill and a flyer announcing sign-ups for youth soccer league. He'd been waiting for it, an invitation to perform at the National Cowboy Poetry Gathering in Elko, Nevada. Pretty big fuckin' deal. He'd gotten invited the year before by accident after he and some friends had gone to a ranch rodeo and one of the big names in cowboy music had been there. When some of that guy's band started jamming, Blake had joined in, played "Milk Cow Blues" on the fiddle. The guy had come up and asked what else he could play. Three hours later, after a great jam and some poems thrown in for fun, plus all of the God and country stuff Blake knew to wrap it up, he told Blake that every year the gathering invited one sure 'nuff ranch cowboy on a kind of scholarship. At the time, Blake had wondered at the necessity of using the sure 'nuff adjective, but after he and Brenna went to the gathering he understood. At the gathering there were quite a few punchers who'd given up the cows and kept the poems, or people who'd found the poems but never met the cows.

Damn they'd had a good time, away from the ranch, just two bumpkins out on the town, childless for the first time since he'd planted Bliss on their third date when they were just kids. It had been hard to scrape together the money for Brenna to go with him, and they'd had to hunt down a bank in Elko to cash his per diem check that first morning before his first session, not exactly a good way to settle his nerves, but they'd needed the money contained in that check to eat on all weekend. Brenna had been stressed out about her clothes, taking two outfits for each day, thanks to Velma Jo's well-stocked closet and head full of fashion sense. Blake thought that half the time she'd looked like a little girl playing dress-up next to the glossy slick rich women and performers all decked out in turquoise and inlaid boots and big-brimmed hats. The other half of the time he'd thought Brenna was the most beautiful woman there, simple and ranch. The real deal. They'd held hands and walked through the dark night with snow coming down from the street-lights – 12 degrees on the bank thermometer – felt a frantic little edge to see everything – until Blake discovered the jam session upstairs at the Stockman's on Friday night. Brenna gave it up by 1:00 a.m., going heavy-eyed down the dark street to their room at the Thunderbird. Blake followed at 3:00 a.m., feeling guilty as he crossed the street in the dark. He'd been too wide awake and jazzed with the music to sleep. He lay there beside his wife and dreamed of microphones and applause.

On Saturday night Brenna had gone to bed even earlier, but had al-ready asked a bewhiskered scholarly folklorist to walk her over to the motel room so that Blake didn't have to give up his place in the circle, pack up his fiddle and guitar. He felt guilty again, not for letting his wife go to bed alone, but for the eyes of the woman to his left in the circle who casually slipped back and forth between her harp and her guitar, picking up the harmony notes in his songs as if they were pretty rocks along a creek bank.

This year, after he was lucky enough to be chosen again, this time from amongst the many people who submitted their material to the selection committee, Blake and Brenna had planned on saving up the airfare for her to go with him again. But today, after he pulled the mail from the box, Blake stared at the preliminary brochure for the gathering and realized for the first time that because of Brenna's due date, he'd be going to Nevada alone. The idea spread itself out before him like a buffet.

He'd signed a contract. He had to go. He was obligated.

Blake sat beside the mailbox on that long red dirt road and imagined having only *his* belongings in the airport, flying away free and light, smiling and laughing and looking and jamming and singing, the notes from his fiddle rising higher than before, audiences cradled in the nooks of the poems he recited effortlessly, going with the Elko flow. A festival that was truly festive.

The hot wind had stopped blowing. Blake stepped out of the truck to pee and breathed in air barely frosted with the hint of fall, leaned back and grinned up at the dull blue sky.

He loved babies. This one would be special. Hooray for babies. He'd play music tonight, and all winter long.

Rattlesnake Dusk

Sunshine Angel Lewis was sitting in the window seat when her new cowboy arrived – his antique truck with stock racks reminiscent of a time when the bunkhouse was full of men, when most of the bottom bunks running down both sides of the long room were occupied. When the men's laundry hung on a line by the bathroom door, and the wood-burning stove was surrounded by chairs at the far end of the room. Boots and bootjacks scattered around. Gear stowed on top bunks. Canvas bedrolls and colorful Navajo or Mexican blankets spread on the beds. Chairs with denim hanging from them. A poker table with worn top that could have told a thousand Western tales.

Having only one man in the bunkhouse seemed a lonely thing to her.

In reality she had only been inside the bunkhouse a few times in her life, even though it was one of the main buildings at headquarters, connected to the cook house by a breezeway with a hollow wooden floor. She'd been in and out as the owner, of course, making decisions about plumbing, reroofing, and maintenance, but those times were few and far between. And for sure, there had been no call for her to go in the bunkhouse when she was a child even if Punch Lewis had deemed it a proper place for his daughter.

The transition from living among and with his hands to living in the Big House must have been a difficult one for Punch, and she remembered an evening when she was only three or four years old, just a baby really, when she had a spat with Mama D. She ran out into the rattlesnake dusk, hunting for the big man with the big voice who always took her side – or so it seemed at the time. Later she saw the illusion. But on that night she went instinctually to where she knew her champion would be, her bare feet slapping along the dirt path across the yard, slapping the boards of the bunkhouse porch, pausing at the heavy screen door, not only stopped by its cumbersome weight, but also by an instinctual feminine hesitance to enter such a blatantly masculine room, one she'd never been inside before. One of the men had pushed the door open, given her a view of her beloved Papa sitting beside the cold stove, a fistful of cards in his hand, a squat brown bottle on the table beside him, a cigarette in his mouth and every face in the room, lit by harsh bare bulbs, turned her way.

Shiney wondered sometimes if she really remembered Punch mashing out his cigarette in the tin ashtray and putting down his cards.

"I'm out, boys."

Or did she just remember pattering down the room, clambering up into his arms and then on up toward the ceiling as Punch rose, bid the men goodnight, and carried his little girl home.

"But I needed you, Papa," she had said, her hands on his whiskery cheeks, turning his face so she could see his eyes. She wondered now if that's when Punch started spending his evenings in the library of the Big House instead of with his men.

When Punch Lewis built the Big House, everyone thought he was crazy. Most of the houses in the area were low and sprawling, more of the Spanish-style that came about from haphazard additions making the homes into long-halled rabbit warrens where the connections between rooms often didn't make sense. By contrast, the Big House on the Tinaja resembled a Swiss chalet. Punch had built up rather than out, solid and old school rather than practical, and perhaps by the design of his eastern bride who spent one summer in the adobe cabin at headquarters before moving into an apartment in town, the one in the back of the hotel, and soon showed herself pear-shaped with baby, entertaining the preacher's wife to coffee on Tuesdays, her husband on odd days when ranch needs brought him to town, and the ladies' book club when it was her turn to play hostess. Her lights were always extinguished early of a night except on the nights when her husband stayed in town, and then the windows stayed lit until almost midnight. Everyone knew he was building the house for her, but they also knew that she left for her father's home back east without ever having seen it.

Shiney knew Papa started building the house for Mother, but she also knew he finished it and the odd extra wing for her and Mama D. And she loved it. She loved every formal room, every cavernous cedar-lined closet, every worn carpet, every stiff piece of furniture, though much of the stiffness had mellowed with time, too many Chavez kids, the vigorous cleanings of Mama D, and memories. Now Shiney lived mainly in the kitchen downstairs and this room, her old bedroom. She had dragged a sideboard and a huge easy chair in here when the old library had become too empty, and now she had her scotch and her evenings in the window seat.

Shiney sat among pillows she had known since Mama D redecorated this room right after Shiney graduated from college, which meant they were now almost forty years old. Mama D had ordered them out of a catalog and Shiney remembered them arriving, vacuum-packed in plastic, all flat and dead, but they sucked in ranch air when she cut the packages open, as if they were being born onto the Tinaja. Time and sunlight and moonlight had faded the heavy, rich-looking brocade, maroon with gold threads, but Shiney Lewis knew every detail of those pillows, had smothered both laughter and tears in them, had slept on them, pummeled them, and idly chewed their tassels as she read. Originally, Mama D ordered four for the bed and four for the window seat, but they all ended up in the deep bay window that looked out over headquarters, a vantage point from which one could watch stories unfold, which is exactly what Shiney did – listening to the ice clink in her glass, listening to her own breathing, picking at her own horny toenails, eating plates of pickled herring and saltines – as she made all that went on down below her own.

She was hidden here in her window seat, curled up exactly as she had as a young dreamy girl, secure in the knowledge that the gold of sunset stuck firmly to the leaded windows that threw it back like a spotlight aimed at the rest of the buildings below – the perfect cover for her observations.

She saw the young man arrive in his old truck, bedroll tied to the homemade headache rack. Saw him stop down at the cattle guard and step out, a small puppy under his arm. While the puppy squatted in the dirt, he stood and looked for a long time at TJ headquarters, stretching his back. She thought how appropriate it was that he was seeing it at its best time of day, not rushing in, taking his time to savor it.

Shiney knew from Monte that this kid was pretty young, only twenty. She watched him park the truck in front of the bunkhouse, put the puppy in the back, shake hands with Monte, unload a war bag, a bedroll, and a small stereo. She watched him pull around to the saddle house and the next day peeked in to see his hand-me-down saddle, a brand new shoeing outfit, and a metal box of leatherworking tools she knew Rafe would be interested in.

This kid might be the real deal.

She paid attention to the portable yard he set up for the puppy, and had still been in the window seat after he'd eaten dinner in the cook house with Sam and Sue. She saw how the boy lifted the little dog out of her pen and sat on the steps playing with her, an old towel the object of her aggression, even when his own hands rolled her gently in the dirt.

Shiney often walked the Big House at night, especially when a full moon lit up the rooms. There was only half a moon tonight. As she walked the faded old carpets, Shiney heard the Chavez kids' laughter and yells, heard her father's footsteps, heard Mama D answering the phone after two rings, "TJs! How can I help?" Heard Mama D screech to Nesto to "Put me down!" when he lifted his fat little wife off of her feet and teased her with wanting to add more chile pepper to something she was cooking, "More hot, Mama, just a leetle more hot!" She heard echoes of the long lazy conversations she had with Papa as he sat at his desk in the library, heard the sound of the crystal stopper sliding from the decanter as he poured their drinks, heard the heavy door thumping in the mornings as he left for the barn. She heard her college friends calling her "Sunny" and the blank silence that marked the years since Nesto and Mama D died, so quickly, within six months of each other. And Shiney saw a big old empty museum with her ghosts all around.

She only smoked on sleepless nights.

She was awake when the puppy began to cry, was standing at the open casement, blowing guilty cigarette smoke out into the night when the bunkhouse door creaked open, and the puppy's cries stopped, presumably and predictably, because the kid took the pup into his bedroll indoors.

On the night of the welcome party, Shiney settled herself in the window seat early. In her office that day, she had printed out an e-mail that pointed out what "land rich, cash poor" really meant. Now it lay beside her on the cushions as she settled in.

Isn't e-mail a kick! So glad to have reconnected with you, dear friend.

Please come to Scottsdale and play with us this winter. I know you love the ranch, but you're getting old! I never thought I'd say this when we were twenty and reading silly poems on campus and dreaming, but we are old ladies now. Come walk through the museums, go to some shows, let's eat out and order something besides beef. Truly, Sunny, I think you've given enough of your life to that place. Don't you deserve to play a little bit now? With long ago memories, Betts

No one had called her Sunny in years and it took her back to being a young woman, such a young woman. Tonight she wondered where that youth had gone as she looked down on headquarters as it came alive.

Shiney had resigned herself years ago to the fact that ranch families could have a party for any reason. It was like a disease. This gathering was to welcome Jody Neil to the bunkhouse.

Shiney felt as if she were counting cattle through a gate, taking a strange human inventory. She saw the Davis kids pile out of Blake's ranch truck. Bliss carried a covered dish and walked inside with her parents while the little boys all went running straight to the hay barn to swing from the ropes hanging from the rafters, only going into the cook house when it was time to eat, rowdy, loud, ragged little guys. She shook her head and let the fact that Blake was driving his company rig to a social event slide off. Some things weren't worth the fuss, but it irked her that his truck was in the shop more than any other on the ranch. And it did not bode well for Blake that Monte had recently taken note of it, too. Monte was having a hard enough time keeping Blake on the payroll as it was. Just two days before, Monte had found a water leak over on the west side that had been going so long as to be growing algae.

"It isn't that Blake is lazy so much as he is careless and oblivious. He just doesn't pay attention. Have you seen the electric bills from that camp? They're shameful! And I can't get him to see that we, or you, are not some endless pile of money!"

Shiney had to agree, but couldn't get as worked up about it as Monte. It felt as if she had been caring about this kind of thing her whole life. And she was tired. Sam had remarked the other day something about his "shiv-a-gitter" being broke. Exactly. Her shiv-a-gitter was broke.

The sun continued to sink and the day continued to cool. Shiney continued taking inventory as Velma Jo and Levi drove in, followed closely by their teenagers in a separate vehicle. The kids were probably going on to town to their own social event later. Shiney guessed by the set of Velma Jo's shoulders that she and Levi were having a tiff. Chris, the newest camp man, and his wife Annie, came in the back way, as did Rafe and Nell. She saw Monte, handsome and lonely, walk down the hill from the foreman's house.

She was grateful for Monte, who was taking things seriously right now, but that's what she'd hired him to do. Things were serious. For as long as she had managed the ranch, she had raised cattle, sold them and they made money. Most years. Sure, some years were tougher than others, some dryer than others, some markets worse than others. There was the beef embargo in the 70s, then that crazy lady on television one year talking about mad cow disease. But things had changed, and Shiney wasn't sure if she was flexible enough to change with them.

"Land rich and cash poor," was the phrase that ran through Shiney's head every day now. Punch Lewis would have risen from his grave and cussed the whole world at that phrase. For him, and in his time, land was wealth, and he would not have understood how things had changed. E-mail. He might have liked e-mail, but he would have cursed every other innovation and every other challenge that Shiney was facing.

Monte was the first manager she had hired from outside since Nesto died. Always before she had let her cowboys work their way up through the ranks – but times were different, the industry had changed. It was her concession to those changes that caused her to seek a manager outside of her tried-and-true cowboys. She chose Monte Wells for his business experience, his and his father's. Monte had been raised with the ranching tradition, and when he approached her about the manager's position, he had been hungry to come back to it. His understanding of the lifestyle, coupled with his respect for tradition, made him more attractive than the other smart men she'd interviewed. And her instincts had been right. He was trying as hard as she was to pick the Tinaja up out of its current financial crisis without being all gloom and doom or hurting her feelings by pointing out her past bad decisions and what she was sure he considered poor planning for the future on her part. He'd explained to her just the other day that while he thought traditions were cool, habits were expensive. Ah, well. She comforted herself with the fact that she had always done the best she could with the information she had at the time. All she knew to do was to keep on going.

She'd lived with this war, sentiment and people and animals taking constant pot shots at accounting and bottom line and practicality, all of her life. It had been interesting for the past couple of years to watch someone like Monte, someone smart and determined to do a good job, be caught by those dichotomies over and over again.

Tonight, from her place on high, Shiney saw her cowboys sitting on the long porch with beers in their hands. She saw them stomp their boots on the boards before they went in to eat, as if they'd been in the branding pen all afternoon instead of freshly showered before they left home.

She saw Jody come outside when it was getting dim to pick the puppy up out of her pen and scratch her ears. Bliss, Blake's girl, the oldest one of his big brood, came out shortly, sent to round up her brothers. Shiney wished she could hear as well as see, wished she could turn the sound up on the scene down below. Shiney started doing math in her head. How old was that girl now? About sixteen, nearest she could figure.

"Hey." The girl spoke to Jody.

"Hey."

"Cute pup."

"Yeah. She might make a dog. Pretty rotten yet." Jody shrugged off cute, though he continued to fondle the puppy's ears.

The girl reached out her own hand to stroke the dog's small skull lightly. "What's her name?"

"Missy. Not too brilliant, I know, but Missy suits her."

"Sure it does. Hey, little Miss." The girl spoke to the dog without lifting her eyes. "Well, I gotta go get the boys."

Jody put the dog back in her pen and rejoined the party inside.

Not too long after, Shiney saw Monte and Blake walk out to the far end of the wooden porch, saw the glow of the white envelope she knew Monte planned on handing off to the cowboy from West Camp, but then she put her drink down and leaned forward to look more closely. It was hard to see in the dusk, but it appeared as if Monte had put the envelope into his own back pocket and crossed his arms while he did more listening than talking. In a few minutes, he stepped down off the porch and started up the hill. She felt guilty for refusing when he had asked if he could escort her over for at least dinner and wondered if the ice made a friendly sound in his glass after he got home, keeping him company as hers did.

Shiney stayed on her perch until all of the extra vehicles pulled out of headquarters, all of her cowboys and their families going back down long dusty roads to camps scattered over the ranch.

That night, Jody had to go get Missy once again and bring her into the bunkhouse to stop her crying. He tried to make her sleep on the floor, but she made him think of what his mom always said, "Give her an inch and she'll take a mile!" Missy wasn't happy lying on the old bathmat he spread beside his bed. She kept whining and trying to put her paws up on the mattress, even though she was too short to make the reach. Finally, so he could sleep, he reached down, cupped her fat warm tummy, and lifted her up onto his own pillow, where, of course, she was content to curl into a hot little ball of puppy breath, but only after thoroughly licking his ear. He guessed he didn't mind too much. "Go to sleep, Little Miss."

He lay there listening to her stomach gurgle and her breathing turn into baby snores, and thought of the party that night, thought of everyone showing up to tell him thank you for coming.

He thought of Rafe Johansen saying that Cash Neil had been a fine man. Monte had mentioned that Jody was going to help Rafe for several days before fall works got cranked up. Velma Jo had explained, behind her hand and off to the side, that Monte had a wife. Jody couldn't remember her name, but Velma Jo said she wasn't around much, and Monte had gone home early. One person Jody had wanted to meet was Sunshine Angel Lewis, but she hadn't come to the party.

As sleep approached, he could hear Del's voice . . . dreamed and remembered that last night before he left, Del saying something about dignity.

Del's cigarette glowed in the night and Missy huffed softly in Jody's ear. The moon glowed over the tinaja, and a deer stepped lightly up to the edge. Del's voice blended the then with the now. They had been in the saddle shed, had yet to turn on a light, but the dusk was comfortable, full of the sound of horses chewing and chickens fussing over roosts. Jody knew that Del wasn't ready to go in to dinner yet, even though his own stomach rumbled.

"Shiney Lewis." Del's smile was audible in the dark. "I was at the Tinaja when she was a young woman. When she shouldered the whole thing – after Punch Lewis up and died. We all wondered when she'd get a husband and who the lucky son of a bitch would be. I guess all the young bucks figured it might as well be him, at least somewheres in his dreams, but really, we all knew she'd pick someone smart, someone who would fit into life in the Big House, or we figured she'd bring in one of Nesto's boys to do the job of running the outfit. None of us ever thought she'd just by Gawd do it herself, but she has! By Gawd, she has! For going on thirty years now. 'Course she's also had the smarts to hire some good men along the way, too. You know she had Lew Forsythe for years, until the Wagon Mound stole him away. She's done a good job, that girl has . . . ." Del's voice faded.

When the threads of Del's thoughts were taken all together, they often made a picture that Jody could carry around in his head. The saddle shed behind them was fully dark, and the horizon's glow had put the rest of the world in shadows darker than they would be after the glow was gone before Del continued.

"I remember once when Shiney was, oh, probably putting her feet on thirty or maybe not yet, we were working that Old Sally country over on the far northeast side. Some of that country is great, and the cows really use it. But some of it is just an armpit. Could have used a good torchin' even then. Well, all us boys was young, pretty full of ourselves. We had a pact that fall. Not to let one cow get away from us – not one – get everything we saw to the hold-up, and we all stood on our honor about it, too. Many was the day that fall when one of us would get to the hold up and say, 'Where's that high-horned old red bitch, the one with that black steer following her?' If she wasn't there, two or three of us would peel off and leave the rest to keep the herd, and we'd go back and trail the old broad up, make damned sure we got her that time. Anyway, by that stage of the works, it had ceased to be, oh, I don't know . . . ceased to be so *light-hearted*. We was pretty serious about the pact even though the crew was already cut down to winter numbers, just a few of us cleaning up remnant. But we was invested, you might say. So there we were over in the Granites, and Shiney was riding that day. I helped her scoop three pair out of a boulder pile, and got her going down the way while I set off on a bull track I saw going up yonder. The bull was no problem, just lazy, just happy to be running off by hisself, and the day was warmin' up, but I got him off down to the tank where we were supposed to meet. When I got there, there was two of Shiney's pairs, but no Shiney. I waited around awhile until the other guy got there. I think it was Jack Beeler. In fact, I know it was because I said, 'Jack, I am gonna go find our Shiney,' and he slung his knee over the saddle horn the way he allus did and lit a smoke, content to wait for a bit, keep the cows we had from driftin' off. I trailed the other cows back the way they come an' sure 'nuff, found where the third had done a little shuck and jive, just walked off the trail and stuck her head in a laurel tree. I saw the wallerin' around Shiney had done 'til she found the right track and then the merry chase that spoiled ol' hussy had taken her on. I got a little worried, but the story was all there in the dirt 'til I come on Shiney's horse hobbled on the edge of one of the most Gawd-awful thickets. I could hear a bunch of crashing around, and finally, out come that cow with her baby at her side and behind 'em come Sunshine Angel Lewis, rock in each hand, her shirt in shreds, her face all red, cussing like a sailor (or a cowhand, come to think of it) 'til she saw me. Then she just got on her horse all quiet, daring me to say a word, and we followed that old cow to the tank. Jack, he says, 'Shiney, what in hell happened to you?' She looks over at me. Looks me right in the eye while she answers him! 'Why Jack, I was just getting everything I saw.' Then with all this dignity, I guess you'd call it, she rode over to give her horse a drink. Dignity. That's what I remember about Shiney."

Jody was asleep. Missy was asleep. They were both too young to know much about dignity. And Del was miles away, getting ready to sleep.

No Apples, Just Bacon

"Goddammit."

Monte slapped the table hard with the palm of his hand.

"Goddammit. She's pregnant! No shit! Brenna is pregnant and how the fuck am I supposed to give Blake a stupid electric bill when he's standing there about to be supporting five . . . FIVE . . . children? Pregnant! And then he says, all off-hand, that by the way did I know he was also invited back to the cowboy poetry gathering in January and he'd be gone whatever the fuck dates he named, and not once did he mention the heifers that will be in the very big middle of calving about then, and do you remember what it was like last year when we had to send Joe over there to handle things while he was gone? Now I am going to have an empty bunkhouse and a hundred and fifty piggy heifers and the camp man off in bumfuck singing songs and his wife just as piggy as the heifers. I know, I know. I am overreacting. Excuse my language, Shiney, but fuck. Fuckfuckfuck. You know, I want to be fair and I want to do the right thing, but dammit! Blake is going to have to meet me halfway here, is going to have to put out a little bit of effort in my direction. If you just could have seen his face, like some little boy who is ashamed that he spilled his milk."

Common Denominator

Why do they ride for their money
Why do they rope for short pay
They ain't getting nowhere
And they're losing their share
Son, they all must be crazy out there.

The song lyrics were stuck in Jody's head. As he rode behind Rafe, climbed in and out of canyons, mounted the ridges of Bride Mountain for the first time, the words began to make sense. Jody guessed that it probably *was* possible to go crazy in a place as wild as that mountain, but going crazy wasn't too bad of a thing if it meant choosing this life over one in town.

Jody had been riding along behind Del for half of his life, just listening, not having to ask too many questions because most of the time Del's nonstop chatter answered them all eventually. But with Rafe it was different. They rode all morning that first day with Rafe saying a total of two words along with a gesture, "Bear track."

Jody didn't mind the silence, though, because they rode up through some of the prettiest country he'd ever seen, and that night, there were a few more words.

"Rare or done?" Rafe was cooking steaks.

And as they filled their plates he'd said, "Now, getcha plenty."

After the meal was eaten and the plates wiped clean, Rafe had said, "Whiskey?"

They sat out on the porch as the air cooled off much faster than it did down below, and Rafe told Jody how Precious Camp got its name. How an old homesteader and his wife had lived up here, how he always called her "Precious," and how she stayed up on the mountain after he died and no one in the country knew her real name, just called her "Precious" through the few years that she lived on after him. And how Punch Lewis wouldn't have the camp called anything else after he bought it when the old lady died. When Jody asked about how Old Sally got its name, Rafe looked sideways at him, "Probably named after someone's durned milk cow."

In a while, his last words for the day had been, "Good night." Jody savored the taste of whiskey on his tongue.

Jody knew, even as they were happening, that he would always remember those two weeks, his introduction to the Bride. They sat high in the wind as Rafe pointed, swept his hand across the horizon and said place names Jody figured it would take years to learn. They worked the fat cows with big calves at side down the slopes. As the nights got colder and Rafe doled out stories and wisdom with few words and a lot of work, Jody knew he was living a gift. This was why men rode for little pay.

Jody discovered that if he'd pick his moments, usually after dinner and with a little splash of whiskey in hand, he could ask Rafe something about the day and find out something about more than that. He could say, "What did you mean earlier when you said it was a myth that the country makes the cattle wild?" referencing Rafe's grin and nod as they sat watching a little group of cows rise and stretch from their noontime nap before gathering up their calves and move steadily downhill, finding the best trail and lining out on it in single file.

"Watch 'em. They're waspy! The country makes 'em wild, doncha know? Old myth."

In the evening with fall coming as fast as the dark, Rafe elaborated.

"Oh, it is the same mindset that riding in heavy brush makes hard-mouthed horses. One of those myths that are tossed about when a man doesn't want to look in the mirror. Doesn't want to identify *himself* as the common denominator."

Then there was the fox. In later years, Jody would think of those early days with Rafe and the fox as something out of a fairy tale, as some sort of imaginary creature that he couldn't share with anyone. And, in fact, he never tried, just kept the memory of that silent sleek shadow privately tucked into his mind. He saw him for the first time on the second morning, and pointed through the window.

The fox was standing with his front feet up on a rock, looking expectantly at the cabin.

Rafe got up from the table where he was writing in his tally book and grinned. "Little devil. Musta heard the cabin door and known I was back."

With that, he picked up the heavy frying pan from the stove. The fox had disappeared, but Rafe walked right out to the rock and scraped bacon grease onto its surface.

As they saddled up, Jody glanced over his shoulder and saw the fox's tail disappearing into the oakbrush. The top of the rock had been licked clean. After every meal, Rafe would put food scraps on the rock as casually as if he were feeding some old hound, and Jody saw glimpses of the fox again and again.

September 21 — Ready to head off down below. Mountain clean, or durn near. And if the old Bride isn't lying to me, a hard freeze is on its way. Jody Neil rode with me this week. Good kid. Kind. But makes me feel old and creaky, too. Looks like his dad.

On their last evening at Precious Camp, Rafe built a fire in the old stone hearth and they sat indoors instead of out as they drank their toddy. Jody asked about the crew and about how fall works would go. Rafe had again used few words, but as the fire burned down and the night turned full dark, he added a few more, almost as if Jody wasn't there, almost as if he were talking to himself.

"You know, working with a crew is a fine and pleasurable thing, a lot of fun sometimes, and you can get a lot done in a little bit of no time. But you really begin to learn something about a cow, about how to work cows, when you have to work alone. You figure out how to get things done. Learn something about a horse, too, when he's your only partner. About yourself some, too. And you see things you'd never see in a crowd of hands all telling cowboy stories. You learn to watch. And sometimes the things you see, well, they aren't the kinds of things you go off telling everybody about."

Rafe grinned across the dim cabin at Jody, making the young man realize that the older man *did* remember his presence.

"You go running off and telling people about some of the things you see out here in the wild and they durned sure are going to think you're crazy. But you know. You will always know how it happened. I've seen some things — lots of things — that I keep in my head. Wouldn't translate around some bullshit fire. I figure they are meant to belong to just me. And I wouldn't have missed them for the world. So don't be afraid to spend time alone, learning how to work alone, Jody. It's not a bad thing."

As they rode down down down the next morning, the cabin

buttoned up for winter, Jody played the words over in his head, hoping he could keep them forever, hoping they wouldn't dim in the light of any bullshit fires.

FIRST FIRE

Monte drove away from the corrals toward headquarters at the head of a line of pickups dragging horse trailers. The dust of the main road sprouted branches as each rig turned off toward home for two nights' rest before they all convened again at West Camp. Jody was quiet in the passenger seat.

Nell Johansen was such a good cook that Monte always felt as if fall works started off pleasant and right. Jody had already been over at Old Sally for two weeks, and when he and Rafe had come down off the mountain, the young man had made himself a little place by the woodstove in Rafe's leather shop. Looked like a pretty fucking cozy place to be, Monte thought. Missy was there, too, in her pen out by the barn when she wasn't at the young man's heels. As he lay in his bedroll every night, Monte found himself wishing he could trade in all his classroom education, all of his knowledge of the markets and economics and personnel management, all of his time spent in front of a computer screen or on a phone for those days that Jody had gotten with Rafe, riding around up on the mountain, trailing up little bunches of cows and assorted yearlings and bulls, bringing them down.

One evening during that first week of fall works, the men had been sitting outside waiting for bedtime. Jody had lain back in the grass and was soon wrestling with that silly pup, all roughgentle and getting wilder by the minute, like a little kid. Monte had thought about how for a young man physical touch is hard to come by. Men just don't touch each other, and when mothers and sisters are far away and lovers are hard to find, the craving for some soft touch is intense. Monte figured cowboys were pretty lucky having something breathing between their knees, a horse's flesh beneath their hands. But when the roughhousing stopped and Missy ceased her little puppy growls to collapse exhausted in Jody's lap, Monte saw her pink tongue reach out and touch him on the inside of the wrist and thought about how it wasn't only the young single men who craved real touch. He wondered if maybe he didn't need a puppy himself.

Fall works were in full swing, and in Monte's mind the easy part was over, Old Sally and Half-way Camps worked, West Camp and Farm Camp and headquarters still to go. He had about sixty things to tend to in the next forty-eight hours, about thirty-two phone calls to make, and if he had anything to say about it, six tequilas to drink, more or less. The e-mail count would be in the thousands. Okay, so he was exaggerating and Pam would call his hand on those exaggerations if she cared to be around, cared to listen, but he knew she didn't and wouldn't. She was working. He bet he was the only married man on the ranch not looking forward to his woman's arms tonight.

Each dawn was successively colder as the year aged. Monte was already tired. Levi was already mad. Blake's jokes and poems were already old. Chris had already broken the leg on a yearling dragging him into the trailer, an unnecessary stunt that had earned Chris a conversation with his new boss. Monte bet that Brenna would serve meatloaf at least three times in the days the crew ate at West Camp. Last year she'd even "iced" one batch with mashed potatoes desperately in need of salt, or something. He made a mental note to ask Sue to stock the supper box and cooler extra heavy this week since the guys rustled their own evening meals no matter where they were camped except headquarters. Thank heaven for Sue who rarely repeated a meal unless someone begged her for something he particularly liked.

Sue and Sam had truly been a gift to the ranch. After going through several families in the cook house, Shiney had been ready to give up on having a full time cook, had about decided to let whoever was in the bunkhouse cook for himself, and to take over all of the yard work herself. Monte had been firmly pulled into her camp on the issue when they'd had to have the inside of the cook house repainted and the floors sanded after he fired the last people with their slovenly ways, gray menus, and indoor dogs. But just at the right time a big summer storm dumped Sam and Sue in his lap.

Sam had recently retired from driving heavy equipment for the state highway department, and Sue had just retired from teaching school. They were both used to being busy five days a week, eight to five, and found themselves too young to sit at home and watch television, too old to want to get new jobs, and too smart to play bingo. For about six months, they'd been driving back roads, discussing the problem of retirement.

A sudden thunderstorm mired them to the running boards in the bar ditch of the county road running through the Tinaja. Pam came along and rescued them on one of her trips home, left them on the porch of the ranch office, covered in mud, while she went on up to the house. Monte was smiling and polite as they tried to get the mud off of their shoes until after a few sentences, the couples' chatter began to register.

Sam asked intelligent questions about the heavy equipment parked by the shop. Sue explained how all she'd wanted to do after she retired was grow a vegetable garden and spend time in her kitchen, but how it was no fun canning and cooking for two. Sam mentioned that if the road had been crowned right, they wouldn't have slid off into the ditch. Sue said something about how much they wished they had bought a place in the country instead of being cheek-by-jowl with their neighbors and how much fun it must be to live way out here. Sam pointed out that one of the ancient trees Punch had planted was going to lose a limb if the wind blew too hard with the next storm. He finished scraping the mud off of his work boots and stood up. Monte was all ears.

By the time the roads were set up enough to pull their truck out, Monte had introduced them to Shiney, and before the week was out, invited them back for a formal interview. It was a match, all the way around. Monte let go of the painting project in the cook house because Sue took over the decision-making and Sam took over.

Sam simply took over.

Within six months of the enthusiastic couple moving to headquarters, a huge kitchen garden was flourishing in Mama D's old weeded-over plot. Ten hens and one rooster pecked in the old poultry run, newly patched with net wire. The shops and barns had been cleaned out and organized, right down to bins of tools and hardware with neatly-lettered labels on them, and many of the roads on the ranch had been reworked. Sam had cleaned out three dirt tanks with several more on the list waiting their turns. He had even cleaned out most of the cattle guards, spray painting them yellow while he had them jacked up out of the ground. He had changed the oil in everything with a motor and hung a precise schedule of the dates of service for each vehicle on the wall of the shop. The bunkhouse and the cook house were in top notch condition, and the cowboys groaned every time they stepped away from Sue's table. The piece of tin that had been flapping on the hay barn for at least three years was silent. The rosebushes around the Big House no longer had aphids.

Monte was glad that Sue was willing to haul dinner to the crew when they were working Half-Way and Farm Camps. Velma Jo made breakfasts at Half-Way, and Annie and Chris managed the breakfasts over there, but because Velma Jo went to work in town at the school and Annie saddled up with the crew, it was a godsend to see Sue and Sam show up at the corrals. Sam had made a cunning chuckbox out of plyboard after carefully measuring all of Sue's favorite pans and bowls. The two of them, cheerful and round and wrinkled, would unload gallons of iced tea, lemonade, and coffee, flip down the lid of the chuckbox and drag out salads, beans, meat, huge bowls of homemade bread and mashed potatoes, pies and cakes. Sue always had salt and pepper shakers, toothpicks, and salad dressings, little touches that made the noon break something to look forward to.

Monte was pretty sure that any of his men would have ridden to hell and back for Sue. Monte sometimes thought of her and Sam as the grandparents of the ranch even though they had only been there a little over a year. He smiled a bit thinking of how two days before a bull had hit a metal gate at the end of the alley, breaking several of the welds, and how after Sam had gotten Sue all unloaded back at headquarters, he had hooked up to the welder and come on back. The sparks were still flying at dusk. Those were the kind of folks Monte wanted on his team.

When he first got to the Tinaja, Monte had considered pulling out a chuck wagon purely for the economics of it, but discovered that the wives counted on their cooking checks during spring and fall works. Besides that, running a wagon really locked the crew into working no matter what the weather since he'd have to hire a cook for the duration, and no matter how many other traditions went by the wayside, how many of them got sacrificed for the bottom line, there was no way Monte could see his way to getting one of the women to cook on the wagon. Still, he felt a bit of sadness every time he passed by the wagon shed and saw the old rig, parked and dusty. Now a relic.

Monte encouraged the men to stay at the camp where they were working to reduce wear and tear on ranch vehicles and the ranch's consumption of gasoline, and for the most part, they did, pitching their tipis or rolling their beds out in the barn, or when they were at Old Sally, in Rafe's leather shop. Everybody welcomed a break now and again, though, and he was glad he'd have two days to catch up in the office, glad his men were getting to sleep in their own beds. It always made them more eager to jump back into the work.

Monte glanced over at Jody, still silent, in the passenger seat. Levi had gotten in a dig early in the day, interrupting a story Jody was telling about Del with, "Would that be Del Lincoln you're talking about. The one and only Delbert Lincoln?" The other men had been highly amused since all of Jody's stories were about Del.

"They're just hoorawing you, you know."

Jody shrugged and tried to grin. "I know. No big deal."

"Well, it is a big deal sometimes when the hoorawing hits close to home. Everyone respects Del a lot, you know."

"Yeah. I guess I talk about him too much." Jody's voice was forced and he shrugged his shoulders again.

"Well, maybe. Maybe not. Every man jack around that breakfast table this morning has looked up to someone who had a big influence on him at some point in his life. But you are an easy target, being the youngest, being new, and are in an enviable position, having grown up riding behind Delbert Lincoln."

"You think Levi is jealous?" This time the young man turned to face Monte's profile full-on.

"Oh, I'm sure, a little, not that he'd probably admit to it. *I'll* damned sure admit to it. Del is something of a legend, and it must have been a great honor to be the one he taught things to. The only trouble is, Jody, it's easy to get closed off to new teachers when you've had a great one."

"Yes, sir." Jody's face relaxed, and he looked a little less pounded on. Monte had been impressed with how the boy hadn't sulled up at breakfast, but had the grace to grin ruefully and laugh along with the crew, even if he had carried the sting inside all day.

Jody spoke earnestly to his boss. "I'm learning from Rafe, too, you know. I mean, he hardly talks, but when he does, I don't know, he always says things that *matter*, know what I mean?"

"I do. And there again, I'm jealous as hell. First of all, that you are getting that kind of experience, and second of all, that you are smart enough to appreciate it."

Jody sat up straighter in the seat of the truck. "And he's, like, a good person, too, you know. Like how he didn't spread it around about Blake's water gaps being down and all of those cows going through up onto the mountain." Jody was almost bouncing in the seat.

Monte drove for a moment in silence. No, Rafe sure as hell *hadn't* ratted Blake out, just mentioned the water gaps in passing. "Jody, tell you what. Why don't you see if Del wants to join us for the last few days of works. Everyone will be sleeping in the bunkhouse when we move over to headquarters, and I'll cut him day wages. Give him a call this weekend, see if he's willing. I'll mount him, too. Just have him bring his bed."

Monte and a smiling Jody pulled into headquarters just as Sue turned on the lights in the cook house. All of headquarters smelled like whatever she had in her oven. After the horses were unloaded, Monte carried the vaccine cooler into the office and stowed it in the refrigerator. He bent down to wash his hands in the little sink, watched pink and gray water slide down the porcelain. His shirt was blood splattered from running the knife, ear marking and cutting late calves, and his hair smelled of branding smoke and sweat, but he needed to talk to Shiney before the evening was over. He glanced up from the sink and into the mirror. There were dark lines of dirt in the creases of his face. Even his teeth were brown.

Fuck it.

He walked up the hill to his house and ran through the shower.

Shiney got out the ice bucket with the silver tongs, an unexpected convention precipitated by having an unexpected visitor. The change from their usual time and setting, coffee and breakfast in the kitchen, to drinks in the library where, at Shiney's request, Monte lit the first fire of the season just for the friendliness of it, felt like a party. When he had walked up to the back door, they had stood for a bit out on the stoop shivering and talking, watching the very last of the sunset. Finally Shiney said, "I know you're tired, but surely you could use a drink." Her foreman was all shaved and smelled good, so Shiney filled the ice bucket, pulled out the expensive tequila, the good scotch, and ensconced him in Papa's chair. Maybe the fire was unnecessary and sentimental, but Shiney liked it. It felt less like business and more like friends.

"Thanks." Monte lifted his glass to her and she lifted hers back, settling into the chair.

"So, what is Levi mad about?"

Monte laid his head back, closed his eyes. "Jody let the sort out two days ago. We spent all afternoon sorting steers from heifers, getting ready for Monterey, you know, to come with the trucks. Jody opened the wrong gate."

Somehow, Shiney's gasp in the high-ceilinged library soothed Monte like nothing else could. He knew she didn't gasp as the owner of the steers that had sold so well, directly to the feeder, but gasped in recognition of the hours of work that had gone into the sort, the dusty, hot, yelling, swaying work. He could have told that story to Pam a thousand times over and never gotten that gasp, no matter how many cutting horses she rode in the arena.

"It was an honest mistake . . . I mean the maze over there at those Half-Way pens is hard to understand. I don't know what the bozo who built them was thinking."

Shiney chuckled. "Oh, he was. A bozo, I mean. I remember when Nesto fired him."

"Anyway, Jody didn't mean to, and Levi knows that. Levi made his share of mistakes when he was that age, but all he sees in Jody is some kid almost the same age as Chad, doing what he's always wanted Chad to do. Levi is a good hand, aside from his temper, but if I lived with Velma Jo, I might lose it from time to time, too." Monte took a long swallow of tequila. "At least he doesn't recite poems and that is one thing to be eternally grateful for."

Shiney didn't just chuckle. She threw her head back and laughed, long and loud.

Monte grinned at her over the rim. "So how have things been at headquarters?"

"Oh, no you don't. You know exactly how things have been around here. Silent except for the geese flying over and Sam and Sue buzzing off to feed you guys and coming back a few hours later. Go on . . . I want to hear more."

"Well, let's see. It's going well. Calves are fat. Cows look good going into winter. There's a lot of feed in the lower country. I am so glad we have Annie around, keeps us from having to hire an outside hand. She works hard, is quiet, and doesn't make an issue of it when she has to go off into the bushes. Blake seems happier now that he's 'drive leader,' and keeps us laughing. It's just that blasted poetry . . . Jody is, of course, a good hand. I'm glad we sent him over to work with Rafe for as long as we did. Rafe really likes him, and they got on well together. It is good for Jody to start learning Rafe's country, just in case he needs to know his way around up there, plus he's used to working with an older man. Used to that voice of authority that is ultimate but willing to listen to suggestions. I guess even Nell likes him. At least it seemed like it. She looked after that silly pup while he was up on the mountain. We'll be longer than a week at West Camp. Longer than last year, and Brenna already looks tired. Some of Blake's cows got through onto the mountain. Rafe is taking the blame though I know good and well who is at fault, who didn't get over and put up the water gaps in a timely manner. But what am I gonna do?" Monte rubbed a big hand over his face, letting Shiney see how tired he really was. "Oh, two things. First, let's split the burger from that broke leg steer between the cook house and West Camp. Also, I want to bounce an idea off of you. What do you think of sending the keeper heifers to Farm Camp, let Annie and Chris take on the calving? I know that Blake and Brenna count on the calving bonus every year, but dammit, with this poetry bullshit and the baby coming . . . oh, hell. I just think this is a change we need to make."

Shiney looked hard at the fire. "Do it."

"I *cannot* believe they are having another kid. That house is too small, you know. It's a shitty, leaky little dump . . . needs a good bulldozing."

"But we can't replace it now, Monte. You know that. We could add on, but should we? Because one cowboy keeps having kids? If there were an attached garage like over at Old Sally, I'd gladly get Sam to close it in. As it is . . . ." Shiney held up her hands in surrender and got up to refresh their drinks.

Monte passed his glass to her. "My opinion? I think we have to let Blake deal with this the best he can. Bliss won't be there much longer. She's what, sixteen? Anyway, I'll be glad when we get out of Brenna's hair so she can throw up in private or whatever it is pregnant women do. I hate to cheat those guys out of her cooking check, but I'm going to talk to Sue and see if she can help out if it looks like Brenna can't handle it, just haul the food to the house the way she's been hauling to the pens. You should join us some." Monte felt the warmth of the fire and the tequila start to kick in and his speech began to wind down. "When we are done over on that side, we'll all show up here and be under your feet for maybe, oh, four days? I think we can wrap things up in four days. And before I forget, I did even more damage to our payroll. Told Jody to see if Del wants to come help us for a few days here at headquarters. It just seemed like the right thing to do."

Shiney nodded in full agreement. "It'll be nice to see Del. Good idea. But, we *are* going to make that pencil-necked geek of an accountant – I mean, nice Mr. Cameron – have a coronary, especially if we keep Jody on through the winter. Blast, but that man e-mails a lot. Got another one today about some wind energy company. I wish I could explain to him that there will always be wind companies. There have always been foundations wanting us to put the land into a conservation easement. There have always been mining companies wanting to dig, and oil and gas companies wanting to drill." She stopped the speech that had been running through her head for days, and shook her head. "I don't discount any of those in our future, but the truth is, though finances are hard right now, they've been hard before. We'll survive. Your phone call to Monterey saved us this year, and we'll find a way every year, I suppose. December to December!" She grinned wryly. "I sure do want one of those gas wells, though. Always have. Just one, tucked into a hidden little canyon where I never have to see it. Maybe for Christmas?"

Monte grinned at his boss. "Speaking of holidays, Blake wants to have a party in the shop, complete with music and dancing for New Year's Eve. What do you think?"

Shiney waved both hands, palms out, at him. "Don't get me involved! As long as I don't have to go, I don't care what you do. Truth is, I am thinking of having a few of my friends from Scottsdale out for a little shindig around New Years. And, also, I am going to be away for a few days next month, going to a friend's house party in the desert."

Monte raised his eyebrows. "Gotta boyfriend in Phoenix, boss?"

Shiney glared at him. "Just run the ranch, Monte, and don't let it burn down while I am gone. Boyfriend. Right."

The clear tequila, the warm fire, the rambling track of the conversation made Monte not want to leave the library of the Big House and retreat to the colder silence of his house on the hill. This simple contact made him more ready and able to face going back to work. Able to face the lonely part of his job. Lonely because he'd never really be one of the guys. A boss can only be so close to the men he hires and fires. He was pretty sure they all liked him, and he liked them, counted them as friends, but there would always be a barrier. He guessed it was the same with a manager and an owner, but he felt like he and Shiney had overcome some of that. Sometimes he thought the harder he worked, the more his marriage suffered, and the more the isolation of his position was highlighted.

He knew that the fatigue he felt was due to obsessing over every detail, worrying about every part of the process. Truth was, he could stay at his desk and let Rafe run the works if he wanted to, but dammit, this was the part he craved. This was the reward for the administrative duties that were a necessary part of his job.

He remembered his father telling him, right after Shiney hired him, "It's a tough spot to be in. You hope that you're a good enough cowboy that your guys respect you. No better feeling than seeing your crew work well together, riding good horses. A good crew runs like the military with the same kind of respect, chain of command, commitment to the job. It all starts at the top and flows downward."

But, oh, to be just one of the soldiers.

Shiney sat in her window seat, watery drink in her hand, her foreman's shadow already blended in with the others as he walked up the hill. Just before he left, Monte had leaned over and grabbed her hand. "Hey. Nice to see you interested in what all is going on around here. There for awhile, I thought you'd stopped caring . . . ." Shiney had felt the weight of her guilt settle firmly into the pocket around her heart. How to tell Monte Wells that her trip to Scottsdale was more than social? How to tell him how tired this ranch was making her? How to explain that "December to December" was dragging on her much heavier than it ever had? How to admit how attractive some of the options popping up sounded?

Headquarters had been so silent, so still, since works started. Sue and Sam had been in and out, of course, and the school bus had continued to make its dutiful appearances. Occasionally a gooseneck trailer rattled in and dumped a load of culled cows, the ones that Monte wanted to feed extra well for a few weeks before hauling them to the local sale. But it never stayed long. Always rumbled back out leaving a little cloud of dust hanging by the gate into the trap and a scattering of alfalfa flakes with cows munching contentedly. Big fat barren cows. Old shelly cows with loose, ruined bags. Thin cows that didn't breed back for some reason or another. And occasionally, an old running off, hiding, filthy-to-gather cow who had shit in her nest with Monte. Or Rafe. Shiney always grinned when she thought of the one time she'd seen Rafe Johansen lose his temper, several years ago when he had granted amnesty to an old hiding bitch several times in a row, only to have her run him all over the side of a rough-assed hill, sticking her head in every tree she could find, earning herself a solid cussing and a quick trip to the sale barn as soon as he had her within eye-sight of a trailer.

Shiney missed the days when she was right in the middle of things. Or maybe she didn't. It had been her decision, about three years earlier, not to ride with the crew anymore. The cold mornings and long days had lost their appeal, and the hours in the saddle made her hips hurt. She still enjoyed showing up some days at the corrals in the pickup, though, and thought she'd go over to West Camp next week. It would be good to get out and about. It was such a relief to have Monte. She trusted him as well as understood the need for someone at headquarters to answer the phone, man the office, listen to the wind blow more than to the cattle bawl, hay the culls, feed the mares, look after the lonely weanling colts.

Every morning, in lieu of coffee with Monte, she bundled up so she could feel her cowboys' discomfort, and walked down to the tinaja and back.

Autumn is when the Bride dances.

No longer self-conscious and shy, no longer blushing, no longer heavy with heat and seed, she wears the fiery jewels she's earned through the year. Her nests and pastures are empty, and cool nights whisper gold into her green.

The Bride in autumn is free, free to rustle her skirts and fling herself into mature color, sure of her age and her gifts. She claps and rattles and sighs. She plays her own music, sings her own song, and dives into entropy as if it were a deep and welcome bed.

The cow tracks on her trails and in her canyons become obscured by the softer tracks of creatures eager to hibernate and sleep, the cloven hoof prints wiped away by those with claws and pads and scales. Her leftover berries wrinkle with crystallizing sugars, and the trees turn golden in her draws. The winds lay the cured grasses down to sleep, and one early morning the clouds frost the Bride's top with snow that disappears by noon. The moon rises round and mysterious to bathe the mountain with vows, vows of tomorrow and tomorrow and tomorrow.

EEYORE

"THE BOY'S GOT RHYTHM!!!" became the anthem for the second half of fall works on the Tinaja. Everyone tired of it eventually, except Blake of course, who could repeat anything and everything *ad nauseum*, and wouldn't shut up with that Peaches poem.

They all knew the little blue horse could pitch because he'd pitched with Joe, the last guy who'd lived in the bunkhouse, but everyone figured he was over it. Even Jody, who'd ridden him a couple of times at headquarters, on warm afternoons in a relaxed kind of way, thought the little blue horse was solid, just young. He left him behind when he pulled out for Old Sally, and it proved to be a mistake, proved to be too many days off. He'd brought him along on this round though, and never thought about how long the little horse's vacation had been until he stepped aboard on the first morning that frost covered the ground.

Jody was glad that all he knew was the simple, "He's a little cold backed," that Rafe had told him and Monte had affirmed because there was no way in holy hell he could have ridden the blue roan if he'd been dry mouthed and hollow stomached with anticipation, or been fed a lot of advice like, "don't let him jerk your rein," or "he sounds worse than he is," or "keep your feet from getting sucked back under you," though every bit of that would have been helpful and true.

The little blue horse with no name made awful sounds as he pitched all over the driveway of West Camp, but Jody never heard them, just like he never heard the shouts of the other men. He was, however, fully aware when Levi on his big bay horse came up beside him just as the little blue was ready to give it up, was aware of making a big wide fast arc out into the horse pasture side by side, and he heard Levi clearly when he yelled, "Don't spur him again now that he's quit!"

When they reined up back beside the barn, everyone was whooping and hollering, and Blake roared, "THE BOY'S GOT RHYTHM!" and Jody realized his hand was cemented to his night latch.

After that morning, the little horse never pitched again, and Jody was never the new kid again.

To Monte's dismay, that week was also the beginning of the run of cartoon and Disney names given to the horses on the ranch. Levi had looked lazily at Jody over his beans and meatloaf at noon and said, "Ah, hell. That colt can't pitch. He's just a slow moving donkey. Like Eeyore!" The name stuck. And it seemed like for the next couple of years, every new colt the cowboys drew got a name like Mufasa or Pooh or Aladdin or Speedy or Tigger or, unfortunately, one in Blake's string named The White Rabbit. When Shiney heard the story her only comment to Monte was, "Cowboys, my foot. They're all just overgrown children."

CARROT CAKE

In her next life, Brenna wanted to come back as a man, except that even the idea of a next life made her tired. So tired. Sometimes she really did wish she were a man though because the idea of sitting down to pee and then having to stand back up again exhausted her. And of course she had to pee all the blessed time. If she were a man, she could just stand there. Which must be what all three boys and Blake did. Just stand there. Not giving any guidance whatsoever, judging from the smell and the yellow stains around the toilet. Brenna leaned against the wall. Maybe if she wasn't having so many dreams at night, she wouldn't be so tired.

She dreamed about two-headed babies. She dreamed about houses with endless rooms. She dreamed about giving birth to snakes or litters of kittens that turned into snakes. She dreamed about having a beautiful baby but being scared to change its diaper because she knew that when she peeled back the wet diaper she would discover that the baby had a tail, a scaly, horrible, awful, long, pointy tail.

Brenna wanted to come back as a man so she could have holidays and weekends off, never have to make a bed or fold socks or clean out the refrigerator. She wanted to come back as a man so that she could plant a baby in someone else and then ride off into the dawn, so that she could do something glorious like ride a bucking horse the way she'd seen Jody do that morning as she looked out the kitchen window scrubbing egg off of the skillet, a mountain of dirty dishes waiting.

She wanted to show up with cigars after the baby was born (sweat, curse, hold the sides of the bed, pant, pant, where is the rotten bastard? and then add in periods, menopause, sore boobs, and miscarriages), tell the nurse the name he picked out, and forget this silly B thing.

She wanted to have a *Playboy* to read in the bathroom (can you say airbrushed, fantasy, probably a bitch, and who the hell leans over like THAT without hurting her back?) and never, ever having to shave her legs.

Brenna was on her fourth day cooking for the crew, and the biggest blessing of the whole fall was that all four kids were at school during the day. She'd been plenty worried about Bliss driving everyone to headquarters to catch the bus, even if it was only dirt road, but Blake had given her several lessons before works started, and now Brenna was hoping the trend could continue, freeing her from the twice a day bumpy commute. She didn't mind doing without her personal pickup since several ranch trucks were parked around if she needed one.

She stared at the packages of hamburger on the cookie sheet where they had thawed overnight. The dark puddle of blood beneath them would have made her retch with her other pregnancies. This time, nothing. This time the aching weariness was worse. She felt as if she were moving in slow motion. Must be age.

But if it really was age, she wondered how in the hell things were going to go from now on. There were wet clothes in the washer, souring, dry clothes in the dryer, wrinkling, more dirty laundry spilling out of the hampers in the bathrooms. There were toys on the living room floor, syrup dripped on the table where she'd need to feed men in a few hours, and every time the heater kicked on she thought with shame of the afternoon before when she was lying on the couch and heard the back porch door blow open. The heating and cooling unit was on the porch, and Monte had told Blake that the door needed to stay closed to give the unit every chance to operate efficiently. But Brenna had felt weighted down by such a huge load that she had just lain there until she was startled by the sound of the door being shut firmly. She got up and looked out the window to see Shiney Lewis climb into a strange truck and go on down the driveway. Blake told her that night that Shiney had been on her way back from the corrals where she and the cow buyer had gone to watch the trucks being loaded and had seen the porch door open. She had stopped and shut it, slammed it really, while Brenna had been lying there like a slug, letting money blow out into the wind.

Brenna shrugged. She figured the old lady could afford it. Some people were born rich. She went back to staring, this time at the list of things to be prepared for the noon meal when she heard a truck drive up. Nell came through the back door without knocking, carrying a big cardboard box.

"Just bringing a dessert for those rotten men. I love making this recipe so it wasn't any big deal. If you don't need to serve it today, it'll keep for tomorrow. How you feeling, honey?" She lifted out a gorgeous three-layer carrot cake piled with cream cheese icing sprinkled with pecans.

No big deal? It was thirteen miles of dirt road from Old Sally Camp to West Camp. Rough dirt road. And Brenna knew for certain that pecans were expensive, $7 for just one little pouch. She shoved a Jell-O cheesecake mix behind some dirty dishes with the back of her hand.

Nell went straight to the sink and started making hot soapy water. "Don't mind me. I just got lonely. Got used to having those smelly men under my feet, had a week to rest without them, and now I came to see what was going on around here. Like my new haircut? Velma Jo talked me into it. You look plumb peaked, girl!"

Brenna started stirring spices into the ground meat, her arms too weak to turn the heavy beef into anything more than a big blob. About the time Nell got the rest of the dishes done, another truck pulled up, this time one owned by the ranch, the TJ brand stenciled on the door panels. Nell dried her hands on a dish towel and opened the screen door for Sue, whose arms were full.

"Brenna! You poor thing! I brought stuff to put in the supper box, and while I was at it, I decided to use up every bit of garden truck I could pick. These cool nights are bringing the spinach and lettuces on again!" She opened a big red cooler and lifted out an enormous wooden salad bowl piled with greens topped with shredded carrots, slivered almonds, mandarin orange slices, dried cranberries, and crumbled boiled egg. She also lifted out matching salad tongs, a mason jar full of home-made vinaigrette, and a big platter of deep red sliced tomatoes with white cheese and some sort of leaf on top of each one. Brenna thought of the slightly browning head of iceberg and the pale soft tomatoes in the bottom drawer of her refrigerator, the half-empty bottles of ranch and thousand island dressing. She'd gotten a wooden salad bowl for a wedding gift, but someone had fed the dog in it a few years back and it had ended up all weathered and with chew marks.

Before long, not only were the kitchen and dining room spotless, but the plates were stacked, the silverware laid out, the living room vacuumed, the brown-and-serve rolls Brenna had bought out on cookie sheets ready to go into the oven when the meatloaf was done, and somehow Sue had taken over the mashed potatoes. They were creamy and perfect, not a lump in sight. Brenna felt tears spring into her eyes and the baby move in her belly.

A cooler wind moved the crew on to Farm Camp and then to headquarters. Monte blessed the contract signed in late summer as the fat calves walked across the scales. Annie and Chris worked as a team frying bacon and buttering toast for the crew. Sue made coconut cream pies, and Levi was sweet for three days. Jody watched the school bus go by on the highway one afternoon. Blake had finally run out of stories and songs and poems. Only Rafe saw the snow up on the highest peak, and only he heard his mountain welcome winter.

KNEELING IN THE DIRT

The computer screen dimmed down to its final star as Shiney turned off the lights in the office. The wagon yard was full of empty rigs, the corrals full of horses dripping water from muzzles and walking out into the trap for the night. They'd fought the war of pecking order earlier in the season, and now they were tired, not anxious to expend energy on the battles again. Good smells wrapped like a cloak around the cook house, accented with the stomp of boots on wooden floors, a smothered whoop of laughter from inside the dining hall, and the crinkle of a silver can smashed flat. A solitary smoker made a stationary firefly at the end of the porch. Shiney saw the real and ancient stars begin to appear as she walked quickly to the Big House, pulling her sweater tighter. Headquarters certainly wasn't quiet and lonely tonight.

Shiney was tired of hard decisions. She was tired of sitting in the office where the hard decisions had to be made. Tired of getting e-mails and phone calls with more hard decisions for tomorrow. Like she'd told Monte, the bounce in the cow market had saved them this year, along with his clever marketing, but the new year was coming, and it carried with it more hard decisions. Rather than decreasing the number of employees, they'd increased, gone the wrong way. Papa and her mother had given her life, and dollars, but the Tinaja was a big drain on both. No one but Shiney would ever know how many of her mother's dollars had gone to keep the Tinaja afloat over the years.

She turned on a single lamp in the kitchen. Sue had put a plate of leftovers beside the stove, and all of a sudden Shiney was hungry. She could have eaten any of her meals at the same table as her cowboys, but she rarely did. Seemed awkward to be there, and the men acted differently, like school boys when the principal walks in. Tonight she filled a tumbler with ice as she waited for the microwave to beep and then carried her meal up the stairs, up to the TV tray in front of the window seat, up to a place where she could watch. Watch as night descended.

Shiney had been watching the evening before when an extra hand had pulled into headquarters. Watched Del Lincoln shake hands with the boy, and then almost hug him, turn it into more of a slap on the back. Watched as Jody introduced him to the men on the crew. Watched her cowboys drink a beer on the porch while waiting for Sue to call dinner. Watched Levi smoke a cigarette with Sam. Watched a card game keep the bunkhouse lights on past ten o'clock.

She continued to watch at different times through the next few days. Watched as fall works wound down, as Pam came home and headed straight up to the house on the hill, watched as those lights burned late. Watched the dust rise from the shipping pens half a mile away. Watched culture and industry bump heads gently while Monte and Rafe decided which cows to cull and which heifers to keep. Watched as the children climbed wearily into Brenna's truck after school one day. Watched Sue pull up tomato plants and stack them on the compost pile, pausing to rub a hand on her back as if it ached. Watched the cookhouse lights come on a few minutes earlier each night. After she signed Del's day working check, taking his gentle joshing as matter of course, she watched him drive away, going home, just as the rest of the men did that evening.

And she was still watching several evenings later. She saw the whole thing happen, sat with her jaws and her soul locked and immoveable while the boy knelt in the dirt.

Since Jody had moved into the bunkhouse, he'd been away more than he'd been there at headquarters, but he'd been around long enough for Shiney to begin to like him, long enough for her to want to know him better.

During their first meeting Jody had said, "I'm supposed to say hello to you from Delbert Lincoln." She supposed she'd been a little ungracious, saying only, "Huh. I hadn't thought of him in years. Damned old cowboys."

Several days later, she'd gotten to know him a little bit better. She'd been in the office all morning and had gone home at noon to eat a bite and was walking back across the grass when she rounded the grape arbor and there was Jody beside a decent-sized hole under the newest lilac bush Sam had planted back in the spring. He was filling the hole back in with a mound of freshly dug dirt. Missy sat off to his right, her head tilted to the side.

"I'm sorry, Miz Lewis. I guess when she saw Sam diggin' she thought she'd be allowed, too." The sight of the tall almost-man kneeling on the ground, looking like he was demonstrating how to dig, even though the little blue and white cowdog didn't seem to need lessons judging from the damage she'd done, made Shiney laugh.

Jody blushed.

"Oh, she's just doing what puppies do. We'll keep an eye on her, and if we have to, you can put her on a leash and jerk her over backwards a few times. But for now, just tell her no." With that, Sunshine Angel Lewis did something she hadn't done in years – she reached down and picked up a soft, fat, wriggling creature in her arms, felt a wet nose touch her chin, smelled the unmistakable baby breath mixed with loamy soil from beneath the lilac.

"No," she said in the puppy's face. Missy licked her on the nose.

The autumn sunshine felt so good, the puppy smelled so good, and the boy was someone she wanted to like.

"So you know Del Lincoln well?"

"Yes, ma'am. Real well."

"How is he? Or I guess, the best question, where is he?"

Jody told her about the ranch Del was on, said he was fine, ". . . sometimes pretty cranky."

"Oh, well, we all get cranky when we get old." The two stood in silence soaking up the midday warmth for a few moments.

"Sounds like you care about Del, cranky or not."

Jody lowered his gaze. "Del is the closest thing to a father I've ever had. He raised me."

Shiney set the puppy down. "Well, then, I'd say you and Del both got lucky."

And so the boy and the puppy settled into life on the Tinaja. And Shiney thought it was good.

From the window she saw Jody do things like hunt up a broom to sweep the porch of the bunkhouse, the puppy pouncing and chewing on the broom straws, and Jody laughing out loud when she got too rowdy and fell off the edge. She saw Jody pick up one of Blake's boys and dust him off when he fell in the gravel and skinned his knee getting off the bus. Shiney noticed that Jody didn't watch television much in the evenings, preferring to work with leather in the saddle house or sit on the porch with Missy as the sun went down, even when he had to put on a denim coat. She and Monte had decided to keep the young man on for the winter to halter break the colts and float around to the other camps.

The past few days, Shiney had seen Jody out by the colt pen where the weanlings stood, missing their mothers. The ranch weaned fewer and fewer colts every year; this year only six. Jody stood in their midst for several evenings until they counted him as one of them. Seven.

And Shiney saw that it was good.

Fall works were well and truly over, plunging headquarters back into a deserted, lonely feeling. The only rig in the yard that evening was a neighbor's. He'd brought a stray TJ bull home and stood talking to Monte in the lee of the barn, the men's hands in their pockets, their collars turned up. Fall had turned to winter, and the wind knew it. Shiney saw Monte shake the neighbor's hand, saw Jody out beside the colt pen button his coat and pull on his gloves, saw Monte wave goodbye and hurry across the wagon yard, up toward his own house, heard the neighbor slam his pickup door. Shiney saw Jody cross the yard, too, headed to wash up for dinner, saw him get almost to the porch before he turned back, calling for Missy. Shiney saw the neighbor pull his rig out of the wagon yard and onto the road, the long gooseneck trailer making a wide sweep, saw the gray shadow of puppy come darting out from behind a low rock wall to nip at the tires, saw the wheel bump bump, barely a bump, not even enough for the driver to think it was anything but a rock. Saw the boy start to run, and Shiney knew, oh, she knew it was too late.

She must have stood up, must have knocked over her drink, when the shadow of dog flung itself into the path of the trailer tires. But now, as Jody Neil knelt in the dirt of the ranch road, knelt beside the crumpled little body, knelt there all alone, Sunshine Angel Lewis did not move. As the sun dipped below the horizon, leaving the head-bowed boy in dusk, she stood there, as frozen as the ice that was melting cold on her jeans. And she knew that she must not have one maternal gene in her body, knew she must be as uncaring and unloving as her own mother.

WINE PAIRINGS

Max Angel couldn't have ridden one mile up the slope of Bride Mountain. He would not have been able to lift a saddle to the back of the gentlest horse on the ranch, wouldn't have understood one word of Rafe and Monte's dusty debate about that brindle cow and her chances of fertility in the coming year. He would never have seen the haired-over year brand on her shoulder. Max Angel's hands were soft and white with trimmed nails and a gold ring, and he bore a glass of very cold white wine which he handed to her by way of introduction.

"Mrs. Lewis, Max Angel. I understand you share my odd appellation, though yours is nicely tucked away between names."

Shiney smiled and sipped at the wine, starting with surprise at how good it was. Her new companion pulled out the chair next to her at Betts Gardner's table at the country club and sat down. "Gewurztraminer. Nice, isn't it?"

Betts had extended an invitation to Max by phone the day before. "She's the real deal, Max. She owns a real ranch with real cows and real cowboys, the Old West kind. Her father was some kind of entrepreneur and left the whole . . . well, spread is the word, I guess, to Sunny. We had a lot of good times in college, but she's really different. I mean, she knows about bulls and crops and stuff. She's spent all these years way out there with the cows! But I guess the ranch is beautiful. Some of us are going to go out there at New Year's for a house party . . . . Are there snakes in winter, Max?"

Max Angel spent most of the evening trying to put his tablemate at ease, but he mainly succeeded in making Shiney feel ignorant. And yet, even with her failure to keep up with some of the conversation, she felt a sense of longing. What if she really had missed out on a whole huge segment of life? What if Mother had been right all of those years ago when she shuddered at the possibility that her daughter would bury herself on the Tinaja with the ignorant and the rough and the unworthy? With her Papa.

Shiney made a mental note to renew her subscriptions to the magazines she used to read. Mother could still afford at least that.

At first the evening was bright with Arizona glare, then stage-lit by the desert sunset, then enveloped in candlelight and an unobtrusive electric glow from wall sconces on the restaurant patio where the dining experience was expected to take four hours. Shiney finally sat back in her chair and drained the spicy, but now rather warm, wine from the glass Max had handed her while the sun was still bright. Then she gazed with trepidation at the array of glasses arranged at the top of her plate. Each time the waiter had brought a new course, he had poured a new wine into the appropriately-shaped glass. She hadn't touched one of them yet, though the meal was over. The last one poured was a rich looking sherry that was supposed to go with the chocolate crème brûlée she had only tasted.

Max Angel watched her out of the corner of his eye. Betts Gardner always brought the most interesting people to the group.

"Wine pairings always make me wonder if we are supposed to taste the food at all." He leaned toward the slight woman with a pixie-ish cap of silver hair, but who gave an air of being larger and stronger than the sculptor intended. "Tell me about your ranch and I'll make sure the waiter brings us some coffee and perhaps a good scotch?"

The wine, the scotch, the light . . . they all must have combined to make her tongue flap. Shiney found herself, sometime later, telling the intense little man all about how caught she felt between Rafe – "What an oddly old fashioned name!" Max had declared. And Monte. "Of course his name is Monte!" Max had actually clapped his hands with glee. Shiney talked about the war between the culture of cows and the economics of the cattle industry. She spoke of her love for the Bride, about her Tinaja, about how the accountant kept sending her e-mails with subject lines like cash flow and capital and overhead. At one point she looked up to see Max with his head to the side as she spoke of her Papa.

And, as she lay in a strange bed that night, scotch still flowing through her veins, she had a vague recollection that she had invited Maxmillian Angel to her New Year's Eve party. As she was falling asleep, she decided she wasn't ready to go home, back to the melting pot of problems and decisions. She decided that she didn't miss one blooming thing about the ranch. Not one! Well, maybe one. She missed that old photograph of Papa propped on the sideboard beside the scotch bottle. It showed Paul Amato Lewis astride the big bay horse he had bought from a neighbor one summer, the one he always said should never have been cut. The one that Punch insisted should have sired many. Papa had loved that horse, and Shiney always smiled at his old fashioned posture in the black and white photograph, at his stiffly proud legs, back and reins. Okay, so it was silly to miss a photograph when she was only gone from the Tinaja for three nights.

Oh, Papa, what am I to do?

Mujer Seca

On the evening of the TJ Ranch Christmas party, Sunshine Angel Lewis was oblivious to the encroaching cold front that would, after midnight, leave a skiff of snow around the edges of the tinaja, leave several inches of true snow piled up against the door of Precious Camp, leave a thin sheet of ice on every puddle, on every pond. She was also ignoring the smell of ham that drifted up the stairs from the too warm, too crowded kitchen, ham she had seen smeared with apricot preserves by Sue's competent hand earlier in the afternoon. She was not, however, indifferent to the sound of the carols that rode the waves of sweet porky odors. She detested Christmas carols.

Shiney ran the bristles of a brush through her hair and tugged the hem of her black sweater down over the hips of her Wranglers. No red or green for her, thank you. No reindeer appliqués or jingle bell earrings. Leave those to Nell.

She heard the kitchen door slap open and shut again, and new voices were added to the din down below, and she looked at the main source of her irritation – an empty, sweating highball glass. She picked up a squash blossom necklace from the bureau and clasped its heavy coldness around her neck. She was only wearing it because Nesto gave it to her years ago, and she thought of him when it lay against her chest. Shiney picked up the glass with its melting ice cubes and cursed her own firm policy stating that she could only pour twice in one evening. Damned stupid policy. She was absolutely sure to need a drink later on in the midst of this fiasco. She sucked at the smoky-tasting ice melt, gazed over the rim at the bottle of scotch resting on a crocheted doily on the antique sideboard in her sitting room. Damn. She set the glass firmly down on a coaster, flipped the light switch off, squared her shoulders, and walked down the stairs.

Deuced silly things, Christmas parties.

This was all Monte's fault.

She was a grouchy old woman, set in her ways, and she liked the tradition of having the Tinaja Ranch Christmas party in the cook house dining hall. She preferred the way they'd always done it, or at least the way they had done it since Punch died, and no one had the heart to try to duplicate his big jolly and jovial, expansive and expensive blow-outs complete with too much booze, a pit dug in the ground with a whole hog roasting, so many chile rellenos that Mama D's hands blistered and peeled, the whole ranch one big festival for over a week. Since he'd left them, the ranch wives would bring covered dishes to the cook house, decorate swags of cedar branches with red bows, make the foreman dress up as Santa, and Shiney would make an appearance, hand out bottles of booze to the cowboys, sometimes with discreet bonus checks tucked inside the boxes, gift certificates to the women, and stockings full of candy to the children. She always stayed long enough to slightly dirty a paper plate, smile at everyone, and leave with a box full of silly food covered in green cellophane that she served when the Chavez brood descended in little drips and dribbles through the holidays. Now her house was full of people, her kitchen had been invaded, and there was a cedar tree in her living room – probably dropping ticks into the carpets – all for "morale."

Deucedly and damnedly silly things, Christmas parties.

Unlike the evening social events she had attended in Scottsdale with Betts Gardner, these ranch things often arranged themselves by gender and, sure enough, the women were moving like a flock of cowbirds or a less-than-graceful school of fish back and forth from the kitchen to the long sideboard in the dining room, setting out food and talking non-stop. Shiney heard bits and pieces.

"Oh, we'll go to Blake's folks' house on the day. Santa always shows up there instead of at our house. Just the way we've always . . . ."

"Oh, you know kids. Tonight is their youth group gift exchange, and I told them to at least eat with us, but they just had to go!"

" . . . bought that new Wonder-kin doll for Kenzie, but didn't know it was going to be so sexy-looking. I wonder at the people who make these things . . . ."

" . . . these great bargains on the . . ."

Shiney smiled and nodded her way through the crowd.

Velma Jo was standing in the archway between the dining room and the library. Mercy, that girl was fluffy or shiny all over. She wore those dark little jeans tucked into furred high-heeled hooker boots and so much silver jewelry that she looked anchored to the ground. Shiney thought it unfortunate that Annie walked over to stand by Velma Jo. She made Velma Jo look overdone, hot and fuzzy. Annie was wearing brand new tight Wranglers, much tighter, of course, than a dried up old woman wore hers, but Shiney remembered a time. She liked how Annie wore her red flannel shirt and handmade cowboy boots with simplicity and class. The underslung heels were of a practical height, and the tops were hidden as they should be. Her long straight hair held back with a silver and turquoise clip. Annie was a big girl, tall, with large capable hands, but no one accused her of being manly. Her black hat hung on the cherrywood hat rack with the men's. Nell went by the two with a dish of scalloped potatoes, and Annie reached over to the sideboard to move things around for her.

When Monte approached Shiney with a glass of amber liquid in his hand, she gave an inner shrug. Oh, well, he didn't know about the two pour policy. Who was she to argue? After all, it was a party.

Nell had on an Avon Christmas sweater, red velour sweatpants, and white Reeboks, candy cane earrings dangling. She must have changed clothes while Shiney was upstairs. She wished she'd thought to offer a place to shower and dress, but somehow things like that never entered Shiney's mind. Nell had been at headquarters all day, helping Sue with the decorations and the food. The two of them had rearranged furniture, vacuumed, cooked and decorated. A few weeks ago, Velma Jo had convinced Nell to go to the hairdresser, and instead of the tight old-lady curls she used to wear, now her hair was all red and gold spikes. Shiney thought it made her look ridiculous, but she had heard Nell say it made her feel "young and hip! And Rafe, he's just hopeless! I asked him if he liked it and he looked like I was giving him some sort of test! He said, 'Your hair? Why I like it fine!' Blind old coot. This is the man who notices if I move his razor six inches to the left, but he never even saw my hair!"

Shiney felt like she'd never left her window seat.

She watched while Blake steered Brenna away from the women, her back already swayed with the weight of this baby. He settled her in a chair and brought her a glass of soda, all fizzy and dark, pulled the ottoman up for her feet. The youngest little boy of theirs – Shiney hated to admit even to herself that she couldn't remember all their names – climbed across the mound of his mother's lap and lay breathing open-mouthed around his thumb, his nose crusty. Shiney wondered if his face was flushed from the heat of the fireplace or the excitement of the party or fever. Great. She must remember to wash her hands.

The men stood awkwardly by the far windows looking like an advertisement for Western wear. A row of cowboys in their newest Wranglers, or Levis on the older men, pressed go-to-town shirts, their hair indented by the hats left at the door.

No one had thought to get Blake's boys something to drink so Shiney filled plastic tumblers with ice and poured soda for them, forgetting to make one for the youngest and causing him to cry. Blake attempted to stem the mini-meltdown with a mini-candy cane and pulled out a handkerchief for the already red nose. The handkerchief elicited louder squalls than before.

Shiney escaped the melee feeling vaguely at fault, but clueless as to what she had done wrong. She walked over to stand beside Monte. No one would mistake him for "just a cowboy" with his buttoned-down look of authority and thick salt-and-pepper hair, more salt every day it seemed.

"Trouble-maker."

"Hush. This was your idea."

"You're the boss around here."

"Sometimes I wonder."

Monte grinned big and glanced over just in time to see Blake's daughter, Bliss, smile at Jody. Bliss was wearing a t-shirt with an angel on it, but the angel's halo was crooked and her eyes were decidedly flirtatious. Jody looked like he didn't know what to do with any part of himself. The whole tableau looked like trouble to Monte, but he didn't want to think about it tonight. He liked standing side by side with Shiney, leaders of the whole band. Shiney looked at the glass in Monte's huge hand.

"Tequila?"

"Yes."

"Pam?"

"On her way." He took a swallow. "Late, of course."

"Hmm . . . well, she'd better hurry. She'll miss the speeches."

Monte choked slightly. "You're bad."

There had been someone once, many, many years ago. Someone who had made her equally uncomfortable, and yet, comfortable. Shiney slipped right back to being that young woman when she thought of him. Thought of how she'd wanted to fetch him cold drinks, hold his hand, clear his path of every unpleasant task or event. She'd wanted to stand close to him, listen to his laugh. Give him the biggest slice of chocolate cake. She guessed now that it had been love, and he'd made love to her, several times. But as their ranch management course neared its end, and she'd considered taking him home, introducing him to Punch, she'd drawn back. Silly maybe, but she was too young to trust herself, much less trust him. Trusting him with her body had been one thing, but to trust him with a whole ranch, a whole mountain, one that was her very life, that was quite another. How could she know that he'd love her just for herself and not for the miles and miles of beauty and responsibility that was the Tinaja? The whole question had been very neatly solved when they'd both been invited to a friend's ranch. During the weeklong house party, Shiney discovered that he couldn't saddle his own horse.

And she didn't care to teach him. Now she'd have been hard pressed to remember his name.

The party swirled around them, and Monte held his glass tightly to forestall the ridiculous and inappropriate urge to put his arm around the slight lady at his side, the one with silver hair cut close to her elegant head, the one in Wranglers that had to be at least twenty years old and a black sweater that was just as dated, the one who signed his paycheck and whose hands looked a little frail tonight, holding her own glass in front of her as if it were a gift. He knew she was uncomfortable with all of these extra people in her space. He gazed at his tequila as if it were to blame for the urge to hug his boss to his side, the way he saw Blake hold Brenna. He thought of the way that Rafe had gone right to Nell when he got here, lifted the hair off of her forehead and pressed his lips there. Monte wondered what Pam would do if he did something like that. Probably look at him as if he were an alien. Or laugh at him.

Everyone had piled gifts on a big table pushed into a corner of the library. From where she stood, Shiney could see foil wrapped loaves of what was sure to be pumpkin pecan bread, each one topped by a factory-made bow with sticky on the back like came in bags of 100 at the dollar store. Nell. Several baskets made of old lariat ropes hot-glued into spirals, each with a bag of tortilla chips and a bottle of salsa in it. Annie. Paper plates of sugar cookies. Brenna and the children must have done those. Slim elegant bottles of lotion, pink for the women, navy blue for the men, tied with fancy silver strands. Looked like Velma Jo was selling Mary Kay again, a fact Shiney was sure Monte told her but she must have forgotten. Velma Jo's entrepreneurial endeavors were a source of amusement for the two of them, but Shiney never could keep up with the current product. Seemed the last one was candles, big expensive candles that smelled terrible, some of them claiming to be scented like leather or coffee, but still managing to smell like gas station restrooms. Also on the table were mason jars full of spiced nuts, sure to be from Sam and Sue, sure to be delicious. Her own contributions to the gift table were small stockings of candy for each child, even the teenagers, a row of Crown Royal boxes, gift sets with a pair of tumblers packaged with each purple and gold bag. There was one odd-ball box with Monte's name on it. Don Julio Añejo with a single glass of real crystal, special order. She knew he did most of his drinking alone. Besides, Pam had a gift certificate to the Western wear store right along with the rest of the women in the neat little pile of envelopes that also contained bonus checks for the men written on Shiney's personal account, the individual amounts a matter of great privacy, and Shiney hoped they stayed that way. Shiney had debated giving a kid like Jody a bottle of bourbon, but when she'd asked Monte he'd said, "You hired a man to do a man's job. As far as I can see, he is doing that. Doing a man's job. You have to treat him just like one of your men." And so, the boy, not even legally of drinking age, would get a purple box like all the rest.

Shiney felt like an imposter in her own house as the cowboys, women, and children gathered in the dining room and filled their plates from the many dishes on the sideboard. The meal was noisy, the sturdy paper plates the same as Shiney remembered from years past. No one had asked her if they could use the heavy pottery stacked inside the hutch, but she'd have said no anyway. From what Shiney remembered, though she couldn't have actually remembered, but must remember from bits and pieces of conversations, her mother had requested that her delicate wedding china be packed into barrels with sawdust and shipped back east to the home of her birth. Punch had complied, promising Mama D something better. It was a bitch to think of things now that she wished she had asked Papa or Mama D about, or even Nesto might have remembered. But there was no one left to ask now.

For certain, there was no way she would have pulled out Mama D's pottery for this party, the pottery that Punch Lewis had given her when Shiney was just a little thing. She was sure she remembered this story correctly. Mama D had said firmly that she didn't want any flowers or ribbons on her eatin' dishes. So, every year Punch had added to the

Wallace China he'd chosen for her, the *El Rancho* pattern with Western motifs and chuck wagons and brands painted around the edges. Shiney thought the name, "El Rancho" had tickled Papa. He gave Mama D big pieces like tureens and casseroles when her babies were born, every couple of years there for awhile, new plates and chargers and mugs, even rope-trimmed glassware, on Christmas and her birthday. Mama D always protested, but she slapped and scolded any kid who was rough with the pottery at the kitchen sink, not talking to Nesto, Jr., for three days once when he broke a dinner plate.

Shiney looked down at the three bites of ham, teaspoon of cranberry sauce, and one bright yellow devilled egg on her plate and blinked hard. There was no comfort in having outlived the family – the ones who defined you. The ones who remembered the summer your nose peeled from too much sun, who knew that you hated cooked carrots unless they had brown sugar on them, who remembered the birthday when Papa hid your present up in the sycamore tree and you stomped your foot at him and spat which made him laugh uproariously.

Shiney usually climbed on top of grief quite handily, stomping any tendrils from her feet, and let the tears drain back down from whence they sprang. But the heavy warmth of Monte's hand on her back, the slip of his arm around her shoulders, was so shocking as to cause two drops of salt to spring forward out of her eyes and land on that devilled egg. She brushed at her eyes. Two gone. Two spilled. She hoped they weren't the last two drops of moisture ever in her dry life. *Seco.* One of Nesto's words when looking at the empty sky or a tank dam in need of replenishing. *Mujer seca.*

"You okay?"

His eyes were not really concerned, not really amused, just full of a comfortable asking. "I'm fine. Silly sentimental old woman." She hated that her voice shook slightly on the last syllable so she smiled, and stayed, leaning two inches like a wind-blown oak toward the man who was her second-in-command.

Her smile. Monte wished she'd use it more often.

The heavy front door slammed back, startling them all, and there was a mighty rustle of arriving packages. Monte sat back against his chair, his arm leaving an oddly cold line across Shiney's back. He closed his eyes and sighed. "Pam."

Shiney smiled down at her plate again. This would make for an interesting coffee-time some morning soon. She and Nell and Sue all three stood up briskly.

"Well, let's go help her!"

Teriyaki Chicken

Nell and Rafe rode along in a silence that seemed profound after the noise of the party, in a cold that seemed extreme after the close air of the Big House. The peace was broken only by the sound of the wind and the occasional ting of sleet on the windshield. When the party was over, Rafe had told Nell to leave their personal truck at headquarters and ride home with him in the ranch truck, and that was such a sweet thing to say. Such a sweet thing to do.

Rafe was a quiet man – so quiet sometimes that Nell wanted to stomp on his toe just to hear him say ouch. Rafe was a gentle man – so gentle sometimes that Nell wondered if he ever wanted to stomp on anything. Her favorite view of her husband was when he sat at his desk in the corner of the bedroom, his old man glasses perched on his nose, carefully balancing the checkbook each Sunday night, paying any bills that had come in during the week, licking each stamp, jotting down notes in his old fashioned ledger. She had a hard time finding those ledgers for him anymore, and she had bought four the last time she'd found some in an old dry goods store going out of business. God only knew she hoped they'd both be dead before he made it all the way through the three still stacked in the bottom drawer. She had bought him Quicken for Christmas last year and while he had laughed and hugged her, he had also said wryly that he was such an old dog, and the software looked like such a fancy trick. If she hadn't slit the box open and begun keeping her Avon books on it, it would still be in the drawer under the ledgers.

All it took for Nell to love Rafe as much as she had on their wedding day was something small, like when the lamp shone on his bald head bent over another of his beloved novels, or when their granddaughter Kenzie climbed up in his lap to share his bowl of ice cream. Or when Nell had opened her birthday present a few years back and found a gift certificate to Dell Computers for $1000. Unlike Rafe, Nell liked modern things. She'd been the first one on the ranch to get a microwave, back in the early 80s. She had insisted on a satellite dish, even though Rafe -

looked puzzled, as if he didn't know the rest of America was watching television instead of reading books and making things out of leather. Nell always tried to dress like she knew what was going on in the world even if she had never gotten a job in town. Just because she was saddled with a name like Nell and had married a man named Rafe and lived on a cow camp didn't mean she was hopelessly old fashioned. She reached up a hand and touched her spikey hair.

She was so glad that she had named her son Lance, a name with a modern ring to it. She did wish, though, that she got to see more of him. Since he broke up with Kenzie's mother, he didn't come out to the ranch as much. Kenzie. She'd misunderstood at first and told everyone, in letters and phone calls, that her grandbaby's name was McKenzie. A dignified and formal sounding name, Nell thought, but no. The poor child's name really was some lopped off version, a halfway name. Kenzie Patra Johansen. Whoever heard of Patra? When she first heard that it rhymed with Cleopatra, she thought it was a joke.

Poor little girl had a halfway life, too. Both her parents seemed too young to be anyone's parents, all tattoos on bare brown skin, baggy T-shirts, no one in grown-up pants, always promises of jobs in the near future. And now Lance and Deidra weren't even together anymore, divorced before poor Kenzie was three years old even though Deidra had Lance's name in script twining around her ankle. When Nell mentioned the tattoo, Deidra had looked all serious as she said something about roads we take and can't go back and how the ink kept us grounded and centered in where we are in life. It gave Nell a headache.

Poor little Kenzie. Broken home, going to Headstart and Nell thought if anyone needed a head start in life, it was that little girl.

She did like to go riding with her grandfather, though. Rafe smiled vaguely at her and led her horse on long rides out in the pasture. Kenzie always begged for them when she came out to the ranch, leaving Nell to stare at Deirdra and her ink until Rafe and Kenzie showed back up, the little girl chattering and happy, Rafe silent and nodding.

Rafe had adopted Lance before he turned two, given him his own name, raised him, supported him, sat at the supper table, made the three of them into family. Rafe was the one who told him not to back talk his mama and kept his Father's Day cards propped on the dresser until Nell put them in the bottom drawer weeks later when she was dusting. But Nell always had a vague sense that he should have done *more*. She couldn't figure out exactly what it was that she thought Rafe should have done. But *more*. When she looked at Blake and Brenna and their brood, and how their kids were a big swirl around them, she wondered why Lance had never gone roping at the arena at headquarters with Rafe, not that Rafe cared anything about roping in the arena. Oh, it was a silly thing, really, but Nell didn't like things she couldn't put her finger on. When she said something once about why Lance didn't go off to work with Rafe, her husband turned his calm quiet eyes to her and said, "The boy doesn't like my job. I like my job. He'll find his own way, in something he likes."

It wasn't that Rafe and Lance didn't have a good relationship. They did. In fact, there were times when she wished she could have that same easy way with her son that Rafe seemed to from the very beginning. Like when Lance got the first of his many tattoos. She knew that if he had shown her first, she would have made a big scene. Still wanted to even now. Nell remembered standing at the kitchen window and looking down toward the barn as the sun was setting. There were Rafe and Lance standing outside the door to the saddle shed. Lance had lifted the loose sleeve of his baggy T-shirt and turned his shoulder and back toward the man who raised him. Rafe reached to move the fabric a bit and then fumbled for the reading glasses in his pocket. Nell could still see him in her mind as he tilted his head up and looked through them and his face broke into a rare wide grin. She saw him say something and the two of them laugh together. She never had asked what was said or why they were laughing. Why would anyone laugh about a tattoo? Such foolishness. When they came into the kitchen, she saw Rafe give Lance a signal with his eyes. And that was when her son lifted his sleeve again, this time showing his mama some strange Egyptian-looking eye tattooed on the backside of his shoulder. And all she could do was say, "Hmmm." She couldn't even tell Lance what a stupid thing she thought it was because Rafe had been so cool about it all.

Later when she'd mentioned it to Rafe, he'd said, "Oh, Nell. It's only a thing. It doesn't change who he *is*."

She'd been holding three-week-old Lance in her arms at a rodeo dance when Rafe stepped between her and Steve. She'd always remembered Steve as a drunken good-for-nothing lout, but years later when Lance drove up to the camp and introduced Deidra, already carrying Kenzie in her flat, pierced, little belly, Nell's memory of Lance's biological father and those odd mixed up months became more sympathetic. Steve had just been young, way too young, and scared, weighted down by the cluster of cells he'd accidentally made, and looking for someone to blame for the wad of silly string his life had become. And she saw herself from years ago in straight-backed little Deidra, only a woman for a few years, but now a mother. For Nell and Lance there had been Rafe, definitely not a silly string kind of guy, more like a rock who stepped between them and the drunken package of fear and frustration Steve had turned into in the months since the day she'd told him she was expecting. It had become common in their fights for Steve to remind Nell that when she had called him and said she had to talk to him, he'd been sure she was going to break up with him and he had been relieved because then he wouldn't have to do it. Instead, he'd ended up married to her and her big belly.

After Rafe intervened in their fight, which was not even one Nell would have considered serious by that time, Steve had disappeared. The last she saw of him was his slim vulnerable back as his buddies picked him up out of the dirt where a local cowboy had knocked him down, almost gently, when he lunged at Rafe. "You don't want none of that, kid," the cowboy had said. Nell figured out later that Rafe had a reputation for silence and one-punch fights, over before the word was given to start.

Rafe had led her away from the crowd, taken Lance as she climbed into his truck, gently placed the baby back in her arms, and drove them to her mama's house, a country song on the radio, Rafe's handsome profile stern and quiet. She wasn't sure how she had made it through a pregnancy, a wedding, setting up housekeeping, and giving birth without reality setting in, but that is exactly what had happened . . . until that moment. The truth of her life finally sank in as she watched from the dark familiar living room of her parents' home as Rafe Johansen drove away, back to the dance. Rafe had simply tipped his hat to her and driven away, which is how and why she found herself at home by 10:00 p.m. on Saturday night of rodeo weekend, her mother changing and feeding the baby behind her in the kitchen. She felt betrayed by her slim fit jeans and ruffled blouse, shipwrecked on the shore of motherhood while her friends danced and flirted and drank wine coolers and gossiped. She had imagined them cooing over the baby and holding him while *she* danced, getting compliments on how her jeans from last July still fit, but instead she was just standing there, nothing left to do but go to bed.

Things improved the next afternoon when a freshly-showered Rafe showed up to check on her. Theirs was a slow, solemn courtship that evolved while her marriage was dissolved and Lance changed from an infant into a bow-legged toddler who stamped his way gleefully across the floor to be tossed in the serious cowboy's arms. Nell remembered the night he'd taken her out to dinner at K-Bob's Steakhouse, one of the few times they went out alone because usually Rafe wanted Lance to go with them instead of being left behind with Nell's mom. Nell ordered the teriyaki chicken and he had asked for a bite of it when he saw the pineapple ring and rice. It had been odd, even after having shared a kiss or two, to let him take a bite off of her plate and watch him chewing slowly, knowing he was tasting her food.

"Hm . . . Good! I will have that next time." Even now, after twenty years, she was still uncomfortable sharing intimate everyday things with self-composed Rafe. But she loved him beyond words.

That evening at K-Bob's, over coffee and a meal-cluttered tablecloth, he told her about a childhood illness that had left him sterile and how he'd like to adopt Lance someday. He said he couldn't give her more children, but if she could see her way past that, he'd be honored if she'd allow him to marry her and provide for her and her son.

The only bumps in their road had been Alix Graham and Shiney Lewis, and time had worn them both down until Nell hardly noticed anymore.

Rafe had dated Alix a few times before that rodeo, and all of Nell's girlfriends shrieked into the phone when they found out that Rafe had come calling on her. Older than the crowd Nell ran with, Alix was one of those girls who was gorgeous even with her hair all jammed up under a ball cap while she mowed the lawn. Nell had seen her once, in her cowboy clothes, sitting in the café with her father and a bunch of ranch hands, laughing long and loud with the men, cow shit on her jeans, looking as if she belonged both there and on Fifth Avenue. And a few nights later she would be out on the dance floor at Shiloh's in a mini-skirt and sparkly blouse like some fairy queen, her hair slick and swinging. Just by looking at her Nell knew she'd never end up living in a dinky trailer, throwing a plate of store brand (three boxes for a dollar) mac and cheese at the man who knocked her up, taking a handful of Rolaids and crying herself to sleep only to have to clean up the mess herself the next morning. When she asked Rafe about Alix, months after they got married, Rafe said, "I like Allie. She's smart. She was smart not to settle for a cowpuncher who can't have kids, too." It was like he was saying that Nell wasn't that smart.

Alix had gone on to vet school, and every few months she called, always talking to Nell as if they were old friends, always asking about Lance, always sending a Christmas card, always keeping Rafe on the phone longer than anyone else ever did. At first, Nell tried to protest those calls, but Rafe had looked puzzled and said, "So I am not allowed to have friends?"

Nell always cleaned something vigorously while they talked.

This year, Alix's Christmas card showed her on a sailboat in a bikini, smiling, waving as if directly to Rafe, and the postmark said Sydney, Australia. Nell thought the sun had not been kind to Alix's skin.

Shiney Lewis was a different matter. She didn't sail off to vet school or Australia. She was always there. Had always been there. And Nell had come to accept that she and Rafe would always be close. Still, Nell liked cleaning the Big House and then coming home to Old Sally where Rafe waited.

Nell sat forward in the seat, clutching her coat around her.

"Are those snowflakes?"

Rafe reached across the seat and grasped her cold hand in his warm one. "Looks like it."

Nell sat back and sighed. "I hope it doesn't stick. I need to do the rest of my shopping tomorrow."

Rafe smiled out through the windshield. "Did you have fun today, working with Sue and Shiney?"

"Oh, I guess. It was a good party, wasn't it?"

"I sure did eat. Full as an old tick."

"That Jody is a good kid, isn't he?"

"Yeah, gonna make a fine man."

"Better than his daddy, I hope."

"A boy shouldn't have to pay for sins that were committed before he was born."

The headlights finally picked up the silver of the cattle guard leading in to Old Sally Camp. They were home.

THE AMERICAN DREAM

Monte thought maybe Pam's haircut was new, and for sure the color was. Red. Yeah, it was definitely red tonight. How appropriate. He set the bag he was carrying down near the kitchen sink and went straight for the tequila and ice.

"Haven't you had enough?"

"Oh, you're home now so you're the drink police?"

"See. Point made." She started pulling things out of the bag. "Yuck. I hate trying to decide what to do with all of this stuff."

"You could say thank you."

Pam rolled her eyes. "Oh. Yes. Thank you for the dry pumpkin bread, exactly the same as we got last year. Thank you for the tequila that will make my husband drunker than he already is. Thank you for the Santa cookies with dirty fingerprints . . ."

"Stop it." Monte's voice held a tone that his horses knew to heed. "Just stop it."

"What are you mad about? The presents I brought? You *asked* me to bring them."

"Whatever."

"What do you mean whatever?"

"Did it ever occur to you that I might prefer for you to be beside me, pretending to be my wife, for God's sake, than all the fancy presents in the world?"

"Oh. My. God." Pam often put periods between her words. "You told me to help you out and do the shopping. That *is* being a wife, Monte. How fucking convenient of you to forget that you asked me."

"Yeah, well, I won't do that again."

"Do what again, forget?"

He rounded on her. "No. Ask you to buy gifts! You are always so over the top. I thought you'd, you know, bring some chocolates or maybe some popcorn cans or even fruitcakes for crying out loud! But no. Not you."

"Look," Pam reached into the cabinet for a glass, "The ropes were already in our main office at work. We passed them out to the feedlot guys this year. The hams were there, too, and we had extras. And you can't give a little boy or a teenage girl a rope or a ham so I stopped at the mall! Come on, Monte . . . really." Pam twisted the top off of a bottle of designer water from the case beside the refrigerator and poured it in the glass, then leaned on the sink. She said she hated the taste of the ranch well water. For the first time that evening, Monte realized that she looked tired.

He sighed. "Fine. So, where's my rope?"

She laughed, but not much. "How can you stand these people? Look at them. None of them have ever owned their own home. Nor do they plan on it. What do they have to live for anyway? Just automatons, schlepping out their days, squirting out babies, tying raffia around jars of junk, singing bullshit songs, talking about bullshit, nothing important."

Monte stood up straight, no longer caring about tired. "How the fuck would you know? You don't even know these people. You haven't taken the time to know them, and now you're presuming to know what their American dream is? Give me a break. They're good people, living good lives, with their own problems, and their own plans. They are my friends and my employees. Some of them know me better than you do."

Pam looked at him, her head tilted. "What happened to us, Monte?"

Monte took a swallow of cold clear alcohol. "I don't know. You tell me. I am sure you've thought it all out."

"You did. *You* happened to us. Speaking of the American dream. I thought we were dreaming the same one. We were headed the same place until you had some sort of midlife crisis and instead of buying a motorcycle and trading me for a blonde you decided to live in bumfuck nowhere among the redneck peasants . . . decided *that* was more important than the life we were building."

"Yeah, Pammy, a life centered on fancy horses in heated stalls, rich men chasing fresh cattle around in the arena and voting on whether the tines of the plow we used on the dirt should be four inches or six inches apart. Me constantly having to fend off advances from bored women with perfect fucking nails." Monte wondered if he could get away with going down the hall and brushing his teeth after this speech. One never knew, in a fight with Pam, if one had the freedom to walk away or not. He decided to try it. He went down the hall unbuttoning his shirt.

"*Pobrecito*. The women all want him. *Que lástima*." Silhouetted in the doorway of the kitchen, Pam looked like some magazine model that had minored in Spanish, a good move for a woman in the Southwest who was in marketing. A good move, but all she had retained were a few figures of speech, some cuss words. "All you had to do, my handsome one, was show them a little attention, make it *seem* like sex, not get your dick out." She was mocking him as he spread toothpaste. Mocking him with her sing-song words that were honed razor sharp on a thousand such fights, mocking him with her nudity, accomplished in a singularly short amount of time. "I do it every day – flash a smile, touch an arm, agree to a drink and dinner. It's a game, Monte, one you are too bull-headed to learn how to play."

He couldn't help it. He always took the bait. "Anyone getting his dick out for you lately?"

Pam laughed. "Oh, you know me. I'm not crazy about all of that. I sleep alone. Or with you." She laughed again, and turned the water on in the shower. Sometimes Pam showered three times a day. Most days, at least twice. She never used the same towel twice.

Monte crawled in bed. After she'd put on cold cream, lotion, socks, long-sleeved flannel pajamas, brushed out her hair – red, definitely red – Pam arranged her bedside table. Tissues, water glass, sleeping pills just in case, ibuprofen, magazine, again just in case, and lip balm. For a woman who hated alcohol because she might become dependent, it took a lot of paraphernalia to put her in a comfortable spot. Monte was glad he self-medicated with simplicity.

The dark was complete, especially on this side of the house.

"Where do you think we went wrong?" Her voice startled him. Usually when Pam turned out the light, that was all. It had been weeks since she came out of the bathroom in the little baby doll nightgown that was a signal for him, kissed him in such a way as to tell him she was willing for him to take care of his needs. For all of her sassy ways, Pam simply didn't like sex and acknowledged the fact candidly. And yet, she usually went out of her way a couple of times a month to make sure that Monte got his. Tonight, the voice in the dark sounded vulnerable, the way she looked when she donned the nightgown that was designed to be alluring, but only managed to make her look like a little girl eager to please.

He held himself rigid, fearing that he'd say the wrong thing. "Oh, I don't know. I guess it's true. Familiarity does breed contempt."

And, of course, that was the wrong thing.

Her voice dripped with ice. "Only if there is something contemptible."

Contemptible. The word hung in the darkness. It echoed off the silence, seemed to repeat itself in each moment that passed with neither of them speaking. Monte guessed the contemptible waves that buffeted him weren't affecting his wife when he heard her faint snore in the dark.

Lariat ropes for all the men. Brand new ropes. Hams, honey cured, for all of the women. Actual hams, heavy and cumbersome, wrapped in gold foil and mesh bags. Fancy perfume, gift boxes, for the teenage girls. Remote control cars, monster trucks, for Blake's little boys, though Monte had to admit that Pam was slick in giving the oldest, Brice, a rope just like the rest of the men. For Shiney, a huge jar, like an urn, of fancy olives. Sunshine Angel Lewis wouldn't eat that many olives in a whole year, maybe in her whole life.

Monte got up and walked through the dark house, rattled three cubes of ice into a glass, poured two fingers of tequila, and sat at his desk, gazing out the window at the snow falling on The View.

THANKSGIVING

Bliss hoped it would snow. Hoped it would snow and snow and snow. Maybe then they wouldn't have to go to her grandparents' house for Christmas. She hoped that the storm would move in and bury the ranch, make the roads impassable so she could lie on her bed and think about Jody instead of being nice and holy and bored, instead of saying, "Yes, school is great, and yes, I love Jesus."

She might have been the only one, you know, watching his face tonight. Right before her dad started playing and singing, when Ms. Lewis had stood up by the fireplace and made this little speech. Bliss thought that Ms. Lewis's top half didn't match her bottom half. It was like her old-fashioned pointy-toed boots and Wranglers was her old lady half and her cute short hair and silver jewelry was her strong real self. Tonight she had looked sorta sweet when she cleared her throat twice before she said, "Well, welcome. Welcome to the Big House. I wish my father could see all of you here tonight. He would have liked it. We've had a good year here on the Tinaja, and I want to thank each one of you for your contribution. Mainly, I am glad that we all seem to have made it through alive!" There was a pause while everyone chuckled,.

Brian-big-mouth was the one who had to pipe up and say something stupid. "Huh uh!" He shook his head, frowning. "Jody's puppy didn't make it alive. She died!"

Bliss wished she could have wiped that, just wiped it. She didn't know how everyone else in the room reacted, because she was watching Jody's face. Instead of all horrible or crushed though, he just looked grateful and sad at the same time.

And Ms. Lewis just went right on. "You are right, young man. We all feel the loss of Missy." Shiney had nodded her head toward Jody, and there it was again, on Jody's face, that strange grateful look. As Shiney wrapped up her speech, Bliss moved carefully around in the crowd until she was directly behind Jody. Even though she knew it was wrong, she brushed up against him, like it was an accident. She was shocked when he leaned back on the chair, trapping her arm, mashing it there. She'd have stayed mashed there the rest of her life. She almost died with the awesomeness. Now if she could just skip the Christmas and keep this feeling of thanks-giving.

For once, Blake left the radio off as he drove his family home. The little boys had fallen asleep, all sticky, clutching their net stockings full of more sugar. Brice and Bliss were on either side of the back seat looking out their respective windows, Brice holding his new rope on his lap while Bliss fingered the elegant box of perfume and lotion that had come packaged with a glittery butterfly ornament to hang in a window. Brenna joined the little boys in sleep, her head leaning against the passenger side window. Blake reached and pulled the jacket that she was wearing like a blanket more firmly up under her chin. This pregnancy wasn't like the others. It had started out better without the nausea, but she was definitely more tired. Maybe that was to be expected with a houseful of other kids. Blake thought of the days when Brenna had moved with more grace than any other woman he knew, like a little child, like a deer. But now she moved heavy, old, weighted down.

With his seed.

And he couldn't think of that any more.

He fell back into the fantasy he had been harboring, embroidering, embellishing, since August. Elko alone. He could see himself driving away from the ranch, bag packed so neatly as to be razor sharp, pristine shaving kit, not the messiness that was some of her stuff, some of his. He saw himself driving away early, before anyone was awake to see him off. He saw the airport, all lit up, waiting for him, saw himself in the solemn line of travelers, a little mysterious, his guitar case a subtle sign that he was a performer. Saw himself on the flight, not worrying about anything or anyone, ordering coffee, a responsible sober man. Saw himself arriving in northern Nevada, free to check in, still clean and starched, fresh and unrumpled. Hotel room all to himself, no one to see who came or went, what he did, no one to coordinate every move with. A small guilty part thought it should be lonely in that room, barren, stark, but instead the aloneness in his imagination seemed luxurious, opulent, priceless. He saw himself playing to adoring crowds, but even his imagination kept it responsible and respectable and reasonable. No cheating, just the guilty freedom of the whole weekend, or longer really. Flying away on Wednesday before dawn, returning on Sunday night, after dark, thank the meridian gods.

Blake fantasized not about houses with red doors, a line-up of Nevada's finest to choose from, not about a private and forbidden flirtation with someone he had something in common with, but about clean lines, freedom of movement, selfishly ordering whatever he wanted to eat, drinking with friends he had yet to make, smiling at whomever looked his way. Not cheating or drunkenness, but about time spent thinking only of himself.

Only he and Bliss were awake as the miles of dirt road slipped away, and the snow began to fall. He wondered how his teenage daughter could stare so long into the night in silence. The coat had fallen from Brenna's shoulders, and she cried out with cold in her sleep.

Later, Blake lay on his side, Brenna wrapped firmly in his arms, the way they were used to sleeping. He'd carried the smaller boys in to bed, stripped off their boots and jeans, put them under the covers. Only Brice had stumbled to bed under his own steam, and Bliss had wandered quietly into her room, helping to tuck a dead-weight Brian under the covers. Now Blake lay with his wife, feeling like king of his castle. Playing music always did that for him. He murmured in Brenna's ear, "Hey, you."

She sighed in return, "Hey, you."

"I think we should let Bliss name this baby."

Brenna moved his hand to rest on her belly where he couldn't feel anything moving at present. "Ok. Bliss can name this baby." Her smile slipped quickly away as she drifted back off into sleep.

The winter Bride wears diamonds.

To those down below, she appears to be sleeping, locked inside a chastity belt of cold. She naps lightly behind her veil of ice and snow that shields her from the sun and throws it back into the sky.

But her chill is only skin deep. Inside her hidden folds and caves and recesses, the heartbeat of her lives and breathes and curls around the seeds of what will be. The winter Bride is pregnant, gestating the future, smiling quietly at the snores of the bears and the mountain lions, allowing all of the fertile places to swell and burgeon with the life that is to come.

The winter Bride is holding a flood in deposit for the sun's withdrawal in spring.

FOR BABY JESUS'S SAKE

Del had decided years earlier that it was easier for a young boy to see things in black and white, good guys versus bad guys, the shirts versus the skins. Easier to see family and friends as being good and honest and decent. Sometimes the truth needs more than one avenue to get to the heart, like water cuts more than one path down the mountain, many small streams coming together in the end, or not, because maybe one big rush cuts too deeply, and small realizations, over time, soak in better.

At least that is what Del had been counting on because he loved Jody Neil, had loved the boy from the start. Loved the boy on the bike with the too big hat. Loved the boy who made a sour face the first time he ordered lemon meringue pie and always ordered chocolate after that. Loved the boy who drank his first black coffee on a very cold morning, camped beside the corrals, shivering inside his denim jacket, but trying not to show it. Loved that smelly boy who disappeared sodas all summer long out on the ranch but who always ordered coffee at the café after that chilly morning when he'd toughed it out and gone on to do a man's job all day long. From the beginning that boy had been an individual rather than Cash Neil's carbon copy, and when Del lay awake at night, he acknowledged to himself that Jody deserved the truth. But first he deserved to be a boy who idolized his father, even if that father had feet of clay all the way up to his armpits.

Del pushed his shopping cart through the too-brightly lit superstore, loading it up with food for his boy's homecoming. The inane music irritated him as he put a plastic domed chocolate pie carefully in the bottom of the cart. He had to rearrange the whole mess to keep from smashing the bread, finally putting the carton of soda underneath the basket

He rested for a moment, his hands braced on the sides of the cart. Shit. Getting old wasn't for pussies, and now he had a stupid Christmas song stuck in his head.

When Jody finally pulled up to Del's house on Christmas Eve, it was already full dark. Del had probably looked out the window twenty times, and still missed seeing the headlights come up the road. Jody carried in the boxes and bags of stuff he'd gotten at the ranch party, and Del acted like a little kid going through the tissue paper, taking nibbles here and there.

"You're late!" This around a mouthful of cookie. Jody lugged in his duffle bag and let the back door slam.

He was home.

He grinned at Del who was fingering his way through the jar of spiced nuts. Picking out the cashews, no doubt.

"Yeah, I didn't know that everyone was supposed to give gifts at the party, so I had to deliver mine all over the ranch. Took all day. Everyone wanted me to eat when I got there." He didn't tell Del that he stood outside in a benevolent morning sun at West Camp for almost two hours talking to Bliss until Blake yelled at her to "Let that boy go and come inside and help your mom!" It irritated Jody that he'd stood out there that long, especially talking to some kid.

"How are you, old man?" Jody gave Del a sort of slap on the back. Del grunted and sat down in his chair, tea glass, ashtray, fly swatter though it would be months before there was a fly to be swatted, reading glasses, *Livestock Weekly*, and phone all scattered in front of him. "I am old, goddammit! I am! Saved some stuff for you to do tomorrow, help an old man out. Heavy lifting and shit. Christmas Day be damned!" The kitchen looked festive with the tissue paper and Jody cluttering it up and, to Del, it finally felt like a holiday.

Del and Jody stayed up so late, catching up, that Del's face seemed to fall in on itself. Del wondered if Jody had talked at all since he left in September, or if he'd saved it up just for tonight. Jody told him about every one of the horses in his string. He talked about each person on the ranch, and so much about Rafe Johansen that Del got tired of hearing about his old friend. Jody told about every one of his pastures and all of the things he didn't get to talk about during the four days Del had been on the Tinaja, the four days that Jody had shared him with everyone else.

Since neither man was talkative on the phone, Del hadn't heard of Missy's death. Jody's words were blunt and his eyes stayed firmly on Del's face. "Got run over. Shit happens. Just part of life. I'll get another dog someday, but probably not while I'm single. Too much trouble, just like you said."

Del's heart wadded up into a ball, but he just nodded his head. "Too bad. Cute pup."

Del sighed hard when he lay down in his bed. Wondered where his boy had gone. Wondered as he always did if he'd done Jody wrong.

Jody lay wide awake for a long time on the little iron bedstead that seemed to have shrunk while he was away. He'd gotten up early that morning, loaded his truck before breakfast. Before he'd poured his first cup of coffee, he'd given Sue the set of leather coasters he'd cut for her and Sam, two intertwined Ss tooled on each one. Sue had made a big deal, fussing over him while he ate, filling a tin full of fudge and rolling up the leftover eggs in a tortilla for him to take with him. He'd spent two days making coasters for everyone on the ranch, embarrassed by the party with its table loaded with gifts. He had tied each coaster set with thin red ribbon that he'd begged from Sue the night before. She had thrown up her hands and waddled her round figure into the living room as she yelled over her shoulder that he could have anything, "just anything!" he needed. All he had to do was "ask, for Baby Jesus sake! Precious boy." He wasn't sure if she meant he was precious or baby Jesus was precious, but he'd taken his ribbon and run. He'd made a keychain for Bliss, but cringed at how less than smooth he'd been in giving it to her. He'd tossed it to her out of the seat of his truck. *Yeah, that Jody Neil, has a way with women, just throws things at them.*

He'd taken Shiney's coasters to her right after breakfast, busting in on her and Monte drinking coffee in the Big House kitchen. She'd looked pretty pleased, though. Her set was the only one he'd tooled with the TJ, figured that was the way it ought to be. She'd said for him to be sure and say hello to Del for her. Gave him a tin with a fruitcake in it to deliver.

He'd made Bliss's keychain in the shape of the sunrise.

What had made his stupid lack of gifts at the party even more embarrassing were the drums. He was used to a tree with piles of gifts beneath it, politely opening them on Christmas morning with Mattie wrapped in her fuzzy robe sipping her coffee, always getting things he needed and had asked for as well as a lot of nonsense that he never even used. Most of the nonsense stayed in his room on Las Lomas and when his mother moved out she must have packed it all up or sold it in a garage sale, since by then he was living full time with Del. The only times he'd been part of a big noisy group at Christmas had been when they'd visited his Nana and all of his cousins were there. The last two holidays he'd spent with

Del, going to see Mattie on Christmas afternoon, staying about an hour, taking her the perfume from the drug store that she liked and that he had been buying for her every year since he was about eight. This year she'd gone to Belize with her new boyfriend, so he was off the hook. He wondered what she would have thought if she'd seen everyone gathered around in the Big House library, Blake playing Feliz Navidad on the guitar and then, as he conducted everyone in shouting "UNO, DOS, TRES, QUATRO!" strolling over, everyone but Jody knowing what was about to happen, ripping back the red cloth from a pile in the corner, and everyone yelling, "The boy's got rhythm!" He had tried to tell Del about it, but it was too late. The old man was nodding off, holding a big glass of water, ready for bed.

Jody lay there, smiling. He didn't know if he had rhythm or not, but he'd sure liked carrying that drum set through the darkness to the bunkhouse with Blake and Levi, laughing and joking about touring with their band some day. The Tinaja Trio.

Jody went through the list of everyone on the ranch, let his mind touch on each person, even all those little Davis boys, even Pam whom he'd only seen three or four times total, saving Bliss for last. That morning the sun had made her head look fuzzy, lighting up individual strands of hair as they flew around her head. Jody flopped over on his belly, and groaned. Pulled his own hair until the roots hurt.

Del didn't get to drink coffee alone very long on Christmas morning before he heard Jody shuffling around. He'd expected his boy to come home. Instead he'd gotten this man in his house. And he didn't like it. Not one bit.

LIKE SO MUCH LUXURY

The night of the Christmas party, Shiney pulled Nell aside and asked her to come clean the Big House on December 27 since the normal cleaning day would fall on the 25th. They both knew that what Shiney meant was, "Come clean up all these decorations and put my life back in order." They had also discussed the special plans for New Year's Eve and the need for some of the bedrooms in the Big House to be opened up and readied for guests.

Since Monte was gone to Pam's parents' house, not due back until late evening or even the next day, Shiney drank her coffee and ate a slice of bacon with a hunk of Sue's buttered banana bread in the dim quiet kitchen before bundling up and walking out the back door.

The tinaja was full, both the upper and lower pools still holding, and there was a glitter of ice around the edges. The morning was cold, but not bitter. Shiney stayed awhile, stayed until she was sure that Nell had driven in and was busy undecorating the tree, moving things back until the legs of the furniture slipped into their accustomed indentions on the rugs.

Shiney was glad Christmas was over and regretted having planned the New Year's Eve thing. She had to admit, though, that she had enjoyed the time spent with Nesto Jr. and his sister Rena on Christmas afternoon. They had left their spouses and children behind and driven out to the ranch, coming in the door of their childhood home giggling like two school children at having run away. The three of them sat in the library by the tree that Sue and Nell had decorated. Nesto carried in a big box of gifts from the family, and Shiney went through them one by one. Finally, Rena asked her about the gifts from the ranch party still stashed under the tree and Shiney opened those as well, she and Rena putting all of the food gifts aside to be carried into the kitchen. When they sat back in their chairs to laugh at the vat of olives Pam had bought and how silly Christmas seemed when you got old, Nesto leaned forward and pulled one more gift, clumsily wrapped in green tissue paper from way up under the branches.

"Hey, *hermana*, you missed one." Nesto Jr. looked so much like Nesto Sr. that at times Shiney was shocked when he called her sister instead of *niñita*. Rena had Mama D's blue eyes, and had been a dark blonde all of her life, but now her hair was silver white and with her brown skin she looked like her father, too. Old age was making Shiney a weepy fool. She looked down and tore the wrapping off the gift without reading who it was from. And there, folded neatly, was the softest merino wool top she'd ever had in her hands. It slipped through her palms and landed in her lap like so much luxury. Rena and Nesto stood to carry the food stuffs into the kitchen, arguing like the little kids they once were over who was going to try the peanut butter fudge first. Shiney turned the green tissue over in her hands until she found, written in ink pen, "To the Boss. Not a gas well, but maybe it will keep you warm anyway."

"M" was written with a dramatic flourish that had made a tiny rip in the tissue.

Shiney had talked long into the night with Nesto Jr. while Rena dozed on the big velvet sofa wrapped in an old afghan of Mama D's. Nesto had gotten tears in his eyes when he spoke of loving the ranch but understanding that its sale would benefit all of the Chavez grandchildren when each of them reached an age to go to college. He leaned over and put his hand on Shiney's knee.

"You can't just ranch until it's all gone, now can you? I'll help, you know. Call up my secretary when you are ready to make a deal. We'll look over the contracts. *Hermana*, you don't carry the whole world on those tiny little shoulders."

Shiney hadn't slept much that night.

Shiney left the tinaja and went to the office. Monte came stomping in sometime in mid-morning. He hung up his coat and looked over at her.

"What are you doing at your desk today?"

"What are you doing home already?"

"Pam drove her own truck so I came on back. Nothing to hold me there. Besides, I missed you."

"Go on with you. I'm busy."

Monte poured a cup of coffee from the pot, and strolled over to his own desk, punching all of the right buttons to make things hum.

"Have a good Christmas?"

Shiney answered this and other sallies with a faint distracted murmur until she said, "Huh! Well, I never! Monte Wells, you should be ashamed of yourself!"

Monte reared back in his chair and looked around his console. "What did I do? I just got here!"

"How in the world could anyone spend $150 on a shirt! And not even a dress shirt! A pull-over-your-head shirt!"

Monte threw his head back and roared his laughter at the ceiling. He hadn't laughed in three days, and damn, it felt good, felt good to be back where he belonged.

"You are not supposed to look up your Christmas presents online! That's tacky!" He could see the black wool jersey peeking over the collar of Shiney's usual denim work shirt.

"Well, I never. I mean, I never! And I *had* to look it up because it's the warmest thing I've ever worn and I wanted to see what else they had and besides the brand name is on it and their website is on the hanging tag, and Monte Wells, stop laughing at me!" She sucked in a breath but couldn't keep from letting her smile move from her eyes to her mouth. "I was wondering before, but I am absolutely sure now. I am paying you too much!"

"Dance with me at the New Year's Eve party."

Shiney was glad her foreman was home. "No, I will not. Truth is, I have a whole houseful of guests coming for New Year's Eve. You keep those cowboys from destroying something, you hear me? And we can't let them mingle with my guests because not all of the people on this ranch are housebroke. Now somebody better order some protein block. Looks like we're gonna have some weather next week."

"Somebody better, but why not you? You going home already?"

Shiney slumped back in her chair and rubbed her hand over her silver hair. "I can't. Nell is over there. Cleaning."

Monte rose and picked up a white porcelain mug, rinsed it out in the tiny sink along the wall.

"Coffee?"

Shiney sat up and nodded.

"Sure."

She moved to one of the big chairs in the center of the room. They drank coffee together and Shiney peered carefully over the rim of her mug. Monte looked like someone had been beating him with a ball peen hammer.

"Did you get to see your sister . . . what's her name . . . Liz? And all of those kids of hers?"

"No, not this time. We went to Pam's mom's house, the opposite direction. Command performance and all of that, you know, smile and clink your glasses! Sheesh." Monte sighed. "I'm glad to be home. Even if you are one of those tacky women who look up their gifts online." Monte grinned over at his boss.

Shiney smiled right back, glad she'd made this pot of coffee.

FISH BOWL

The new year brought cold winds and dry, too dry, days. Monte stood on the porch of the office and looked at the gray skies, wishing for moisture, even snow.

Rafe put another stick of blackjack oak in the wood-burning stove in the leather shop and turned back to his work. He knew that looking and wishing wouldn't bring spring. It smelled like Nell was making apple cake.

Jody pushed hard against the gate stick and slid the wire loop over, ducking his head to keep his eyes from watering in the wind. Eeyore stood, hip cocked, tail streaming between his knees waiting for Jody to remount.

Shiney picked up Punch's pearl-handled letter opener and began to go through the stack of mail – bills, advertisements, a letter about group health insurance. She opened an invitation from Southwest Wind and Power to attend a spring field trip or barbecue or some such nonsense, tossed it in the throw-away pile.

Brenna turned up the thermostat as she moved along the hallway, another load of laundry in her arms. The bus would be at headquarters soon.

Jody turned his horse east, gave him his head and leaned into the wind once they hit the trail. All through January, Jody tried to be at headquarters every afternoon when the bus pulled in, but he hated himself for it. He lectured himself about getting to town more often, going over to the Double H headquarters and getting with those boys in the bunkhouse, going out to the bar, finding some real women, tying one on. Instead, he found himself around the barn at four o'clock each evening, waiting for some high school girl. He should have his head examined. Bliss had started driving to headquarters to meet the bus during fall works, herding those little boys around. After the party on New Year's Eve, Jody had vowed to avoid her, but then he got to worrying because, after all, what if that piece of shit truck didn't start the way it had on that really cold, almost dark evening when the coil wire had jiggled loose and he'd had to go find Sam to put it back on for her? He'd made damned sure he watched, though, so he could fix it himself next time. Some evenings, all Jody did was watch Bliss walk to the truck and load the boys up, make sure they made it over the cattle guard okay, but more often than not she let the boys swing on the ropes in the barn for five minutes while they talked. Jody liked it when she put her hand on the door or the hood and he could rest his next to it, just barely touching. Being at headquarters was like being in a goldfish bowl, so that's all they ever did. Just talk.

On days when she didn't bring the family truck, when she and the boys had to wait for Blake or Brenna to pick them up, she sat on the cook house porch and pulled out her homework or stood out of the wind beside the saddle house. At night, Jody thought about how no one was looking after Bliss anymore, what with Blake and Brenna having so many other kids and the new baby coming. He thought about how earlier in the fall she had taken a picture of Missy with a cardboard camera, and after Missy died, she'd had it developed and put a copy in an envelope and slipped it under the wires that criss-crossed the screen door of the bunkhouse. He was pretty sure he was the only one she'd ever kissed, and he liked to think about that the most.

It would have shocked almost no one, except maybe Blake, to have seen Bliss taking small, almost-not sips, from Jody's bottle of Crown on New Year's Eve. Every time he saw the empty bottle, months later, slowly filling up with pennies on his bedside table, Jody would think of how Bliss's lips had tasted as if she were wearing bourbon lipstick. She wasn't the first girl he'd kissed, of course, but she was the first one who gave him a lump in his throat just as firm and uncomfortable as the one in his jeans.

Brenna was spared her daughter's first kiss because she'd skipped the New Year's Eve party. She sent along a plate of tortilla, cream cheese, and green chile pinwheels she and Bliss had made earlier in the day. It had been a good day all the way around actually because, between her and Bliss, they'd cleaned both bathrooms, mopped the kitchen and dining room, and done all of the laundry. Bliss had even vacuumed the whole house while Brenna sat on the couch and folded as much laundry as she could reach while Brian read aloud from one of his school books. She'd wanted to start the New Year out at least halfway decent, but by the time the sun went down, Brenna knew she had no business walking her belly around and being sociable. She could barely move with fatigue.

"Just go on without me. I will sleep my way into the next year. Really, Blake. Go play some music. I'll be here when you get home. The kids would be disappointed to miss the party, and you and I know that one missed kiss isn't the end of the world!"

Brenna lay on the couch amidst the sweet-smelling, freshly-folded laundry and listened to the chaos of her family getting ready for the party, didn't comment on her daughter's heavy eye make-up, and heard the back door slam, the pickup doors slam, and everyone disappear off into the night. And her tears leaked out onto the couch pillow, not tears of sad, but tears of relief, relief at being left alone to rest. This baby was weighing on her, was taking all of Brenna's energy to grow into what it was going to be.

Brenna ate a bowl of cream of wheat with brown sugar and butter, made her slice of toast come out even with the bites of cereal. She lay in a hot bath until the water cooled. She drank a cup of tea and lay down in her bed, fast asleep by nine o'clock. It had been one of the best evenings of the last few months, to tell God's honest truth.

Bliss knew that if her mother had been at the party, there was no way she'd have been able to walk off toward the colt pens as the music played, her jacket pulled tight, staying in the shadows. No way would she have been able to stand and talk to Jody until he asked if she was cold, opened his blanket-lined denim coat, and pulled her in. No way she could have been gone from the circle of light that long, no way she would have sipped the bourbon, which she didn't like much.

And so, Brenna slept soundly while Blake chose song after song to blast over Velma Jo's boom box. Everyone had brought their favorite music, and it was piled in stacks on the pallet of salt blocks in the corner of the shop. Chad had made a sort of table using the welding horses and a big piece of plywood. The women loaded it up with every kind of finger food – sweet, salty, gooey, cold, hot, comforting. Just right for absorbing alcohol and keeping kids happy.

Sue and Sam stayed until after ten o'clock, which was testament to a good party. Shiney showed up right at the beginning, drank one beer, and danced one dance with her foreman.

"Having fun?" She felt both fragile and unbreakable in his arms.

"What? Have fun with no wine pairings? I wouldn't know how."

"Am I still to come up to your shindig later?" Monte knew he'd need an excuse to leave this one.

"Yes. Please. There is someone I want to introduce you to."

"A hot chick?"

Shiney snorted. "Just bring your sassy self up to my party. I promise you don't have to stay longer than fifteen minutes. I'll pour you a tequila to dilute the beer."

Pam was on the road again.

People flowed from the shop out into the wagon yard and back all night long. Chad and Haley had invited several of the high school crowd out, so Blake never noticed his own daughter's absence in the excitement.

For the last set before the New Year, Blake turned off the boom box and played the fiddle and sang, played the guitar and sang. He promised everyone a real band next year, gesturing around for Levi and Jody. Levi, several beers into the evening, bowed and clowned and promised to outdo Blake if the other cowboy would just clear the stage. No one thought to look around for Jody. Blake told some funny poems and everyone counted down.

At one point, Monte walked between parties, through the dark to the Big House, and stood with an uncomfortable drink in his hand in Shiney's library.

This party had been catered and therefore, in Shiney's mind, was too expensive to justify a bunch of old people sitting around talking about subjects far removed from the songs of weather, seeds, cows, and numbers that made up her life. She introduced her foreman to a plump little man named Max Angel who examined Monte like an archeologist with a rare specimen unexpectedly encountered.

"And so, uh, Monte," Max stumbled over the name, "what exactly is your capacity here on the ranch?"

His tone made Monte want to kick shit and spit on the floor, but he caught a glimpse of Shiney out of the corner of his eye as she drifted through the crowd, her head cocked so as not to miss his answer. So he cocked his own head and grinned at the bald little man.

"Crisis management, mostly." By the time the conversation got to the Citizens United Supreme Court decision, having brushed on the commodities market, danced on top of the Euro trend, debated whether or not natural gas was a good investment, Max had changed his posture and was leaning forward into his words.

And Shiney was listening openly, smiling at how interesting life could become even at the tail end of a year.

At the noise from the shop at midnight, a curtain upstairs in the Big House twitched. The entwined couple over by the colt pen stopped kissing and held very still.

And Monte Wells, absent from both crowds, looked out over the canyon, kept his eyes away from the Big House windows, and raised his glass of Añejo to the moon.

And Brenna slept on.

LEAD POISONING

Take today, subtract fifty years, and no one would have thought a single thing about it when Enid Trent drove up to Tinaja headquarters, expecting a hot meal and a bunk, asking about any work that was to be had. He would simply have been riding the chuck line until gainful employment presented itself. But the problem was that Enid Trent didn't want a real job, had no intention of actually doing any work, and in these modern times the chuck line was broken, abused by cowboys like him. Monte agreed that he could stay in the bunkhouse, and eat at Sue's table, but only for the weekend.

"You're welcome here, Enid. I've got a couple of gates needing to be rebuilt on Monday, several head of horses that need to be shod, and on Tuesday we'll be digging up a water leak over in the mare pasture. Sure am glad you came along!" Enid sighed big and gave an equally long list of reasons why he'd be pulling out, early on Monday, though he durned sure wished he could stay around and help, and did Monte know of anyone who'd had rotator cuff surgery because he was purely sure that was what was going to have to happen to him, this bum shoulder giving him fits and all.

But Monday was too late. Maybe Del was at fault for having loved Jody too much. Maybe Mattie was at fault for having loved Jody too little. Maybe no one was at fault except Enid Trent. But whatever the case, Monday was too late.

On Sunday Levi and Blake came over to headquarters so "the band" could practice. The idea was to be able to play for ranch parties like the one on New Year's Eve, to have learned enough songs to be able to spare the boom box for a couple of hours. On this afternoon in mid-January they cranked up the wood-burning stove in the bunkhouse, and Jody started learning to keep time while Levi played simple, if boring, chords on the guitar. Blake fiddled his heart out and sang into an imaginary mic. Sometimes Blake took over the drums or the guitar, "showing" Levi and Jody how it was really done while Enid Trent manned the fire.

As the cowboys plodded and halted their way through several songs, the visitor rocked back on the legs of the chair by the stove and looked unhappy. Enid Trent preferred being the center of attention.

When the music making, if it could be called that, wound down, the old bum started telling stories as the cowboys stood around the stove. Enid had been on every outfit, ridden every horse, roped every cow, built every good hog trap, tracked every lion, and loved every woman. Of course, he was not currently employed by any outfit, didn't own a horse or a trailer, and had been worked over soundly by all of his ex-wives, bitches every one. To put it mildly.

Jody excused himself right before he expected Sue to call dinnertime and walked to the barn to feed the horses. When he got back to the porch of the bunkhouse, Levi and Blake were driving away. Enid jerked his chin toward Jody's rig.

"Where did you get the truck, kid?"

"Del Lincoln had it out at his camp when my dad got sick and died. He gave it to me when I got my license."

Enid Trent's laugh sounded like a bark. "Got sick and died? Yeah, right. Of lead poisoning!"

Jody excused himself from the table before dessert, and when Enid thumped his way over the wooden floors to his bed, the kid still hadn't come in from the dark.

Was it only youth that had imagined nothing but illness taking someone young away?

When Jody looked back, he realized that his mom had never lied to him, but the only way he ever experienced death was almost not at all. A mouse died beneath the rosebush, and his mom said, "Don't touch it. It must have been sick." It was sickness that made people die.

The truth wasn't hurled at Jody. It dawned on him slowly.

Cash Neil did not get sick and die.

Cash Neil died.

After Jody crept into the dark bunkhouse and slid into his bed, he lay there with the same feeling he'd had the night that Missy had gotten run over, only that night he'd skipped dinner altogether. On that night, after he'd buried Missy out behind the kitchen garden with Sam's silent help, he'd been totally alone in the bunkhouse. On this night he had to listen to Enid Trent snore. On that night he'd wanted to sob into his pillow like a little child and on this night he didn't have one single tear, only anger, only a feeling as if he'd been the butt of a bad joke or the object of every person's pity in his whole world.

A week later, Enid Trent long gone, the forecast threatened the area, especially Bride Mountain, with a major storm, but Jody Neil didn't even notice. He was locked in winter both on the inside and the dry cold outside. With her computer humming with the weather website, Shiney answered the phone in her office and scribbled down some words before walking over to the base radio in the corner.

"HQ base to unit 3, Jody. HQ base to unit 3, Jody."

"Unit 3, go ahead."

"Where are you, Jody?"

"I'm over here in the mare pasture, Miz Lewis, on my way in."

"Come by the office when you get here, please."

"Yes ma'am. Unit 3 out."

"HQ base out."

Shiney went to the Big House for her coat and purse and met Jody as he pulled into the wagon yard. She got in the passenger side of the ranch truck, the page from the message pad clutched in her hand. On it were written words she didn't know how to say.

Diabetic coma

loss of circulation

ICU 202

"Jody, we have to go to town. And let's just take this rig, okay? Go get your wallet or what have you."

"I've got it with me, Miz Lewis. Is something wrong?"

"Del's sick, Jody. Very sick. He's in the hospital. I think I'd better go with you."

It was a small county hospital, the kind that was having a hard time staying afloat financially, but at least parking was not an issue, and the lady in the pink coat at the front desk had gone to high school with Shiney. She clucked at them both and led them toward Del's room saying he was much better now, had actually eaten some soup! When she left them, she went straight to the head nurse to let her know that Sunshine Angel Lewis was in the building.

Del didn't look so much like a black man as an old man, one who had somehow lost his big and his loud and his Del-ness. The first time he'd gotten sick, several weeks before Christmas, the doctors had released him to go home pretty quickly and he never told Jody. This time, Jody was the only person Del knew to have the hospital call.

Now Jody filled the room, bewildered and awkward. He didn't know whether to put his hat on or take it off, ask a lot of questions or sit down and be still, take charge or take orders.

Shiney went off with the head nurse for a bit, and she came back looking grim. She sat down in an uncomfortable orange chair beside the bed. Del had been trying to tell Jody how much bullshit it all was, confusing him even more.

Shiney shut him down. "Delbert Lincoln, they won't tell me anything except sugar diabetes, and I guess you know that because this is not the first time you've been here. Is that right?"

Del's face lit up with almost his old smile. "Why, Shiney Lewis! You sound like yo' daddy! Gettin' right to the heart of the matter. It shore is good to see you. You look just as beautiful as always."

"Don't talk nonsense. Now tell me, do you have medical insurance?" Shiney looked stern but Jody could see she was a little bit pleased.

Del sighed. "Shiney, I mean, Miz Lewis, you know these ranches. What an ol' black man like me needs insurance for?"

"For just such as this, Del! You are a sick man, can't work, and now you are going to need care!"

Del's face got almost as hard as Shiney's did sometimes, and Jody sat back in his own weird plastic chair. He knew that look.

"Miz Lewis, I can work. I am mighty sorry they bothered you. I just wanted Jody to know I was feeling poorly. Now if you will excuse me, I am sure they are getting ready to let me go home. These hospital gowns are none too decent, and I'd hate to offend you when I rise from this bed. I shore do thank you for stopping by." With that, Jody started to stand up, but Shiney let out a whoop of laughter and stayed right in her chair.

"You stubborn old coot! You aren't going anywhere. You've had a major diabetic episode and will have another if you don't learn some new ways. I won't be offended by your wrinkled old backside, but I will be offended if you don't accept the hand of friendship from a long time back and learn to take care of yourself!"

One of the ways Shiney extended her friendship was to loan Jody to Del for the week so he could help him get home and back on his feet. Later Jody went out in the hallway and found her talking to someone in a business suit. He stood back, letting them finish, but he heard the words and knew that Shiney was fighting Del's battles, fighting things that weren't hers to fight, but he also felt certain that she was going to make it all right. Jody walked with her out to the ranch truck in the parking lot.

Shiney stood looking into the approaching storm. "Take care of him and see that he understands about his diet, you hear? No more sweet tea."

"Yes, ma'am. You paying his bills, Miz Lewis?"

"Mind your own business, Jody." Then her voice softened. "Just get him home and call the ranch when it looks like he's okay to be alone. I'll send Sam over to get you."

"This is my fault, you know." Jody stood with his hands in his coat pockets, his head low.

Shiney put her hand on the door of the truck. "No, I don't know. Please tell me. What did you do? Invent a disease?"

Jody's head jerked up. "No. What I mean is, if I hadn't taken all those sweet things to him at Christmas. And Del *is* my business."

"Ha. You young people are so arrogant. Think everything is about you. Del's a big boy, Jody. Buys his own sweets. You know that."

"Sometimes you are a mean old lady."

Shiney snorted. "Damn right I am. And don't you forget it." She saluted him with a jaunty wave, crawled up in the red truck, and started it with a roar. Jody watched her drive off toward the ranch. He felt like he had just been saluted by a queen.

Shiney loved people who could make her laugh and that young cowboy made her laugh in spite of seeing her longtime friend gray and helpless and old.

The lady with the diabetic educators program left a whole sheaf of papers in the hospital room, and Jody read every single word, most of it aloud to Del's annoyance. Buried in them was the perfect diabetic meal plan. After they checked out of the hospital, Jody made Del stay in the truck while he went into the Safeway. That evening, Del sat in his chair intending to watch a Western on the television, still gray, still breathing hard after walking from the bed, but looking like he was going to live. Jody scooted an old metal tray over beside the chair. Sleet ticked against the window. They'd have five or six inches of snow before morning.

"Here. Vegetable soup. A turkey sandwich." He had also arranged a sliced apple on the plate with the sandwich made on the whole-est whole wheat bread he could find. He had measured the mayo carefully, one tablespoon, no more. He'd cut one sweet gherkin in half lengthwise, put the other half back in the jar. It wasn't on the meal plan but he figured half a pickle couldn't hurt.

He went back into the kitchen, returning with a glass of unsweet iced tea and a box of pink packets of artificial sweetener. Del stirred a couple of packets into the glass and tasted it. Grimaced. He made a gesture as if to push it all aside. "Don't want to live if that is how I have to eat."

Maybe the timing wasn't right, but one thing about life, timing is rarely perfect. We don't always get an overture to introduce the sound-track or a predictable build up for the drums or an accurate forecast for the storm. Sometimes there are little mini-explosions along our way and we deal with them, even if we lose a limb.

Jody'd had enough. First, he'd had all fall being the button on the crew and taking their shit, being called "the old lady's pet" and "Rafe's new boy" by Levi, taking the low man jobs and making a slew of mistakes.

Then Missy.

Then this thing with Bliss.

Then Enid Trent.

Then Shiney being mean in the hospital parking lot.

Then his oldest friend and almost-father looking all weak and help-less in an open-backed hospital gown.

"Just eat it! Fuck you! Why can't you just eat it! Hard headed old man! Go ahead and kill yourself with sweet tea. Go right ahead and eat bad things! Ignore the doctors and all the people who care about you. Me! I care about you! If you are going to starve yourself or sugar yourself to death, then at least tell me the truth before you do it. How did my dad die?"

Del ignored the spastic motions Jody was making. Had ignored him since the fuck you. Now he picked up half of the turkey sandwich and pointed it at him.

"Someone shot him. Shot him for stealing cows, which he had been doing for quite awhile. He'd been going around with cake sacks and chummin' other people's cows until he could get a trailer load. Pretend-ed to be lion hunting, even had a bunch of hound dogs and dog boxes on the back of his truck. He was selling the cows he stole to a couple of crooked ranchers down south, making those runs late at night. He was trying to buy your mother everything she wanted. Everything. Do you understand that? He tried to give Mattie everything he thought she wanted and deserved. And you know what?" Del took a bite of the sandwich, before he pointed it at Jody again, talking around the food. "He got caught. Someone shot him, and I found him three days later.

Think about that, kid. Three days later. You ever wanna be mad, you think about that. So there. You've got the truth." Del bit into the sandwich again, "Hmmm . . . not bad."

The truth was finally off his mind and his heart, and Del thought maybe it had been the holding back of that truth that had made him sick, not too much sugar and not enough insulin.

Jody stood like a statue. "What happened to the dogs?"

Del stopped chewing. "Son of a bitch shot them, too."

PART FOUR : HOLDING BEAUTY

SOGGY CHEERIOS

Blake didn't do anything wrong that week, but he didn't do anything right either. He started getting irritable on Friday and was in a completely foul humor by Sunday. The cold wind blew like a mo-fo, making everything outside difficult and unpleasant. The boys were dripping and coughing in the house. It was the perpetual snot that made Blake cranky, the constant sniffles, the red-rimmed nostrils, the crusty shirt sleeves.

Monte had called on Thursday night with some last minute bullshit things on his mind, details that Blake had already gone over with Jody who was assigned to look after West Camp while he was away. Blake felt dry and crumpled inside while he tended to Monte's old woman list, most of it just jackin' off, and the foreman ought to trust his cowboys to tend to business anyway. It was just like Monte to make him look bad by moving the bred heifers over to Farm Camp. Fucking cheated Blake out of his calving bonus, but more than that, Monte kept making it look like Blake just plain wasn't doing his job. Plus, every month he put a blasted photocopy of the electric bill in the envelope with Blake's paycheck. What a chicken shit thing to do.

Brenna didn't feel well, so on top of everything else, Blake ended up doing the cooking all weekend in the too-hot kitchen. He stomped around, trying to iron his dress shirts, mutter his poems to himself, and carve out time to play the guitar

"Mother of Christ. It is roasting in here!" He knew Brenna hated him using Jesus-name-in-vain expressions. It's what he got for hooking up with a preacher's daughter – a suspended license where cussing was concerned. "No wonder everyone is sick! We keep breathing each other's germs!" He stalked over to the thermostat and turned down the heat before throwing open a kitchen window. A few minutes later, Bliss walked into the living room to see Brenna shivering on the couch. She stalked over with a stride identical to Blake's and slapped the window back shut. "Good going, Dad."

Blake had to admit, as the wind slapped against the north side of the house that perhaps he had overdone airing things out. But a man had a right to be a little edgy. After all, going to Elko was a big deal. He had shows to prepare for. And did he have a whole garage all warm and clean, a man's haven from the rest of the house, the way Rafe did? No. And Rafe wasn't even a musician. Just did leatherwork in his! This little house was barely big enough to house the family, and it didn't have a garage, only a carport filled with boxes and tubs of hand-me-down clothes, charity from Brenna's father's congregation, and plastic ride-on toys that faded and cracked with the weather.

Blake laid his list of songs out on the sticky dining room table, trying to get all the way through one before Bliss burned the potatoes frying on the back burner. Brenna lay still and watchful on the couch. Her face was pale and her eyes huge and dark. She'd been coloring her hair in the years since Brian was born, but now, what with being pregnant, the roots were dark and an inch long. Blake had been startled, a few nights back, to see the gray threaded through them.

But of course he didn't make it through the song. Bliss splashed hot grease on her wrist and cried out with pain. Right then Brice came in from the barn, along with the latest kitten that insisted on scooting in the door every time someone opened it. When Blake jumped up to tend to Bliss, he stepped on the cat who yowled as if it were dying. Brian began to cry about the cat. Blake yelled at Bradley to catch the god-damned thing. Brad gave chase, and just as Blake stood holding Bliss's bubbling skin beneath the cold tap water, he knocked Blake's guitar off the chair where it was propped.

Bliss lay listening to her mother's footsteps all night long. Up and down, never finding a comfortable place to light. Brian coughed hard and long every few minutes until Brenna tilted him up on extra pillows. "Here, sweetie. Drink this. No, wake up and drink it." Brian gagged on the thick syrup, but the pillows and the medicine helped quiet the night. Bliss's wrist burned.

It was better in the morning, but it was the only thing that was. She got on the bus with Blake's voice echoing in her head. "You've got to be fuckin' kidding me."

Brice's eyes were red-rimmed, not from his head cold, but from their normally easy-going father's slamming exit from the kitchen and the silent pickup ride to headquarters to catch the bus, Brice's milk-soaked math homework drying on the dashboard. When Brice's bowl of Cheerios got tipped over, thanks to Brad's elbow, Brice had said, "Hey!" in dismay.

Blake, helping clean up the mess, asked, "Why are you just now do-ing your homework? You had all weekend!"

Brice looked up at his dad, "Because no one said . . ."

Bliss would have laughed at her father's bewildered face as he stood holding the dripping worksheet if there had been anything at all funny about the last three days, anything at all lighthearted the way things usually were with Blake around, the way things used to be.

Blake was calm and quiet enough to make everyone stop and look at him. "No one said what?"

Brice's voice was very small, even quieter than Blake's. "No one said do your homework."

The phrase Blake uttered was the only thing he said from then until the four children got on the bus at headquarters. "You've got to be fuckin' kidding me."

Blake worked all morning. He put music and poetry and kids and cooking and dreams out of his mind. He saddled a horse and rode the fence around the bull trap. He hauled another round bale out to them and cut the string. He drove over to the Breakdown mill and chopped ice on the drinker since it was the shallowest one on his country. He threw a sack of cake onto the flatbed of the truck before he went into the house for a sandwich. He hadn't eaten much dinner the night before in all of the hot chaos, and he sure as hell hadn't eaten any soggy Cheer-ios that morning.

The house was dim and quiet, most of the mess from the morning cleaned up. Blake noted mop marks on the floor, and the air smelled vaguely spicy. Brenna must have been up and about for awhile. He walked down the hallway to the bedroom where a little lamp burned on the dresser. The lamp was one that he had bought for too much money when Bliss was born. That was back before they knew to count the idea of a nursery as a luxury. This baby was going to be tucked into the corner of the master bedroom in a crib with a previously chewed rail, thanks to Bradley who had been part baby, part beaver. The lampshade was painted with the bucolic scene of a mother rocking her newborn. The sight of it always made Blake want to write a brand new lullaby that had never been sung. The lamp threw soft light over the mound of sleeping Brenna. Blake eased down on the edge of the bed and watched her eyelids lift.

She smiled. "Hey, you."

He smoothed her hair back. It was greasy and limp. "Hey, you. How ya feeling?"

"Better."

But Blake saw the shadow cross her face — like a fast-moving cloud across the land — making you doubt that a sunny day will make it all the way to sunset without the forecasted cold front moving in.

"Sure?" Brenna put her hand on her belly, not massive yet, just round and hard. She wrinkled her nose.

"Six more weeks." Then she struggled up to sit against the headboard. "Ah, well. Just a baby. We've done this before. Play me some songs, cowboy."

So Blake played them all — played the ones he'd lined up for his daytime sessions and the ones he planned to play for his show in the little theater on Thursday night. Played every one of them and sang 'em good, too. By the time he was finished, and his fingers were just moving on the strings, a mind and a melody of their own, Brenna was asleep again, her face golden in the lamplight. Blake let his fingers ramble on for a bit longer, slips and measures of songs spilling around them both, some begging for words, some content to sing on their own. He laid aside his guitar, unharmed by its tumble the night before, and turned off the lamp. Cold afternoon sun filtered through the curtains, turning Brenna's face to gray instead of gold. He turned the lamp back on.

There wasn't any lettuce in the fridge so he contented himself with white bread and bologna, or he would have been content if there had been more than a smear of Miracle Whip in the jar. His search through the pantry made him pause. He thought of his wife and her gray-gold face, of the long week ahead, and switched gears. He left the barren sandwich beside the kitchen sink, changed his work boots for his dress boots, put on a clean shirt, grabbed his town hat and his wallet, picked up his sandwich again and headed out the door. He left a note, a big one, taped to the fridge.

Gone to buy groceries. Have the kids with me. Rest. FYB

They always used to sign their notes to each other, "Forever your girl," and "Forever your boy." He wondered when they'd stopped. Maybe when they didn't feel so much like a boy and a girl anymore.

Blake ate his almost dry sandwich, poured cake out for some cows using his personal rig, and felt a little self-righteous to be tending to his job while on his way to supply the larder for his family so they'd be comfortable in his absence.

His "Elko alone" fantasy had a new element. Two weeks before, Blake had gone into a thrift store after delivering some late steers to the sale for Monte. Pawnshops and thrift stores were Blake's biggest weakness after music. He loved to treasure hunt and had, in the last few years, added a cornet, a xylophone, and an accordion to his collection of musical instruments, all for around $50 each. Plus the set of drums for Jody. But on that day, two weeks before, it wasn't a new instrument he'd found but a "like new," hell, might as well have *been* new, wool Pendleton coat, red and black plaid. It fit as if it had been tailored for him. Twelve dollars. Even now it hung on the outside of the closet door in his bedroom.

The year before, Elko in January had been almost balmy, the streets clear, only mounds of old snow in the corners of the parking lots getting smaller every afternoon, a reminder that it really was northern Nevada in mid-winter, but the deep dark early nights had been very cold with snow flurries around midnight. Blake was proud he'd have the coat this year.

In his current fantasy he was wearing it as he left the dark silent camp on Wednesday morning, closing the door carefully behind him, ruefully shaking his head with affection for his loved ones, sleeping and oblivious as he drove toward the airport. What did his slumbering family know of plane rides and performances looming? He imagined wearing the coat while parking the truck and walking into the brightly lit airport dragging a simple rollered suitcase (that he didn't own) and his guitar, which he would not check, of course.

From smiling at the flight attendants, female of course, to entering a crowded restaurant, to draping it over a chair in the green room and sitting in the spotlight on the stage, Blake saw the coat in every scene.

He was smiling with fantasy when he got to headquarters. He poked his head into the office to tell Monte what was up before the bus got there.

"Hey, Blake! Come on in! Me and Jody, we're just doing a little googling . . . . What do you know about diabetes?" Blake sat down in one of the big chairs, watching Monte and Jody tussle slightly over the keyboard, both of them saying, "Click here. No, on that!" every so often with Jody taking notes on a yellow legal pad. At one point Jody looked up at Monte.

"Hey, how come Mr. Unitas isn't, like, taking care of Del? Like helping him out or whatever. I mean Del's been there a long time, something like twenty years. He's made him a good hand and all."

Monte sat back in his chair. "Oh, I don't know. Only Mr. Unitas can say for sure, I reckon. Maybe he doesn't know that Del needs help, or maybe he doesn't think it is his problem. And, you know how it is, cowboys are a dime a dozen, right?" The silence stretched out until Monte was uncomfortable under the eyes of his youngest employee and Blake. Finally he put his hand on Jody's shoulder. "That last was a joke. A poor one. I don't have a good answer for you, Jody. I don't. I'm sorry."

The school bus rumbled across the cattle guard.

The boys were bewildered at the idea of getting in the truck and heading back down the long dirt road, back to the little town where they attended school, making a hard left onto the freeway, going to the city with the supercenter perched in a vast parking lot on the edge of town on a school night. At Blake's cheerful suggestion, Brice and Bradley quickly pulled their homework out of their backpacks, studious and quiet in the atmosphere of unexpected evening plans and in the echo of their father's early morning outburst. Blake, on his part, would have been hard pressed to remember what had set him off all of those hours ago. Brian stared blankly out at the already darkening sky. He looked wrung out like a cheap dollar store wash cloth, like he did every weekday evening. Blake realized guiltily that it has been several weeks since he had asked his youngest how kindergarten was going.

"Did Mom give you a list?" Blake looked at his baby girl, the one he had held in his arms over sixteen years ago and felt that all of life was worth living – the current expression on her face the greatest evidence that she was slipping away. Or Daddy was slipping, rather had *already* slipped down several notches in her estimation, losing his star status.

"Nope! No list! Your mama was sleeping and I realized we were low on stuff. I'm gonna be gone for several days, and your mom doesn't feel that good. Just want to make sure you guys are going to be okay."

"Mom always has a list."

"Well, pardner, how about you and me wing it? I'll bet we do okay."

Bliss loved it when her dad called her pardner. She didn't know what was afoot, and didn't entirely trust this plan, but she grinned at her dad anyway.

"'Kay, pardner."

They threw things into the cart until Bliss began to worry about money, but Blake told her no big deal. He had it under control. And he did. He was using the credit card with a vow to pay this whole grocery bill off with his paycheck from the poetry gathering. Four loaves of bread. Peanut butter. Two jars of Miracle Whip, pancake mix, mac and cheese (several boxes of the three for a dollar kind), more vegetables than Bliss was used to her mother buying, five boxes of Hamburger Helper because she said she knew how to make it and the freezer was full of ground beef. Oreos. Honey Nut Cheerios instead of the plain kind and none of the kids said a word to correct their father's mistake. Potatoes, eggs, bacon, canned beans, a box of powdered sugar donuts that made Brian's eyes get bigger still.

Blake stood in front of the fruit juice with Bliss, and father and daughter had a serious discussion about snotty noses and vitamin C. Blake got quite an education when they got to the jarred spaghetti sauces, and Bliss informed him of what all she needed to make a complete meal for the boys some night while he was gone.

After all of the groceries were loaded into the truck, they left Brice in charge of the two younger boys while Blake and Bliss went back in to get McDonalds for everyone. This time Blake used the "real money" account to pay. He and Brenna referred to the credit card as fake money and their actual checking account as real money. Again, Blake promised himself to pay back the fake money he had spent that night, but he was a little shocked at how much the total had been. No wonder grocery shopping made Brenna look so grim every month.

As the kids rustled the paper and cardboard from their meals and Brian spun the wheels on some toy that didn't look remotely like a car, Blake's virtuous-father feeling rose to full ebb. Here he was, tending his family before going off to perform for the crowds. The boys fell asleep almost as soon as they finished eating, and Bliss unbuckled her seat belt to turn around and gather up all of the trash from the meal, reminding Blake of how many tasks she did lately, tasks that she performed just like Brenna.

"Dad, can I have a cell phone?" They drove through the dark.

"No, you can't have a cell phone, Bliss."

"Yeah. Did you know about Jody's dad? That he stole cattle, I mean?"

Blake smiled. Damn he loved this girl.

"Pardner, everyone heard rumors about Cash Neil. We all heard how he died, and we all believed Delbert Lincoln when he brought him in. Shot for a thief."

Bliss was silent for a long time. Finally she turned sideways in her seat. "Jody knows."

"I'm not surprised. The cowboy world is small. You know the saying, 'Telephone, telegraph, tell a cowboy?' But the fact is I would have thought that Del or Jody's mom would have told him long ago."

"Yeah, that would have been the right thing. Don't you think so, Dad?"

"Oh, I don't know. We can't decide what is right for other people sometimes. How did he find out? Not Del?"

"No. That old guy that came to the bunkhouse, Enid? He told him."

"No shit?"

Bliss looked at her dad.

"No shit."

Blake laughed and reached for his daughter's hand, gave it a squeeze. Maybe watching your kids grow up wasn't such a bad thing after all.

"Did they find the guy who shot him, Dad?"

"Well, I don't remember all of the details, kiddo. Seems like they made a stab at it, but you know, the law frowns pretty hard on cattle theft, so it wouldn't surprise me if they didn't look that much. It was a big scandal though."

Bliss gave him the hardest look he'd ever seen from his daughter. "Doesn't seem fair, Dad. And don't tell me life isn't fair."

She had a point.

It was almost midnight before Blake got everyone bathed, tucked in bed, and all of the groceries put away, some a little haphazardly.

Brenna came in to sit at the table and watch him. "Nell was here this evening. She brought her cell phone. She wants you to take it with you on your trip."

Blake looked around from putting the spaghetti makings all together on a pantry shelf. "Oh? Nell? A cell phone?"

Brenna persisted. "Yeah. In case something happens. Like with one of the kids or the ranch or maybe even the baby."

Blake was trying to fit all of the cereal boxes on the right shelf. "Uh huh."

"So I can call you if I need you."

Blake wondered who had put the bag of iced animal cookies in the cart. "Right."

Brenna raised her voice. "Blake! I want you to take the phone."

Blake looked up, "Okay, sweetie! If Nell loaned it to us, of course I'll take it! Not sure I know how to use the durned thing, but I'll take it."

He gathered up the mound of plastic sacks and stuffed them under the sink. "I'm beat. Wanna snuggle?"

In bed he held his wife close up under the heavy quilt, mashed his nose into her hair, and thought about the end of the week.

Blake loved to fly.

"A Message for you, Mr. Davis"

Four weeks after the National Cowboy Poetry Gathering, an envelope arrived in the mail, "Photos Enclosed," and "Do Not Bend," written on the outside in block print. It was two days before Blake got around to opening it after Bliss dropped it on the dining room table with the rest of the mail. The enclosed note said, *"Big time was had by all! Hope you got home safe and sound. Happy Trails! Mac and Grace Peele."* Blake wondered who the fuck Mac and Grace Peele were and who in the world that guy in the photos was. He didn't even recognize himself, all smiles and beautiful coat and casual guitar. The glossy photos were lit up, bright lights glinting off shiny people, all laughing, all clean, all swimming in a sea of happy.

It was six months before Blake looked closely at the photos again, remembered who everyone was, allowed himself to think of that week. Very little of his trip, if any, had turned out to match his daydreams. Rather than leaving a peacefully sleeping quiet house, he left in a rush, his duffle bag not fully zipped, every light in the house on because Brenna was up caring for Bradley who had been vomiting all night, a virus making him retch long after there was nothing left in his stomach. Finally, they got him settled on the couch with a big bowl beside him, sleeping, with beads of sweat up under his hair and a sour smell on his breath. Brenna was sitting in the recliner, her face gray again, gray enough to match the old sports jersey that wrapped tightly around her belly and rode up to show her pale thighs.

"I hope you don't get this," she said to Blake as he snapped his guitar case closed. "Doesn't look like too much fun."

For someone who loved words, Blake was having a hard time finding his. He was angry. Angry at Brenna for looking gray. Angry at her for not even asking him to stay home and help. Angry at her for being pregnant, for how unappealing she looked with her stained panties showing, for her quiet smile as he kissed the top of her head, for her stupid "break a leg, honey," as he abandoned her. He hated her even more as he went out the door, and didn't get it all the way closed before he heard Brice come down the hall. "Ma, I don't feel so good."

He had to drive too fast because he was running fifteen minutes late, and he hated to do that in the ranch truck. Monte had said, "Yeah, take it," so that Blake could leave his personal rig for the kids to get back and forth to the bus. Sue and Sam brought *their* personal rig over the night before so Brenna wouldn't be afoot during the day. It was fruit basket turnover of vehicles just so one man could get off the ranch.

When he got to the airport, he took a deep breath out in the cold dark parking lot, hit the reset button on his attitude, and found a glimmer of his errant excitement for the trip. He shrugged into his new coat, used a fast food napkin from the door panel cubby to wipe the vomit splatters off of his boot where Bradley had missed the toilet while Blake was brushing his teeth, and finally got his duffle bag zipped around his shaving kit and the cell phone charger. He let the lights of the terminal act as a magnet to pull him into his fantasy. Which would begin soon, of course. Always soon.

Since he'd returned to the ranch from Elko, he'd corrected more homework, cooked more meals, done more laundry, read more bedtime stories, driven more miles, listened to more medical words than he had ever imagined possible. He'd never played so little music, not since he picked out his first tune on his mom's piano when he was six years old. His guitar was locked in the case just exactly as it had been since he got off the airplane and retrieved it from the luggage carousel. All of his poetry books had been shelved together in the living room, by Sue he supposed.

Blake got up at five every morning, worked hard, worked every moment, worked at everything until he crashed into bed at night, usually by eleven, but never with any laundry left unfolded or dishes left unwashed. And that was just inside the house, not counting his job. On his job he saw more things undone that he had ever seen before. And he worked to correct them. And he couldn't look at Bliss.

He hadn't meant to stay up all night on that snowy Saturday in Nevada. First there had been the relief that his official shows and sessions were over, that he had done his job and earned his applause. Then there was the jam session, a little louder, a little longer, a little bit frantic with everyone knowing it was the last night. Then there was a midnight breakfast that went on for two hours, dirty napkins and ketchup bottles and empty highball glasses littering the table. Then a nightcap. He'd meant to get a couple of hours of sleep, but before he knew it, he had ten minutes before the bus arrived to shuttle performers back to the Salt Lake City Airport. He never saw the telephone message light blinking on the nightstand as he threw his things into the duffle bag and grabbed his guitar. Nell's cell phone had been silent since he'd called home on Friday morning, surprised at hearing Bliss's voice. She had taken the boys to the bus, but had come home because Brenna had the stomach flu now, and she was taking care of her mother. She sounded worried and distracted. Brenna took the phone and assured him she was fine, just achy and pukey but she'd been there before. Blake ended up slapping the phone shut after saying goodbye, a little petulant that no one asked how *he* was doing, tossed it onto a pile of clothes where in the wee hours of Saturday morning it blinked off, battery empty, and had remained mute ever since.

Blake stashed his duffle and guitar in the belly of the bus, clambered aboard, folded the wool coat carefully on the seat beside him, leaned back with his hat over his eyes, and slept for four straight hours.

Once in Salt Lake City, he hunted up a little boy's room, and then went straight to a coffee shop where he very gratefully paid most of a ten dollar bill for a large hot cup and a pastry. He didn't feel debonair or suave or anything but awkward and wrung out as he stood in line in front of the airline counter. He let his bag and his guitar rest at his feet as he gobbled the sweet, washed it down with the bitter coffee, and looked around for a garbage container. Blake wondered vaguely why he wasn't ready to go home.

Standing behind him was a brown sparrow of a woman, her feathers of hair done up in a roll, a neat little suitcase at her feet. She smiled, "Hi, Blake!"

Damn. He knew her. Right? He smiled as he looked around, still seeking a trash can. "Well, hello there . . . ?!"

"Carmella," the woman supplied helpfully as she took the garbage from his hands and walked over to a silver cylinder.

Blake leaned down to pick up his luggage and shift it forward along the chute to the ticket counter. "So, Carmella, thank you. I saw one of your sessions and I really like your poems. One about barn cats, right?"

The little sparrow smiled at him. She had on the tiniest snow boots he'd ever seen. "Everyone calls me Mel," she said, and he thought he could hear chirping in her voice. The line moved again and they shuffled along with it.

"You have a good voice, you know."

"Thank you, Mel!" He winked at her.

"Don't you have a sweet little wife? Wasn't she with you last year?"

Blake felt itchy. "I do. Where do you live?"

"North Dakota. That's why I so admire your coat, it looks so warm. What was your wife's name again?"

"Uh, Brenna. My coat?"

"Why, yes! Last night I couldn't sleep and when I looked out my hotel room window, I saw you walking along the sidewalk and that coat just glowed. It's a beauty!"

Last night. Shortly after dark, it had begun to snow millions of heavy flakes. Blake had walked along the streets with Sophia, laughing. They had sat at the jam session and made conversation with their music. They had clinked glasses and told their stories to each other. They had drifted from one hot party to the next through the cold corridors of snowy nighttime streets. Sophia. He thought of the way her fingers moved across the strings of her harp, of her voice as it lifted and supported his, of the way she laughed and waved him aside. "Oh, I don't know cows and ranching and stuff. I was an attorney for years, but don't practice anymore. Always had horses, of course. Now, I just play music! Some of us, you know, need the spotlight."

His coat had glowed as he walked with another woman.

The line moved. He was up to the ticket counter, and the minute he said his name, the airline employee started rustling papers to hand him an official-looking envelope. "A message for you, Mr. Davis." Divested of his bag and his guitar, Blake walked toward security, carrying only his coat and the envelope. He ripped it open.

Baby girl born 1a.m., come straight to hospital. Please turn on phone.

Blake turned back as if he could retrieve it, retrieve his bag, retrieve the dead phone inside, retrieve his world, retrieve the night, retrieve the day. But it was gone.

PAPA SAID SO

Punch Lewis started coming to Shiney the night after the ranch Christmas party, as if the crowd in his library had awakened him, made him restless. Shiney wondered the next morning, over coffee, why he had waited thirty years. On the nights he came, they always sat in the big red leather chairs, sipped scotch, and talked about the ranch, the modern-day ranch, the current employees, the here-and-now problems, not the simpler ones he had left her with way back then.

By the time Christmas had become a month-old fruitcake in the pantry and the wintertime cold had ceased to be of note, Shiney had grown accustomed to her father's ghostly presence at night, even if she always assured herself it was a dream. So it was quite startling to realize that he was standing beside her, in her upstairs sitting room, as she knelt on the window seat on the afternoon of the day Brenna's baby was born. In broad daylight.

Monte spent Sunday in his home office, the television in the living room chattering a build up to the Super Bowl. Pam had invited him to the big party a friend was throwing in town, but he'd turned her down and invited Jody and Shiney to come up and watch the game with him instead. He was in the kitchen compiling a platter of sandwich makings when Shiney drove up the hill. Monte answered the door in his sock feet, and grinned at his boss, glad she'd agreed to come.

But she didn't come all the way in the door.

"Get your coat . . . we are going to see that baby."

They stopped at the cook house where Jody, just back from feeding at West Camp, was rustling around in Sue's kitchen for the last of the fudge to carry up to Monte's. He looked tired, but he got his coat, too, and climbed in the backseat. He didn't care much about the ball game anyway. It had been a long month, surely longer than thirty-one days.

As they drove toward the highway in the very beginnings of dusk, Shiney answered Monte's unspoken question, "Because Papa said so."

The drive was quiet, only the occasional remark between Monte and

Shiney floating over the back seat. Jody had been tending to West Camp every day since Wednesday, driving over and back instead of staying. The afternoon before he had kissed Bliss in the stall beside the saddle house, out of sight of the kitchen window, kissed her long and hard and without the tenderness he should have felt. He wanted to run rough hands over her softness, wanted to push her up against the wall. Wanted something to make himself feel better, some kind of relief. Wanted something to drive the broken record replays of truths and lies out of his head.

Today he wished he'd just put his hands in her hair and whispered in her ear and touched her lips softly with his.

"Pam?" Shiney turned her head toward Monte.

"Super Bowl party." Monte drove his boss's SUV even more carefully than he drove the ranch trucks.

As they went by the little dirt tank almost at the highway he nodded toward it. "Ducks."

"Yeah, lots of them this year. And some antelope."

"Saw 'em."

"Who's playing?"

"Don't know . . . Cardinals?" This question was tossed back toward Jody, but he was looking out at the changing sky, not listening.

"When do you fly out?" Monte was puzzled by this unexpected trip Shiney had only told him about the week before. She seemed tense about it, not in a holiday mood which is how she had billed it, just a lark to a warmer climate for a few days like she had done right after fall works.

"Not until next week . . . Thursday. Next. Not this Thursday. Not leaving for several more days." Monte turned his head to look at his boss. She was sitting up straight in the seat, her leather purse clutched in her lap like a little old lady at church.

They were away from the ranch, on the blacktop, the world feeling like an unlit tunnel.

"Down's Syndrome."

"Yeah."

"Know much about it?"

"Not a lot. I called my sister Liz. You know she teaches special ed. She is going to send me some links on e-mail. Nell said something about a heart condition."

"Well, I guess we'll find out."

They bypassed the little town, bypassed the little hospital where Del and Shiney had clashed. Shiney looked longingly at it, wishing they were stopping at that warmer, friendlier place. By the time they got to the big hospital, it was dark, only a faint band of color marking the western horizon.

They met Sue and Sam coming out of the front doors. The five of them made a little huddle, as if they were unpadded players, deciding on strategy, no coaches on the sidelines. Sam gave Monte directions to Brenna's room, put his hand on Jody's shoulder. Sue explained to Shiney that the Davis boys were with Velma Jo and Levi and it had been decided that it was best for them to go on to school and keep as normal a routine as possible. They could come see the baby at a better time, perhaps when their daddy could bring them. Sue had a list of things to retrieve from West Camp and bring back the next day.

"So they're keeping her for awhile?"

"Oh yes. She's too little. Poor thing, there's just not much to her! But a more beautiful baby I never did see. Except for mine, but that's a mama's and gramma's bias talking. Such a sweet little round face." Sam took his wife's arm and led her toward their truck while Monte held the door open for Shiney, passing it off to Jody who came behind. When they got to the quiet wing, the lights were dim, but Brenna was sitting up in bed, looking better than she'd looked for several weeks. Nell was sitting in a chair beside the bed, and Bliss was standing like a ramrod in the corner of the room, her back so straight she looked like she was guarding something. She didn't look at Jody, so he hung back by the door.

Shiney went in, patted Brenna's shoulder, and sat down beside Nell. Monte stood up against the wall, his hat in awkward hands. The talk was quiet.

"When does Blake get here?"

"His plane lands at eight. He called from a pay phone in DFW. I guess the cell phone battery ran out and he forgot to charge it. Seems all of our messages missed him until he got to the airport in Salt Lake City this morning. He's coming straight here when he lands." Nell's voice had an edge to it that made the whole room seem defenseless. Shiney saw Bliss get even stiffer, if possible, and quickly changed the subject, asking when the doctor planned on releasing Brenna.

"Tomorrow morning. But I don't want to leave. I want to stay here with her..." Brenna's voice rose and then trailed off like a little girl's, a little girl who doesn't know how to make things happen.

Shiney leaned over, got hold of Brenna's hand, and made the younger woman look at her while she spoke fiercely. "Of course you do. Of course you want to stay with that baby. You are staying right here where you can be with her all you want. I will make sure you do *not* have to leave her." Shiney glanced to her right and caught Nell's eye. "And so will Nell. Those boys are in good hands. Velma Jo and Levi are the perfect people to take care of them, and I am sure that when Blake gets here we can figure all the logistics out. Jody's done a fine job at West Camp this week. We are purely glad to have him on board for just such a crisis."

Monte looked up from the square of floor between his boots that he had been contemplating. Well, Shiney Lewis! Stepping up to the plate. Other than in her own kitchen, he'd never heard her talk this freely about anything.

A nurse in scrubs with teddy bears and balloons all over them, a clipboard in her hand, walked past Jody into the room. "Well, good evening! Sure is a busy place in here!" She nodded in a way that seemed to include all of them, but her eyes were fixed on Brenna. With her free hand she turned on a brighter light.

"How are we doing? You ate your dinner, and your color looks good. The cardiologist is scheduled to see the baby at 9 a.m., and Dr. Jimenez is rarely late."

All the time she was talking, the nurse was moving around Brenna's bed, putting things to rights.

"How is she, how is the baby?"

"She's doing fine. Now don't you worry. She looks all scary in that incubator and with the ventilator helping her breathe, but babies like her . . ."

Bliss's voice burst all the calm in the room, "Her name is Beauty! Stop calling her 'the baby' or 'babies like her!' Her name is Beauty and I don't CARE what you think, Nell, and I don't care what all of those prissy nurses think. Daddy told me I could name her and her name is Beauty! And she IS beautiful!" Bliss stomped a foot on each repetition of the name and on the word beautiful. Her voice hung at an apex, trembling a little with the last word as if it wouldn't take anything for Bliss to fall from that point.

Brenna, the nurse, and Nell all started talking at once.

"Bliss!"

"It's okay, honey, I didn't mean to upset anyone."

"I'm sorry, Bliss." This from Nell who earlier in the day had expressed her opinion that Beauty sounded like the name of a horse or a dog or a fairy tale princess.

Bliss did not hear the apology, but instead turned and looked at Nell with all of the wisdom of a grown woman who knows what beauty is, with all of the pathos of a heart-broken little girl who has had a dream taken away from her, but more than anything, with the fury of a teenage girl who realizes without doubt that life is not Disney and that there are no real princesses.

"She is *beautiful!*" With this, Bliss's voice rose to a soprano wail and she bolted from the room. Monte moved to go after her, but saw that Jody had it covered and that was plenty.

Brenna's labor had started after dark on Saturday night and it was Bliss who drove the boys to Half-way Camp, Bliss who drove her mother to the small town hospital and then had to drive by herself to the city where the doctors had airlifted Brenna when they couldn't get her labor stopped. The theory was that the bigger hospital could give the premature baby better care. And it had been to Bliss the doctors had delivered the news of trisomy 21 in her new sister. It was Bliss who had sat beside her sleeping mother through the long hours before dawn, before Nell arrived.

Monte figured Bliss was due a meltdown.

In the quiet the kids left behind, the nurse murmured some things about how the whole situation was going to take some time to sink in for everyone, and then said she'd be back to walk Brenna down to NICU before bedtime. She refrained from saying "to see the baby," and everyone heard the omission. After the door closed behind her, Shiney once again rose to the challenge, and in Monte's mind, hit a double.

"Beauty. I like it. I know what it's like to have an odd name, and Beauty is better than Sunshine, believe me! Besides, we can all use a little bit more beauty in this world. What does Blake say?"

"He doesn't know yet, but I know he'll agree. He's so much better with her than I am." Brenna laid her head back on her pillows, and Shiney wondered if she was thinking about starting all over from square one, with another girl to raise. Made Shiney want to shudder.

Always the mother, Brenna turned her head toward Monte and smiled. "Monte, Bliss hasn't eaten all day, I don't think. And then, could you maybe take her to Sue's to sleep? She needs a break, but I couldn't get her to go earlier. Maybe Jody can."

Monte left the women to talk about women things and went to hunt up Jody and Bliss. When he saw them at the end of a corridor, he paused and looked out of a window at the rooftop of the adjoining building, he looked back down the way he had come, he looked up at the ceiling, giving the two huddled in an embrace a chance to realize he was there. Next time he looked toward them, Jody was walking his way, Bliss following, using the sleeve of her hoodie to dry her face, looking even younger than she normally did. Monte tossed the keys toward his youngest cowboy. "Bliss needs to eat something."

Jody grabbed the keys out of midair, "Yes, sir."

"That's the boss's rig, remember. Got some cash?"

"Yes, sir."

"We'll meet you out front in a bit, okay?"

Jody nodded, looking at Monte with the questions of the whole world in his eyes.

A few minutes later, Monte followed the little group of women, looking like so many slow moving birds, down the hall to NICU. It was times like these that he wished Pam would be a true partner. But she wasn't. And she didn't intend to be. So the foreman of a large ranch told himself to make the best of it. Monte Wells lifted his arms, put one around Shiney and one around Nell as the three of them watched through the glass as Brenna greeted her daughter.

And they smiled. They smiled in spite of everything at the tiny girl with the round head, the helpless limbs, the tubes and tape and, somehow, something beautiful under her skin.

SNUFFED

Blake's plane was over an hour late. He joined the quiet, tired travelers filing through the chute into the airport. Behind them, the pilots and flight attendants closed up shop. It took Blake almost another hour to retrieve his bag in the empty soulless belly of the airport, only a few people coming and going like ghosts. The ranch truck sat like a lonely island in the parking lot. The glow of the last few days had been snuffed, obliterated, made nothing, denied. The walk through the cold dark felt like a punishment from God. By the time he got to the hospital, its parking lots were almost empty, too, and the front desk was dark, no kind-faced volunteers to guide his way. The gift shop was closed up, the flowers in the cool case glowing in the distance, impersonal, inaccessible, not available even to the empty handed. The popcorn machine was quiet, clean, and fragrance free. Blake wandered the vacant halls until he found a man with a mop and blank eyes who directed him to the right elevator, to the right floor. He was headed straight for what looked like an unpeopled nurses' station when he saw B. Davis on a pink removable tag beside one of the doors. And there lay Brenna, her back to him, sleeping with her arm up over her head the way she was wont to do. Blake knelt on the hard floor, laid his head on the edge of her bed, didn't pray, didn't cry, didn't sleep.

ROUTINES

When Nell walked into the hospital room the next morning, Starbucks in her hand, Blake was sitting by the window having showered and shaved in the early hours. Now Brenna was taking her turn, a long, slow, careful, postpartum shower.

Nell stopped in the doorway. "So you made it."

"Yeah. You slept in town?"

"At my sister's. I'd have asked you if you wanted one of these," she gestured with the cardboard cup, "but I don't have my cell phone."

The last two words hung in the room. "Oh. Yeah." Blake dug through the mess in his duffle and handed the phone to Nell.

"Charger?" She put her coffee down on the bedside table and turned to face Blake.

"Oh." He leaned down again to his bag, but he knew it was futile. He knew exactly where Nell's charger was. Could see it in his mind. It was plugged in, on the far side of the bed, in room 307 of the Stockman's Hotel and Casino, Elko, Nevada. "I think I left it in the hotel room."

Nell picked up her coffee again. "No big deal. I'll stop by Target. Just $17."

"Sorry about that. I'll pay you back."

"No big deal." Nell turned away from Blake and looked out the window to the parking lot. "So you know the pediatric cardiologist is going to be here soon."

Blake didn't know anything other than at three a.m. Brenna had put her hand on his head as he knelt beside the bed, and they had stayed that way until five.

"Cardiologist?"

"Yeah. Beauty," Nell's voice stumbled a bit, "needs to be checked out. Half of all Down's babies have a heart defect. We need to see if she has it." Her use of the word "we" grated on Blake, but he knew it was the least of his penance.

Over the next few weeks, Blake did more laundry, cooked more meals, bought more groceries, made more decisions, dried more tears, mopped more floors, made more beds, flung the lash of self-discipline more firmly over his shoulder than ever before in his life. It didn't matter that Sue came over twice a week to clean the house more thoroughly than it had ever been cleaned before, that she brought meals each time she came, or that Velma Jo was tending to the boys at school and making sure their teachers knew what was going on at home. It didn't matter that Shiney had said for Blake to take as much time off from the ranch as he needed, had volunteered Jody to move onto the camp if necessary. It didn't matter. Blake worked. Worked as hard as he could as if sheer physical labor could somehow make up for his sins.

Routines establish themselves quickly in times of crisis, and before a full week was gone, Tuesdays and Thursdays had become the days that Blake picked the kids up from school and drove them an additional sixty miles to visit their mom and their new sister, who though she did not exhibit the heart defect present in 50% of babies with Down's Syndrome, was having difficulty eating and swallowing and gaining weight. Failure to thrive, in addition to being premature. Blake knew those terms by heart, and they echoed in his head the way his poems and songs had always done before.

Blake and the kids also went to the city on Sundays so they could take Brenna out to eat and, by the second Sunday it had started to feel like a little party, like perhaps there could be some healing, if only Blake could reach Bliss. But from the Monday morning she had walked into the hospital lobby with Sue, she had kept herself apart from Blake, and he felt her absence like the winter wind.

The doctors said they expected Beauty to be in the hospital for at least a month, so Brenna had settled in for the long haul with Nell firmly by her side. She looked at her boys as if they were little strangers, as if she wondered where they came from. She and Blake talked about hospital routines, Beauty's health, what the doctors were saying, but they never touched on the 100% Bradley got on his spelling test or how Brice had outgrown his boots again or Brian's questions about why Beauty couldn't come home and sleep in the baby bed he had filled with his stuffed animals for her. They talked about how Brenna was sitting with her breasts exposed for upwards of six hours a day, either pumping her milk or trying to get Beauty's funny little mouth to latch on now that she was weaned from the ventilator, how a home health care nurse and educator was being scheduled to come out to the ranch once a week after the doctors released her to go home. But they never talked about their other daughter, the one who was silent, watchful, and turning into a woman in front of Blake's eyes, the one who was spending every moment she could with the boy in the bunkhouse.

The Palm Tree

Shiney hadn't been able to get a window seat. Instead she was folded into an aisle seat which made her feel like Jonah sitting on a whale rib, tucking her elbows in close to keep from getting banged by the drink cart. Silly to think that if she had been two seats over she might have been able to see at least the white of the Bride's crown, though how that was going to make her feel better was anyone's guess.

At least her hair looked good. She'd seen Alma the day before. Mama D had always cut Shiney's hair until she got too weak to stand, and then she suggested that one of her daughters-in-law come out and trim it. Shiney would never forget Alma's gentle hands as she sat beside Mama D's bed and got her hair cut, the kind old eyes watching and making whispered suggestions. Every time Shiney went into Alma's shop, it brought those final days of Mama D's life back to her.

Sunshine Angel Lewis had not rejected this trip out of hand when Max Angel had suggested it. She knew she needed to check things out even if they sounded like a fairy tale. She had even been gracious when he had gifted her the plane ticket, but she wasn't such a rube or country bumpkin that she couldn't see how it wasn't due to friendship exactly, more of an advantageous business deal. Shiney Lewis leaned her head back against the seat and closed her eyes. She was tired. Tired of every-one thinking she was rich, tired of trying to find her way through one more year, tired of the look in Monte's eyes when she played devil's advocate day in and day out. Tired of keeping this secret that felt like a thorn under her skin ever since New Year's Day when Max explained it all so clearly over coffee and pastries. He had it all worked out, and it seemed to Shiney as if it would be a relief to let someone like Max pull it all together, plan her whole life, right down to how she would word her will and where she'd play golf. If she played golf.

It only took four houses before she got a headache. Even in winter the sun in Scottsdale was a summer sun, blinding her and bouncing off all of the noise. It was the last house that did it with its gravel landscaping and the palm tree. She didn't even go inside, could not face walking on that blinding white path past that ridiculous looking tree and through the pink (pink!) wrought iron fence. Could not imagine living beneath those shaggy and bedraggled fronds. She sat still in the slowly warming interior of the car, looking out at all of the bright white and contrasting browns and angles. "Max, I'm sorry." She touched his sleeve, preventing him from getting out of the driver's side door. He'd seen this coming and smiled gently.

"I know. But you can't blame me for trying." And he was right. If she sold the Tinaja to his client, invested in one of these homes, she would have enough to live on for the rest of her days, enough to drink good scotch, and leave a pile of money to educate Chavez offspring for several generations. And she would sleep at night. Who the hell knew what she'd do with her days, but at least she wouldn't see balance sheets and hay trucks in her dreams.

"It doesn't feel right. Not right now."

"But it might someday, Sunny. And I don't want your final answer now. Go home and put out all of the little fires you've been telling me about. Take care of your people. I admire that about you. Let this offer sit awhile longer. Truth is, it isn't going to go away any time soon. My client isn't in a hurry, and can appreciate what a big decision this is. Now, how about I take you back to the hotel, and I'll come back later, treat you to the best pasta you ever ate?"

She ended up in a window seat on her early morning return flight, and she never took her eyes off of the horizon, searched out the landmarks that led her home even from the air.

Rafe only had to say one word to hush his barking dog when Shiney's SUV pulled up to Old Sally Camp. She exited the car in a headlong rush; she hadn't stopped moving in three days. She'd checked in with Monte via cell phone, had heard the good news of Beauty's increasing strength, gotten a rundown on news of the ranch, but she had bypassed headquarters in lieu of this old camp tucked up in the Bride's skirts.

Rafe's smile said her visit was welcome and a surprise, but his words were simply, "Come on in this house." His reading glasses were perched on top of his head, and his index finger marked his place in a book he put down as he moved slowly to the stove, putting on a kettle, and pulling cookies out of a jar.

"Don't go to any trouble. I am so sorry to just bop in on you, didn't even call. I don't know what's gotten into me lately." Shiney sat down, close to tears she could not explain.

Rafe looked so dear in his slippers and sweater, his lined face and thinning hair somehow as she had always known him, but that couldn't be true. It was only his shoulders, a little more stooped than seemed right, that made her think of his age.

"So, I was wondering if I could talk to you."

He smiled. "Always, I hope."

Shiney remembered with a start that Nell was in town, tending to Brenna. Rafe put a cup of hot tea on the table in front of Shiney. She wrapped her hands around it gratefully.

"You are going to think I've gone crazy. I think I did go crazy there for awhile. I don't know how to tell you, and I am tired of holding all of this. I wish Papa were here..."

Shiney felt her shoulders begin to relax as the words began to flow, and the whole story came sliding out, the whole story of not caring anymore, not wanting to change and yet not wanting to stay the same, the scary cliff of knowing that if she sold the ranch, she could live comfortably if not with passion. The story of how passion sometimes seemed like too much work. Rafe sat still and absorbed it all. He never once flinched, though Shiney's decision would affect him, this lifetime cowpuncher, more than any other person in the world. The two friends talked deep into the night, about the past, about the present, about their mutual love. They talked about the Bride.

BREAKING THE TWO-POUR RULE

Pam was making one of her rare layovers at home. Their carefully prepared dinner felt like so much playing house, as if the two of them were going through scripted motions. They were both being so careful of each other, and Monte couldn't find the reason why.

They sat at the dining room table, cloth napkins and all of the dishes that would need to be washed later, eating Caesar salads while steaks and asparagus waited on a platter.

"You seem distracted."

He shook his tumbler of tequila on ice hard and wondered how long they were going to make nice tonight, "Yeah, a little bit, just work stuff."

"Ha! Your work? Can't be that earth shattering."

There wasn't enough tequila in the world.

Monte stood up and walked out onto the deck leaving his meal un-eaten. He didn't need Pam's shit tonight. He'd had enough. First of all he'd made a big mistake early in the afternoon, asking Shiney if she was paying all of Del Lincoln's medical bills in addition to the hotel room for Brenna and Nell.

"Why do people keep asking about my personal business? First Jody and now you. If I want to help an old friend out, that's my business. You won't ever see it on your books, your spreadsheet, I mean."

And the conversation hadn't gotten any better. He had known for some time that something was wrong, and when Shiney got up from her desk, walked around to the front of it, and perched on the corner, she looked older than he'd ever seen her.

"Monte, I need to tell you. Max Angel, my friend who was here New Year's Eve? He was here to present an offer from a client who wants to buy the ranch."

"An offer." Monte had gotten up from his own chair and gone to the window. The Bride looked blank and dull in the hard afternoon light, nothing like the beautiful woman she was when the sun slanted across her gently. He'd wondered about this "friend," even after he met the bald short guy with soft hands and knew that Shiney wasn't interested in him romantically. Not that it was any of his business.

"Yes, an offer, and I don't see how I can dismiss it out of hand."

"An offer on the Tinaja."

"Yes. You know how hard it has been. You know that I have made no plans for the future, no plans for this ranch beyond the next few years, no consideration of my heirs."

"Your heirs."

"Yes, the Chavez family. My heirs. I can't just piss this whole ranch away trying to make it work. And I'm old, Monte!"

"Not that old!"

"Old enough."

"So you'd sell. Sell out and go buy a house somewhere, grow you a little garden, and play solitaire. Abandon this whole thing!" He knew he sounded petulant at best, bitter more likely.

"I didn't say I was going to. I said the offer was there. That is why I went to Scottsdale, to see what kind of life I might have there, to talk more with Max about this buyer."

Monte turned to face her. "You are just now telling me." He'd handed her the projected shortfall that morning, the one that had been keeping him awake for nights, the one he had imagined them working out together.

"I am. Maybe I should have done so before. When I was telling Rafe about this . . . ."

Monte felt like he'd dropped into winter at one of the poles. Everything that was warm inside of himself froze into ice. "You told Rafe before you told me?"

"Look. Rafe has been here a long time. Before I could find my way forward, I had to talk to him, hear what he thought Papa would have said. Monte, sit down. Let's talk about this."

But ice doesn't bend.

"No? Okay. Well, facts are facts and I've seen insurance costs triple in the past five years. I've watched feed costs triple in the last five years. I've opened electric bills that have tripled in the last five years, and this isn't about Blake, so don't start. It makes me tired. You've been here for part of that, and you've seen how just when we figure one thing out, here comes another. It's never-ending. I love this ranch. It has been my whole life. But I need to be clear sighted. Because I love it, I'd like to see it get an infusion of cash by a new owner. I'd like to see it taken care of by someone who might not have to care so much about the bottom line."

"So you'd walk off. You'd sell out and walk off. How convenient for you, you with your little pile of money. Maybe we'll all get a nice severance check."

Shiney took the hit. "I am not going to address that with you at this time." She reached for her jacket on the back of her chair. "There are a lot of people with money out there who could give this old ranch a facelift. Think about that."

"No guarantees that's what they'd do though."

"Well, why don't you stick around and tell them what to do. Seems to be your strong suit."

His boss had left the office, and now he realized that he really hadn't given her a chance. He had reacted instead of responding, and reacted poorly.

As soon as Monte heard Pam's shower start running, he went into the kitchen and snagged a steak from the platter and a dish towel from the sink. He stood on the deck and gnawed the meat from the t-bone, tossing it over the rail and mopping himself up with the towel when he was finished. He sat with a second drink in his hand, his back to the corner of the Big House visible from there. He thought of how tired Shiney looked, and how, yes, old she had looked before she left the office, closing the door firmly behind her, a period to put an end to the discussion. How her computer was still on when he came home. He knew she had to have turned it off now because when he looked out before dinner the office windows were black and still.

She'd already told Rafe.

He slapped his glass onto the railing. Well, the new boy had some ideas of his own.

Shiney was startled by the harder than necessary banging on her back door, but still, when she went to open it, she wished she'd put her shoes on before coming downstairs.

"You're drunk."

"Not very. I just realized that I overreacted. I'm sorry. I want to talk about this."

This time they sat at the kitchen table, not in the cozy library with a fire. This time felt more like a council of war than a party, though they both sat with amber liquid in short glasses, though they both broke the two-pour rule.

"I don't like solitaire."

Monte didn't smile.

"And I've never lived anywhere but here in the shadow of the Bride. It might not be the only place in the world to live, but I suspect that it is the only place for *me* to live. I don't know that, though, and I owe it to myself, after all of these years of taking care of everyone the way Papa would have wanted me to . . . I owe it to myself to find out. Can't you see that? Now don't get mad again. You wouldn't listen to me earlier. But when I talked to Rafe, he said he thinks you are the one to save us, year in and year out, December to December. I went about it wrong this afternoon. What I meant to say was that I have not made a final decision, and I want to hear your ideas. Help me, Monte. Round up all of your numbers, all of your contacts, everything you've got. Let's try some things we've never tried before. Help me turn this over to the Chavez grandchildren someday. Help me keep this thing together. Or, show me a graceful way out. Can you do that?"

Monte found himself, that night, and for many nights to come, back in his office, numbers blinding him from The View.

WONDER OF IT ALL

Jody wondered who thought up the idea of copper rivets. Soft metal tips smashed into submission to hold leather in place. This afternoon in the leather shop with Rafe was the first time he'd been able to breathe since the New Year that had come in a rush. He'd either been looking after West Camp plus his own country at headquarters or he'd been trying to take care of Del long distance, and he was *so* failing at that.

On this Sunday afternoon, he was glad to be doing something that was quiet. Rafe was focused on his work, and Jody was focused on his, but he knew the older man was glad he'd come over and happy to share his tools and his long wooden workbench. Rafe had put his hand on Jody's shoulder three or four times as they worked around each other. Jody was repairing his pulling harness, redoing the piece that went between his horse's front legs and clipped to the ring on his girth. The whole shitarit had broken a couple of days before when the horse he was riding had lunged up a bank, so he was trying a new and improved version, Rafe's design.

He wished he knew how to ask Rafe things the way he used to ask Del. Things were different with Del now, and while Jody wanted to blame it on knowing the truth about his dad, he also thought it might be because for the first time, Del was depending on Jody. Their roles were shifting, and Jody wondered why things couldn't stay the same.

Plus there was this thing with Bliss. Every day seemed to be full of expectations he couldn't get a grip on. Right now she was mad because he had been talking to Haley at headquarters the other day. He wanted to explain to her that Haley was one of those girls a guy thought of when he jacked off but was poisonous to date, but he didn't. He just shrugged and said it was no big deal. Didn't help a lot. She was still mad.

Then there was the talk he had with Monte right after Beauty was born and Bliss was staying with Sam and Sue. They had been graining the horses, a normal morning chore that usually passed wordlessly before Jody went in to eat breakfast and Monte walked over to have coffee with Shiney.

Monte poured a long line of grain into the chewed-on wooden bunk. "She's too young for you, you know. At least right now."

"I know. Jailbait."

Monte wondered if he'd been able, as a young man, to sound as bitter as Jody managed to, but he couldn't keep a little laugh out of his own voice. "Damn the bad luck."

But Jody wasn't listening, just trying to figure things out. "I keep telling myself that. When I am working, or in the round pen, I tell myself 'Bliss is jailbait.' But then I see her and she isn't jailbait. She's Bliss. She's this girl I like, or love, or whatever."

"Fuck." Monte stared at Jody, unable to say more, just fuck what a fucking mess and how fucking great was life and how fucking cool was it that he was here to witness it, and fuck had he ever felt this way about Pam who had called late last night demanding to know where he had been and saying, "Figures," when he told her about Beauty and the diagnosis. He'd hung up on her.

Jody stopped, bucket in hand. "What are you saying?"

The two of them stood in the morning and laughed. The grown man laughed at the wonder of it all. The young man laughed at the look on his boss's face. But Monte went away with an ache in his chest, and Jody went away hoping Bliss would be at breakfast.

And then, even worse, had been the day that Shiney had caught him down at the barn.

Jody wished he knew of a good way to tell his lady boss that he and Bliss weren't having sex. It was bizarre that they were even having the conversation. He'd been giving a bay filly a refresher course on hooking up in the round pen when Shiney had walked up, and pretty soon he found himself listening to an old lady say things like "being careful," and "know how it is," and "young and all," and "implications." Finally, he stepped through the gate, latched it back in place, and faced her. "Shiney, I know that Bliss is too young for me and that the law says I can't lay a hand on her. I know. Trust me. More than anyone, I know. What with you and Monte and even Velma Jo hinting around about it, how could I not know? We won't . . . uh . . ." Jody was running out of vocabulary and steam. "We won't . . . you know."

Shiney had blushed bright red, first with Jody's use of her name instead of his usual careful "Miz Lewis," and then with the idea that she wasn't the only one getting into his business. She gathered her composure and tilted her head to the side. "So, that's what the young folk are calling it nowadays. Hmph. Well, as long as you don't *you know*." And with that, Sunshine Angel Lewis beat a retreat.

Jody wished he knew how to tell people that all he and Bliss really did was hold each other. They didn't talk much. Didn't kiss much. Mainly they just held each other, long and hard, and somehow it was enough.

The smell of R. M. Williams would make a good perfume for a girl, he thought, as Rafe opened the door to let the warmer breeze into the shop. Jody felt like there were doors inside of himself. Behind one was his mother. Behind one was Missy. Behind one was his job and his determination to make a hand, his dreams of what his life would be like. Behind one was Women, and now Bliss. Behind another was Del which was now all smeared up with the door that was supposed to be Cash Neil. Father. Dad. Jody couldn't help but carry around the weight of the pictures that had bloomed behind that door. Cash Neil stealing. Cash Neil lying. Cash Neil bleeding in the dirt. Cash Neil dying.

He whacked the rivet tool with the mallet.

"You knew my dad."

Rafe had been wondering when Jody was going to stop fidgeting and pounding and clearing his throat.

"I did. You know that."

"It's okay, I mean, I know the truth about him," Jody shrugged and started gathering up little bits of leather to put into the scrap box.

Rafe looked up from the spur leathers he was cutting out, his head tilted to the side, "The truth?"

"Yeah, you know, how he didn't get sick and die. How he got shot. For stealing cattle."

Rafe returned to his work. "Ah. Well, yes. That truth."

"Well, what other truth is there? Isn't there just one truth about it?"

"Oh, I don't know. Seems to me that truth always looks different depending on where you're standing."

"My dad was shot for a cow thief. You can't tell me that isn't the truth. Del told me himself. Del found him." Jody knew he sounded more like the little kid in the too-big hat, waiting to be seen by the men in front of the sale barn than he did the strong young man who rode the bucking horse and that Monte was relying on really hard right now.

Rafe put his knife down, walked over and stood in the doorway, looking out at the newly arriving spring. "Truth is a tricky thing, seems to me. Sure, Cash Neil, your father," Rafe turned back and looked at Jody, "was a cow thief. I guess that is the truth of that situation. But there were a lot of other things about Cash *that* truth doesn't sum up at all. I'd keep those things in mind if I were you. And I've found the old saying about truth setting you free doesn't always hold up in real life. Sometimes, we let the truth mire us in a kind of trap. I have no idea how you get past this, Jody, but I do know that you'll be a better man if you do. You'll live your life, and not your father's, if you do. And you'll make your own mistakes if you do. You aren't your father, Jody. But you are a lot like him, and a lot like the man who raised you, too. More importantly, you are someone brand new, and you can look at this truth you've learned as a definition or just another piece of a grand ol' puzzle that makes life interesting. It's up to you." And Rafe went back to his knife, his leather, his work – his words for the year all used up.

March 8 Light snow, melted by noon. Early grasses coming on. Turned on the windmill at Baker Corners, hated to oil the squeak out of it. Friendly sound.

Blake was late getting to headquarters to meet the bus. February had been unusually balmy, and the warmth of early March lifted his spirits a few inches off the bottom where they'd been living for some time. Spring was on its way, and he saw brand new baby calves each time he fed cows. The day before, Brenna had been able to hold Beauty up to the nursery window, the tiny little girl only connected to one wire as far as Blake could see, not the thousand they'd seemed before. The problems the doctors were talking about now were how slowly she was gaining weight and her sleep apnea.

One doctor, a small dark-skinned woman in a white coat, had come out of the nursery to speak to Blake. She looked at the boys lined up along the window. Brice's back was arched in a bow as he lifted Bradley up to see in. Brian was breathing on the glass, making a little cloud of condensation and then sticking his nose in it. Blake turned his back on them while the doctor talked about how fragile Beauty's immune system was, how easily she could get sick, how important it was that the rest of the family stay well and not bring germs home from school. The doctor peered around Blake one last time just as Brice dropped Brian down with a thump, and Brian turned around to sock him.

"Five children . . . ." She looked in wonder at the boys, having just met Bliss sitting in a rocking chair while Brenna placed Beauty in her arms.

Blake could almost hear the words the doctor was too polite to say. *"Five children is a lot, Mr. Davis."* No shit.

He'd been wishing that the doctors would send Beauty home, mainly because Brenna's side of the bed was so empty, but all of a sudden he caught a glimpse of how hard it was going to be. Maybe it was better if they kept the baby for awhile longer. *Five children is a lot, Mr. Davis.*

But today was Wednesday, not a Tuesday or a Thursday, and he didn't have to face his new daughter's translucent skin, her head that looked too big for her body, her creased little hands, her slack mouth that made it so hard for her to take in nutrition. He didn't have to see his beautiful wife in the shapeless scrubs that Nell bought and kept washed and said were so much more comfortable for Brenna right now. He didn't have to wonder what he should be doing next.

He knew what he had to do next. Sue had cleaned the house today so Blake had to pick his children up, listen to them chatter about school, drive to the camp where good things to eat waited to be heated on the stove thanks to the Goddess-better-known-as-Sue, help everyone with homework, make everyone do his or her own dishes, bathe the little boys, make sure everyone had clean clothes for the next day, and read two bedtime stories before collapsing in his chair to watch the tapes of the National Finals Rodeo that Levi had loaned him. It drove the boys crazy that he watched the tapes without them and they could hear the announcer's voice from their beds, but he promised they could watch them all day Saturday if they did their homework faithfully with no nagging on weeknights. Blake felt the nearest thing to a smile nudging his heart that he'd felt since he checked in with the airline that Sunday in Salt Lake City.

Bliss got off the bus without any intention of causing trouble. She had felt hot and cold all day long, had wondered idly in history class why she didn't masturbate anymore. No time, probably. Things were all jammed up. She wondered if she could masturbate to the thought of Jody. To the thought of his kisses. She liked making out with Jody, and they did some stuff, but not a lot of stuff. He always stopped. Especially lately.

She hadn't been thinking of anything when she got off the bus, but the minute she saw her dad's truck, the moment her foot touched the dirt, she was almost blinded by hot. She'd had enough of home lately. It didn't feel much like home without Brenna there anyway. Bliss was tired of being the little mama, and tired of seeing Blake work so hard and never play his guitar. She felt downright bitchy with the need to do something besides her homework on this Wednesday night.

Shiney fingered the tassel on a pillow as she gazed down at the father and daughter facing each other in the wagon yard, facing each other the way Shiney remembered sometimes facing her own father, and she wondered if Punch's face had looked as bewildered as Blake's did now. She stood to the side of the window seat and watched as the look turned from bewildered to firmly angry. Set itself in father lines. And Shiney grinned in recognition as Bliss tossed her hair with a defiant fling.

Shiney felt a shock, like cold water, when she realized that Punch Lewis had not come to visit his daughter in her dreams since her trip to Scottsdale. She slipped her shoes on her feet and went downstairs, thinking in wonderment that she was joining the fray.

Everyone's attention was diverted by the windmill truck clanging over the cattle guard, up from Half-way where Jody and Sam had gone to fix the red rod on a mill that had gotten left on during the last cold snap. Shiney crossed the lawn thinking, "Poor lad. About to get sucked into the drama and not a thing anybody on this earth can do to keep it from happening."

Sam backed in under the shed and Jody stepped down from the truck, greasy and hungry. Bliss turned back to Blake. "Jody will take me." He'd been up since five that morning, had worked on the mill all day long, but Bliss hooked him into the conversation, repeating herself loudly.

"I don't want to wait until tomorrow to see my mother and my sister." She put a lot of emphasis on mother and sister. "And I don't need *you* to take me, Dad. I can get Jody to take me, and I am *sure* he won't mind. After all, he *is* my boyfriend." Jody looked over at Blake as if to apologize. Things seemed to be on fast forward. But Blake wasn't looking at Jody, even when he spoke.

"Will you take her, Jody? Take her to the hospital?"

"Uh, sure. Yes, sir."

"You going to Rafe's tomorrow?"

"No. He is working here at headquarters tomorrow." Everyone turned to look at Shiney Lewis striding across the lawn. "Bliss, you can spend the night in Sue's guest room. Blake, when you bring the boys to the bus in the morning, bring her a change of clothes. Jody, better go take a shower, wash some of that grease off, and tell Sue you won't be to dinner. Fill your truck up from the gas tank if you need to, or take the ranch truck."

"Yes, ma'am."

Blake finally looked over at Jody. "I sure appreciate this."

"No problem." Jody thought he should have said more, but didn't know what. Damn he was tired, and now he had to take a shower and haul Bliss sixty miles. Women. A lot of trouble, but in a way it looked like he was doing this for Shiney.

Velma Jo passed the school bus as it rumbled its way back toward town. It was faster to go around to Half-way Camp the other way, but today she had to deliver some Mary Kay to Sue and decided it was worth the extra ten minutes or so to get the delivery off her list. Headquarters looked like a busy place when she came across the cattle guard, but then she saw Blake's truck. Just a couple of Davises could make a place look busy. She pulled up and stepped out, waving to the Davis boys. "Hey!" she yelled across to the hay barn. "I miss you silly rug rats!"

Velma Jo turned to Blake and Shiney and now Monte, who had walked over from the office.

"Blake! Who pissed in your Post Toasties? Got an update on the baby? How's Brenna doing? I was going to drive in today, but figured I'd better wait until Friday when I have *plenty* to do in town, trust me."

"Well, we were there yesterday . . . ." Blake stopped as Jody came out of the bunkhouse and Bliss, who had been sitting on the steps after talking to Sue jumped up to walk beside him to the antique truck. As Jody and Bliss drove past, Blake raised his hand as if to stop them and said, under his breath as if they could hear, "Do your homework . . . ."

"Where are those two going?"

Blake looked at Velma Jo. "They are going to the hospital."

A lot of words and a lot of worries were bottled up inside Blake. He took a deep breath and then directed everything that spilled out at the three people standing there. "Bliss doesn't like me anymore. I miss my wife. I want her to come home, but if she does and the boys bring so much as a cold home from school, it could kill the baby. *So much as a cold.* And Brenna doesn't even care about any of us anymore, just about the baby. And Bliss hates me, you know, and what if she is sleeping with Jody? He's too old for her. And I know that Shiney is going to end up with a huge motel bill, and it's way expensive for Brenna to be eating in town every meal, but she's nursing, you know, and she has to eat. I mean, at least she's pumping, not really nursing. Beauty can't nurse. Something's wrong with her mouth or the way her tongue is or something. And that Indian doctor, or Himalayan or something, she doesn't want to let us bring our daughter home, I know she doesn't. I saw her looking at the boys as if they were big old germ pots. And they are! No matter how much I wash them, or how much juice I make them drink or how much sleep I insist that they get, they still are just walking germ balls. Are all children like that? Because if so, we are going to have to keep Beauty away from all children, and I am so tired. So tired of trying to fix all of this, and I don't have any idea what to do. Do you think Bliss and Jody are doing it? Because I'll kill him. I mean it. I'll kill him. And she's the same age as Brenna when we got pregnant with Bliss, do you know that? And what am I going to do about bringing that baby home? And . . . ."

Velma Jo laid her hand on Blake's arm. He stopped talking and stared at her with eyes that looked as if they hadn't quit travelling in several weeks.

"Blake. Your boys are not germ balls. They are just kids who go to a public school where we all pass germs around, especially in the winter. I am pretty certain that Bliss is not sleeping with Jody, mainly because I think Jody is smarter than that, but I will talk to both of them. Or make sure someone does." She held up her hand as the desperation started to return to Blake's face. "Ok! I'll do it. Now, are you going to the hospital tomorrow? Good. You tell Brenna and Beauty's doctors that until Beauty gets big and strong, the boys and Bliss are going to live with me and Levi. I'll schlep them back and forth to school every day and we'll sterilize them before visits to West Camp. Sue is cleaning your house, right?" Velma Jo looked at Shiney for help and Shiney stepped up.

"I'll get Sue to rent a steam cleaner and suck up or boil any germs lurking around. Sue will know the magic. And, we'll send Sam over there to start doing all he can with weather stripping and . . . what, Monte? Something, right? To keep that house warmer?"

Monte nodded vigorously. "Sam's the guy."

Shiney nodded. "He is. Now, Blake, you take the little germ pots home before I have to re-upholster my truck. This will all work out." The boys had climbed in Blake's ranch truck out of the wind.

In that moment, Blake felt that winter was over.

As Velma Jo went on to deliver gossip and cosmetics to Sue, and Blake and the boys disappeared in their dust cloud, Monte stood beside Shiney.

"Still hoping to desert us all?" His voice was tight even as he attempted to smile.

"Stick with the numbers, Monte. We're gonna need them." Shiney looked up the side of the Big House to her vacant window seat. Yes, she had entered the fray.

"That colt Rafe handed over into your string. Think he'd be okay for me?"

Monte tried again to smile, and this time he made it.

March 13 Still early, but the Bride is turning just barely green. Filled the last of the leather orders. Oiled my saddle. Shod Poncho. House felt too hot tonight.

Bliss bounced on the springy seat and said, "Where do you want to go?"

Jody stared straight down the road. His hair was still wet from running through the shower, and both hands looked like brown maps with tiny grease roads running through the creases. "I thought we were going to the hospital."

"But really, if you could go anywhere, where would you go?" Bliss gave another little bounce and rolled down the window, sticking both arms and her head out into the cold evening air.

"I'd go to the bunkhouse and go to bed. Roll up the window, Bliss. It's cold."

Bliss rolled the window up slowly, adjusted the heater vent to blow right on her. "But don't you want to do something fun, eat somewhere special, do something wild and crazy? I know! Let's have lobster!"

"No, Bliss. I worked all day and I wanted to eat what Sue had already cooked for me, maybe watch a little TV, and go to bed. I'm tired."

"Well, excuse me for interrupting your exciting evening! Turn around!"

"No. I told Blake and Miz Lewis I'd take you to see your mom and your sister. That's what I am going to do. I don't know what's wrong with you."

He shifted the old gears down to go across the cattle guard into the Highway Pasture. Bliss crossed her arms and sat in silence until they reached the other side of the pasture and the gate that had to remain closed through the spring until they shipped the calves Monte had held over the winter. The calves kept walking the cattle guard otherwise, getting on the highway. Bliss got out to open the gate, and Jody pulled through. He arched his back, his arms braced against the steering wheel. He'd wished he'd had an extra arm most of the day. Had actually caught himself wanting to turn a pipe wrench with his teeth when the wind picked up. Now he was driving to town for Christ's sake. He looked in the rearview mirror. Looked in the side mirror. Maybe she had to pee. The dust in the headlights swam and settled. Still no Bliss. Jody finally got out.

She was gone. The only thing he could see were the tail lights turning the white gate pink.

Jody called her name into the darkening night. Just the chug of the old truck and cold wind.

By the time he got turned around so the headlights would show Bliss' tracks in the dirt, tell him which way she went, Jody wasn't mad so much as scared. What the hell was she thinking? He pulled a flashlight out from behind the seat and walked down the fenceline in the direction her slim footprints were pointing. When he finally caught up with her, he grabbed her arm. The wind blew his entreaties away into the darkness.

Bliss turned with the force of his grip and beat her fists against his chest, tried to knock away his arms. Helpless to break free, the girl sent her grief for Beauty into his skin, buffeted the night with frustration and anger. Wailed about never enough and not fair.

For the rest of his life, Jody Neil stumbled, fell, messed up, lost his temper, felt sorry for himself, and lived like a human, but right there, two hundred meaningless yards down a barbed wire fence at darktime on a chilly spring night, Jody saw something very clearly. He saw, earlier than most people, that we all have something. Later on he would fail to see it as crystalline as it was in that moment. There were whole years in his life when he would lose sight of it altogether, but right then, he saw. Saw that every human being has something. Cash Neil had something. Mattie Neil had something. Delbert Lincoln had something. Monte Wells had something. The President of the United States had something.

No one is immune, and we are all isolated from the rest of the universe by that something that holds us back and down, whether it is a diagnosis from birth, a dead father, an intrinsic lonely, or a hurt heart.

Jody Neil folded Bliss Davis into his arms, gave her all he had to give at that moment, and vowed to use *his* something to make things better, not worse. Vowed to use his mother's indifference, his father's sins,

Del's love as gifts. He couldn't have said any of it out loud, couldn't have said why in that moment he knew how to live, but there was a moment of brightdark clarity when he knew something, something of beauty.

The next morning Sunshine Angel Lewis walked down to the tinaja. She knelt at the edge of the lacy pool, dipped her hands into the water and splashed its springtime iciness up onto her face. She thought of a lifetime committed to this place, to this land, to this battle. And she renewed her vows. She stood and looked up at Bride Mountain. At her mountain.

"For better or worse. For better or worse."

Rain

They were an unlikely pair, but Nell considered that she really was the right one to stay with Brenna while Beauty was in the hospital. After all, Sue had Jody to feed. Velma Jo had a job. Annie, well, what did Annie know about anything, and she was calving out heifers besides. All considered, Nell felt that she was the only person to be with Brenna, especially after she met Brenna's mom, a little mouse of a woman who fluttered her hands about and said, "Praise Jesus" or "My land" at everything.

For weeks the two women shared a long-term hotel suite, courtesy of Sunshine Angel Lewis. Nell helped Brenna grow strong, toted her to the hospital three times a day to hold the fragile newborn that all of the nurses were in love with, made shopping trips for things like nursing pads and warm socks and the miniature peppermint patties that the two women discovered they both loved. Since the room had a kitchenette, Nell went to the grocery store for food she could prepare so as to spare their mutual budgets from always eating out, though Shiney had eased that burden with an envelope of cash that only the two of them ever knew anything about. Nell bought cases of bottled water, magazines full of celebrities, and discounted flowers to make the room more cheerful. She made pasta with fresh vegetables in cream sauce with garlic toast. She crocheted pastel potholders while Brenna watched sit-coms and the Home Shopping Network for hours each day, hooked to the breast pump while the milk flowed from her body. A Special Needs Infant Coordinator explained how to care for Beauty.

Nell was the one who took Brenna to the outpatient surgery center for her tubal ligation, the one her ob-gyn had been going to do after Beauty's birth but had postponed until "things settled down." Nell was the one who drove a groggy Brenna back to the room and convinced her that it was okay not to go to NICU for one day while her incision healed.

One afternoon Brenna and Nell got free facials at the mall and haircuts from a cheaper place down the way. Nell got hers colored again, like she had before Christmas, but when she saw Brenna looking at the price list with a furrowed brow, she leaned over and whispered, "Clairol. $7. Walmart. Tonight!" And they did, too, staining the hotel sink a dark chocolate brown. Brenna shook her wet hair out of the thin white cheap towel and grinned at Nell. She looked ten years younger.

When Beauty could finally go home, Nell escorted the mother and daughter to West Camp, helped tote in all of the luggage and baby stuff and the sleep apnea monitor. She was grateful to Sue for the odor of pine cleaner in the air. Nell unloaded the groceries they had bought and made Brenna a sandwich before she drove home to Old Sally.

That night, after she crawled into bed beside Rafe, tears leaked from her eyes until she was sobbing, wrapped up in his arms. She cried because she was tired. Cried because she had missed Rafe and was just now realizing it. She cried because Brenna hadn't really wanted to go home. She cried for Beauty.

To: Monte Wells <montewells@msn.com>
From: Pam Schaffer <pam.schaffer@hortonvetsupply.biz>
Subject: One last shot

Well, I thought we might try, anyway. I'll meet you at Donovan's for dinner, Sunday night, 7ish? For old time's sake? I know you like their twice-baked. I'll have iced tea, you'll have Hornitos. And we'll see if there is anything left of us. me

Thunder tore the page of winter from the year, and rain fell for three days, making spring.

The spring Bride wears pastel lace. She is shy and blushing, bathing in crystal clear run-off. She is slowly being revealed as her white comes and goes with late storms.

She wakes, gazes quietly with sky-blue eyes until her avian hand-maidens create a chorus of "let's party, let's party." Still, it takes a long time for her to change her clothes. She's loathe to give up her white dress in exchange for this year's colors. She dips herself in the palest tints each dawn until finally she wears a full gown of tender growth.

The Bride ducks her head with a virgin blush until the sun and bees light fires in the throats of her flowers. She's born anew, and she never tells us that she has done this before.

QUITTING TIME

The beginning of April didn't feel like spring at all. It was gloomy, wet, and cold. No matter how it felt though, wet was the promise of grass, and everyone knew it. But in the office, things were still gray. Monte wondered if anyone else was aware that it was almost time to crank up for spring works. Seemed like they just got done with fall.

Jody was off with Sam, on the windmill truck again. Jody'd taken Monte seriously when told what a great opportunity was lying at his feet. First of all, he could learn to windmill and drive heavy equipment from Sam, and no, it wasn't punchy, but it was valuable, and he might need it later on in his life when things didn't work out as planned. Plus, Monte had pointed out that if he'd start hanging around the shop on Sundays, he might learn a thing or two from Chad before he went off to boot camp, might be able to start drawing a little extra pay if he could learn to do for the ranch what Chad had been doing the last few years. This past Sunday, Bliss had come along too, and Monte wasn't so sure *that* was such a great idea, the girl with her long pale arms and legs, hanging around where the guys were welding. Hot sparks and all.

But spring really had arrived. Sam was digging in the garden, picking early lettuce and giving bags of it away to anyone who would take it. Sue was keeping the road hot, running back and forth to West Camp. Rafe had mentioned last week that he was going up on the mountain, taking some pack animals, would be up there awhile going around all the fences. Velma Jo and Levi were still taking care of the Davis boys and Bliss, and Monte couldn't imagine what kind of chaos their house was in.

Monte wasn't sure what had gotten into Shiney since she'd written that e-mail to Max Angel, turning down his offer with a firmness that must have been delivered into her genes by Punch. Then she had taken over almost all of Jody's country while he was bouncing around between Blake and Levi and Sam plus starting all of the colts, and dammit if she wasn't actually in the round pen with Jody half the time! Heaven help them all if she got hurt. She had also been making noise about going up on the mountain this spring, had mumbled something about sleeping beside a waterfall and being glad for her merino wool. Monte thought Rafe might be in on some of those plans.

Monte glared at the computer screen, trying to figure out if he should order more cow cake or hope that the rains that had fallen last week could be counted on to get the green up enough.

Pam had looked beautiful last night at dinner. He'd driven all the way to the swankier side of town, met her there. Her hair was very dark this time, and she had something bright red on her lips. She'd closed her eyes and leaned across the table to show him her permanent eyeliner.

"Tattoo? You let them tattoo your eyelids?"

"Shhh! It is permanent makeup. Everyone is doing it!"

"Give me a break. That sounds like high school." Monte resigned himself to always saying the wrong thing to her. He had a gift for it. The tone of the evening had gone downhill from there, and he hadn't been surprised when, after dinner, skipping their habitual coffee and desert, she had handed him a large yellow envelope.

"I really am sorry, Monte. I just can't see my way clear to your dreams, and you can't see your way to mine. No harm, no foul. Or at least that we need to talk about." She shrugged her shoulders, shook her head.

Now the envelope lay like a hibernating snake in the kitchen up at the house.

It hissed in his mind as Pam's empty closet and dresser had been doing for the last few weeks. Just as the Bride's slopes turned from white to brown to tan to the palest green to emerald so slowly as to be imperceptible, so had Pam moved off the ranch, out of their marriage, without Monte noticing. He'd even sat one evening and watched her paw through her jewelry box, putting the best pieces in a soft bag and dropping it into her suitcase, hadn't thought anything of it other than she was packing for another trip. Didn't realize that clothing and belongings left the Tinaja but never returned. That evening he'd been preoccupied by ideas of value and worth and budget. He'd thought of how silly it had been to spend all of that money on things that were glittery but inedible, shiny but producing nothing of value in the end. How the stones and metals were beautiful, but how much he'd come to value simplicity. He almost wished he could have turned all of that jewelry into a truckload of hay and cake, or several.

Shiney stuck her head in the door of the office. She smelled like the gentle drizzle and barn lot.

"Time to quit, Monte. Day's done."

He tried to smile, tried to exhibit the smallest amount of good humor. He used to have a sense of humor; he remembered having one. "Oh? Well, you're the boss. I'll close up in just a bit."

"I am going to drive over to West Camp, take those guys their mail. Would you like to come along?"

Monte rubbed his hand over his face, hard. "Uh, no. I've got a headache. You go." He turned back to his computer screen where he had too many tabs open. Applications for an operating line of credit, LLC docs and deeds of trust, budget proposals, records of expenses for previous years. All ready to be printed and hauled in to the meeting next week, a meeting at which every suit he could think of would be sitting on the opposite side of the table from himself and Shiney.

Taped to his monitor was a quote by Albert Einstein: "The definition of insanity is doing the same thing over and over and expecting a different result." Good thing his marriage was over. Ha ha. He started closing the tabs, one by one. Wished he could close down the things going on in his personal life with as much ease.

Spring. A time for new beginnings. Monte wondered if he was up to a new beginning. He walked slowly up the hill to his house and did a u-turn at the door to his home office, opting to go out onto the deck, picking up the yellow envelope on his way out.

Sunshine Angel Lewis did a u-turn at the shipping pens, headed back his way.

Monte sat on the deck, blind to The View. What was it a guy did at this point in his life? When faced with such a situation at his age? Did he join eHarmony or Match.com or go out to Midnight Rodeo on Saturday nights hoping someone who'd read a book and ridden a horse showed up? And that he'd recognize her when she did?

Shiney stepped harder on the gas. She could take the mail to West Camp tomorrow. Tonight she was going to butt in where she didn't belong. Tonight she was going to sit beside her friend.

Monte was drinking cheap tequila when Shiney walked up the side steps of the deck. She walked past Monte into his kitchen and poured her own tequila, not that she had ever liked the stuff.

The clouds had cleared, and the moon rose with the dusk while Monte and Shiney sat side by side. At one point she reached over and touched the yellow envelope on the wooden table. Monte rose and poured her tequila into his glass, came back from the kitchen with a glass of scotch, two cubes of ice, just the way she liked it.

It got almost dark with still no words. In a bit, it was Shiney's turn to rise. She picked up the yellow envelope, carried it into the kitchen, and left it there. She got Monte's canvas work coat from the hook by the door and shrugged into it. When she sat back down, he reached for her hand, and she squeezed his just as hard. And it was good.

"Did you know they chose a middle name for that baby? Lew. Short for Lewis. Beauty Lew." Shiney swallowed her laugh valiantly, but was secretly rewarded when she saw a little glint begin to shine in Monte's eyes. She took a deep breath.

"I am going to make a speech, and I don't want to make it twice, okay? I got your e-mail about taking a cut in pay or investing some of your something-or-other-K in this ranch. And I appreciate it, Monte, I do. But I want you to understand that my temptation to sell the outfit wasn't totally about money. That's an old story and I have faith in what I saw on your computer screen this afternoon. I wanted to sell mainly because I was tired. And lonely. I'm too old for a lover now . . ."

Shiney turned her head away and cleared her throat loudly, gulped at her scotch, almost bolted and ran. But she wasn't finished.

". . . and if I had been smart, I'd have had a son. You are too young to be one and too old to be the other, but you are perfect to be my friend, my partner."

The hard part of the speech over, Shiney rushed on.

"So my counter offer is this. How about I give you a 5% share in this mess of a ranch, you earn some sweat equity for the job you are doing? You'll be invested even more then. I may do the same for Rafe."

Monte hadn't struggled with emotion as his wife slowly left him or even when she handed him the envelope the night before, but now he turned his own head away and swallowed hard.

"Sounds good, boss." It was only a whisper.

"Ha! Sounds like a trap! It's a bitch to be married to her." She saluted the mountain that was quickly dimming before them.

"At least this way you'll have a dowry." Sunshine Angel Lewis touched his hand again. "Deal with that packet of papers in there," she shrugged toward the house, "and I'll have another for you after that."

Monte gazed up at the Bride. "Yes, ma'am." Neither one of them knew for sure who he was talking to.

"Oh, and another thing and then this old lady is done speech-ifying. Come up on the mountain with me and Rafe. We'll ask Sue to sit in the office for those days, answer the phone. I know she can't enter numbers into your spreadsheets, but maybe they'll be here when we get back. The three of us will sleep beside a waterfall. Make a little circle. Forget about the computer and the bankers and the accountant and the lawyers for a few nights. It will cure what ails you." She sat in a little pool of silence before grinning sideways at him. "Damn, I should have brought olives with me to this party. I have several."

When their laughter stopped echoing from the rocks, they sat in silence again.

The cow elk that had frozen with the sound of their hilarity thawed her wait and walked slowly, methodically along the far side of the canyon, headed toward the tinaja, head held high, watching, always watching. Both humans sat absolutely still as she moved gracefully over the rock. After she was gone, they lifted their glasses to the almost-full moon that made the night seem more like day.

Beauty had come to them.

Long Enough to Toast the Moon

The older Rafe got, the shorter the summers seemed and the longer the winters stretched out before him, so he'd taken a bigger bite than usual out of spring and headed up onto the side of Bride Mountain while the wind still blew down off of the snowpack and last year's grass still stiffened at dawn.

He was plenty tired of the hot, close leather shop, the never ending casseroles Nell cooked with too many noodles and not enough beef, the incessant sound of her television, having to move his feet at breakfast so she could sweep under them, tired of throwing hay to hunchbacked, heavy cows. Perhaps he was even tired of his grumpy old self.

He sure did like seeing that new baby, though. She was, truly, a beauty.

He was up here on the mountain three weeks early and didn't mind having to cut some extra wood. In fact, Rafe Johansen breathed deeply of that first smoke as it cleansed the old cabin at Precious Camp while he swept the mouse shit out the door, rolled his bed out on the cot, unloaded coffee and canned goods from his canvas panniers.

He smiled to see the fox when he looked out that first morning. They'd both made it through the winter.

For many days, Rafe rode the snow-sagged fences, dug out the choked-up springs, stayed long enough to see the first cool weather grasses begin to show beneath the trees, long enough to blow the winter's stink off his old hide, long enough to have all of the mountain's affairs in order before the crew moved the pairs up here where they'd summer, he and the cows right here on the slope of Bride Mountain. Those cows didn't know anything about who owned the brand they wore or who pocketed the money when their calves were sold. In many ways, they were Rafe's cows, and in many ways, this part of the ranch was Rafe's ranch. Shiney sure had given him a scare. He'd worked for pay all of his life, and he guessed he was too old to change now.

He stayed long enough to walk out on the rock porch late one evening in his socks, on an evening that was warm enough to leave his coat hanging on the hook, a tin coffee cup of Pendleton whiskey in his hand, long enough to toast the moon.

April 12 — Snow flurries this morning, warm sun this afternoon. Patched corrals at camp where that old oak finally fell. Chainsaw sounded rude on the mountain. She's gonna be a beautiful Bride this year.

Tough Up

Brenna had Sue buy some manila file folders which she carefully labeled in pencil first and then traced over with pen. She put every single piece of paper that a doctor, a nurse, or a social worker gave her into its proper folder. If she didn't have one for that subject, she made a new one. She also carefully filed the huge stack of information Monte had printed out in the ranch office, handing it to her solemnly, as if it was all he had to offer. In one of the folders, labeled *Italy/Holland* was a story that Brenna hated, a story that some volunteer outreach mother had given her when she'd come to sit with Brenna in NICU. Brenna suspected that she was volunteering to escape her own special needs child for awhile, for a good cause, doncha know. It was an essay about how having a special needs child was like having booked a vacation to Italy only to end up in Holland. Every time she thought about it, she got angry. Brenna didn't care about having ended up in a different place than she'd been headed, but now that she had Beauty, she knew she'd never see Italy or Holland or France or anywhere else, the metaphor or analogy or whatever it was be damned.

Beauty was sleeping, propped up so that she wouldn't drown in her own reflux. She had eaten about half of what she was supposed to eat that day, and Brenna opened the drawer where her folders were so she could get out the one labeled "Nutrition." She'd labeled it "Feeding" in pencil first, but erased that and used the other word instead. After all, Beauty wasn't a cow. As she pulled the folders out, some old mail came with them and the envelope of photographs from the poetry gathering spilled onto the floor. Blake might not have been able to really see them, way back when he got them in the mail, but Brenna damned sure could.

She could see the woman always standing somewhere close to Blake, Brenna's husband, a beautiful woman, all fancied-up in a swirly skirt paired with cowboy boots (a dumb fashion if there ever was one), wearing a big silly cowboy hat like a costume. She was in every photograph. And Blake looked so handsome, like he belonged around all of those lights, all of those bright people. He was smiling, seemed so happy. It had been a long time since Brenna had seen him look that happy. She laid the photographs out on the dining room table, all of them, flat on the surface so she could look at them.

The spotless house hummed around her. How dirty could it get with the boys gone, and her with only one tiny baby to tend, one tiny baby who rarely cried? With Sue coming over to clean every few days and bringing food? With Nell coming by with food, too, and doing all of the shopping as well? Brenna walked away from the pictures that glowed so warm she could almost put her hands above them and feel their heat. She walked away from the beautiful woman with her hand on Blake's arm. She knew what he would say if she asked who that woman was. He would say her name. Sophia Arenya. It was printed on the back of one photo. He would look like someone had been kicking him the way he did so much of the time lately. He would tell her that "nothing happened," and Brenna couldn't bear that, couldn't bear to hear those words. Something did happen. Fun happened. Light happened. Music happened. Those photos happened.

She prowled through the living room, into the hallway, peeked in at Beauty propped bolt upright on the foam wedge the physical therapist had said she needed. Brenna went into the dim bathroom, turned on the light, gazed at her own grayness in the mirror.

It was a good thing Beauty slept a full hour that afternoon because it took Brenna an hour – an hour to shower, shave her legs and under her arms, pluck her eyebrows that were more than stray, use the whole skin care regimen that Velma Jo had given her as a welcome home present. All of the tubes and bottles were in a wicker basket, and until now, Brenna hadn't even removed the pale pink crinkly plastic gathered around the basket and tied into a poufy topknot with a darker pink silk ribbon. It took her awhile to find a nicer pair of jeans behind all of the sweats and scrubs stacked in the closet, find a button-up-the-front teal shirt that put some color in her face.

She fluffed on her hair until she heard Beauty's little gaks that passed as cries, so much different than Brian's roars as a baby, roars that caused the whole household to rush to his side and do anything it took to make them stop. And in that moment, Brenna missed her boys and her Bliss more than she could have ever thought possible. The missing empty part of her wasn't silent, either . . . it roared just like baby Brian once had.

She had always heard that a mama's heart expanded with each kid, but up until that moment, she'd felt divided and conflicted, as if the best, most concentrated parts of her love had to go to Beauty. All of a sudden, her heart felt enormous, the multiplied and expanded parts ballooning up inside of her. Brenna picked Beauty up and held her too tight and then went into the kitchen and put the latest Nell casserole in the oven at 350 degrees.

When Blake came in, he was met with two things: a display of photos on the kitchen table and a strange ghost who looked like someone he had once known. But the ghost with the shiny hair and glowing face could talk, and talk she did. She said, "No! Don't take your boots off. I want you to go get our boys. Go get our Bliss. If Beauty isn't tough enough to make it in this family, then she'd better *tough up*! Bring them home, Blake. It's time."

And the ghost, who he could see wasn't really a ghost, could kiss, too. Brenna walked up to her husband, wrapped him in her arms, and kissed him full on the mouth. "Looking forward, cowboy. Looking forward."

She smelled good.

When he showed back up with his ebullient boys and his finally smiling Bliss, the photographs were gone, tucked back into the drawer only to fall out again from time to time, but no one cared. No one thought anything of that time when Daddy was gone and Beauty was born.

HOME RUN

Bliss liked to watch people hold Beauty. She liked how calm Brenna got, how Blake got a small smile on his face and closed his eyes, how even the nurses, doctors, and social workers couldn't help but look right down into Beauty's face.

All of a sudden, the boys stopped slamming doors or wrestling at the breakfast table or wiping their noses on their sleeves. It was as if, with Beauty's arrival, someone had given them sensitivity lessons. They went to bed when they were told, picked up their toys so Brenna wouldn't trip, ate the food on their plates, and did their homework on the living room floor gathered around Beauty's swing as if she were a campfire keeping them warm. When Brian held her, he always petted her bald little head and muttered nonsense words, and though it worried Bliss some because of the soft spot, she thought maybe Beauty knew it was him and liked his simple touch.

Nell had given them all lessons on hand washing, and Bradley became the hand washing dictator of the Tinaja, repeating the lessons almost verbatim to anyone who came to the house. Brice had voluntarily gone home with Velma Jo a couple of nights the week before when strep throat was going around in his classroom.

Bliss had watched Shiney Lewis hold Beauty. The old lady who'd never had a child carefully held Beauty's head that seemed like a too-big flower on a too-fragile stem, and the glow of Beauty's face shone up from the little girl and onto Shiney. It was as if she had a warm light inside of her, and it reflected on other people's faces. Monte had leaned over them both and made noises about how even his nieces and nephews couldn't match *their* Beauty.

Even Jody held Beauty. The first time he sat stiffly upright and put his arms and hands just like Bliss showed him, but he made it look as if the dainty infant were so heavy that he would burst from the effort. He got better every time, and even let her sleep on his chest while they watched a movie on Saturday night.

Rafe was the one who acted like it was completely normal to walk in the living room and pick her up, even when she had the feeding tube in her nose. When he came over with Nell, he always asked Bradley to remind him of the proper hand washing techniques saying, "Thank you, young man," when Bradley explained every time that "snot is bad for our baby."

Chris and Annie had both gone through the hand washing routine, and then Chris sat in a rocking chair, laughing sheepishly, while Brenna handed Beauty into his arms.

"I've held babies before, you know, but it's always such a long time between! A feller's bound to forget a thing or two! My, she's a tiny little thing!" And then the big cowboy had pushed off with one foot and started the chair to rocking. Bliss smiled to herself because there was something about Beauty that made people just naturally want to take care of her, make it all better, sing her a song.

April 18 Took Nell to town for her birthday dinner. Don't know what I ate, but liked the little red peppers in it. Leaving for Precious again in the morning.

When the phone rang, Monte took notes and then walked up to the Big House.

Shiney answered the door with a book in her hand, and her reading glasses perched on her nose. "I am doing what you said and acting semi-retired."

Monte handed her the paper and stood while she read.

"Oh, Monte. Where's Jody?"

"Playing music at West Camp."

"You go get him, and I'll meet you at the hospital."

When Blake was needed at home to help Brenna and couldn't come to the music, Jody and Levi took the music to him. They started meeting over at West Camp on Friday nights, and it was a good thing Beauty didn't care about noise, because it really couldn't have always been called music.

Monte stood in the door to Blake's saddle house and fought the urge to cover his ears. Surely these guys were going to get better than this. Jody looked like a robot, biting his lip and trying not to falter with the drum beat. Levi looked like he was memorizing a eulogy, his eyes on his left hand, his brow furrowed. Only Blake looked as if he was having any fun at all. When the song was over, all three cowboys looked up at their boss.

"Jody. Del's sick again."

This time he wasn't sitting up ornery in bed when they got to the hospital. He'd driven himself to town, thinking he was having a heart attack, and lapsed into a diabetic coma in the seat of the truck at the door to the emergency room. He was conscious by the time Jody and Monte got there, but he looked like he shouldn't even be breathing. Because he had listed Jody Neil and Sunshine Angel Lewis as next of kin on papers filed weeks before, they got the full scoop from the doctors just by asking.

Shiney and Monte waited with Jody in the lobby while the doctors made a decision about moving him from ICU to a room. Shiney sat down, and gazed into her Styrofoam cup of coffee. "I am tired of hospitals, how about you?"

"Yes, ma'am. Sick of 'em." Jody hadn't wanted coffee, but held a cold can of Coke in his hands. The taste made him think of those sale barn sodas in the red plastic tumblers, a straw in paper lying alongside. He could see the chocolate pie and hear the auctioneer's voice. His throat was too tight to swallow. He put the can on the table, still full.

Monte held a cup of coffee for no other reason than to keep his hands busy. He had seen Shiney in crisis before and he wondered how she'd do at bat this time.

"We can't leave him alone anymore, Jody. He's going to need care, and I can't imagine that he can continue to hold down his job alone."

"Yes, ma'am."

They sat in the almost quiet, listening to the pneumatic sound of the front doors as people soft shoed in and out.

When he could talk, Jody held his hands out helplessly. "But, Miz Lewis, I can't quit you right here before spring works, and those colts don't have enough days, and —"

"What the hell are you talking about?" Sunshine Angel Lewis interrupted. "Of course you can't quit! I need you! Monte needs you! I am talking about moving Del out to the ranch, not you quitting. My Gawd."

Jody bent his head down, put his hands over his face while Monte listened to his boss hit a home run.

"You'll have to share the bunkhouse with the cranky old bastard, and we'll have to talk to Sue about not making so many desserts, but I was noticing that Sam could do without a cherry pie or two on his waistline anyway."

Shiney stood up and stretched her back. Damned hard old chairs. She looked down at Jody's bowed head, reached out her hand and laid it on his hair, that dark blond hair. Felt its thickness wrap around her old lady fingers.

"We'll take care of him, Jody. That's what we do. We're family."

Her words echoed down through the years, all the way back to Punch Lewis who threw them forward again along the tunnel, and she heard him loud and clear.

"Family! Family is what you make it, and by Gawd, this is a family!"

ACKNOWLEDGMENTS

This book could not have happened without the ideas, advice, and perspective of some dear friends and counselors. I want to thank Ron Lane for countless phone calls during which he talked and I took notes. Without Ron, the character of Monte Wells would have been a stick figure and the story would have been lopsided. I am indebted to Ron for the years he spent spurring his desk chair around his office and going out to rope the dummy when he couldn't stand being indoors any longer. I am glad you are back in the saddle, my friend.

Thank you to Elliot Cox, proofreader extraordinaire. I got tears in my eyes the day he sent me a photograph of himself reading this manuscript with his newborn in his lap.

Thank you to Molly Swets for helping make my female characters more sympathetic and for loving the ending. Will Hale, I don't think all accountants are pencil-necked geeks, and your words of advice gave me a vocabulary to discuss parts of life I tend to ignore.

Thank you to the people who read this manuscript (sometimes more than once) while it was still gross and freshly hatched: Gail, Janice Gilbertson, Lily Rose, Molly, Ken Cook, Ken Rodgers, Shellie Derouen, and Margo Metegrano.

Thank you to Gail Steiger for putting up with me while I talk about my current writing projects in strange loops that make no sense. Thank you for putting up with me, period.

There is a little place on the web where I write unguarded. I owe a huge debt to the amazing and talented writers over there: Bill, Gita, Mike, Teresa, Jamie, Kristine, Bolton, Ed, Travis, Michael, and others. Keep showing up at the page, my friends. And I'll see you all under one roof from time to time.

Thank you to my children, Lily Rose and Oscar Jake, for sharing me with my work, both writing and riding.

And thank you to all of the readers of *Rightful Place* who asked me when my next book was coming out. Writing and publishing are two different animals, and you gave me hope.

This is a work of fiction. Inasmuch as our imaginations are made up of fragments of each moment we've lived, these characters are collages of every person I've ever encountered. They, and the scenes and settings, are not meant to resemble any persons or places or events in real life.

I hope you find yourself, coming and going through these pages.

Amy Hale Auker

ABOUT THE AUTHOR

Amy Hale Auker lives, works, and writes on a ranch in Arizona where she is having a love affair with rock, mountains, piñon and juniper forests, the weather, and her songwriter husband who is also foreman of the ranch.

She guides her readers to a place where the bats fly, lizards do pushups on the rocks, bears leave barefoot prints in the dirt. Where hummingbirds do rain dances in August, spiders weave for their food, and poetry is in the chrysalis and the cocoon.

She tells stories about the real world where things grow up out of the ground, where the miracle of life happens over and over and over again, where people can and do survive without malls or Arby's.

Her first book, *Rightful Place* is a collection of essays about ranch life and its lessons and won the 2012 WILLA Literary Award for best creative non-fiction and the Foreword Book Reviews' Gold Medallion for essays. This is her first novel.

Amy believes that what you put out there is what you get back, and that if you do the good, hard work you will be rewarded. Come, visit the world she lives in. Come to *Winter of Beauty*.

Also from Pen-L Publishing

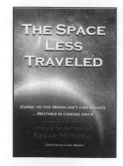

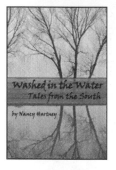

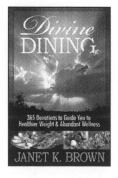

Visit Pen-L.com for more great books!

32860568R00151

Made in the USA
Lexington, KY
05 June 2014